FABLE'S FORTUNE

Sue Johnson

First Edition: Fable's Fortune
First published in Great Britain in 2011 by:
Indigo Dreams Publishing Ltd
132 Hinckley Road
Stoney Stanton
Leics
LE9 4LN

www.indigodreams.co.uk

ISBN 978-1-907401-46-6

British Library Cataloguing in Publication Data. A CIP record for this
book can be obtained from the British Library.

Designed and typeset in Minion Pro and Monotype Corsiva by Indigo
Dreams.

Cover design by Ronnie Goodyer at Indigo Dreams.

Papers used by Indigo Dreams are recyclable products made from
wood grown in sustainable forests following the guidance of the
Forest Stewardship Council.
Printed and bound in Great Britain by Imprint Academic, Exeter

Previous Publications

The Writer's Toolkit:
banish the curse of writer's block
ISBN: 978-0952 1165-4-7

The Writer's Toolkit 2:
how to create magical stories
ISBN: 978-0952 1165-4-5

The Writer's Toolkit 3:
how to create sparkling novels
ISBN: 978-0952 1165-6-1

The Writer's Toolkit 4:
the rainbow body – chakra balancing for writers
ISBN: 978-0952 1165-8-5

Published by Greenwood Press

To my partner and fellow-poet Bob Woodroofe
and my daughter Vicki Martin with love always.

CHAPTER ONE

My life began like a fairytale – I was born under a roof of stars in the plum orchard at the bottom of the garden. It would've stayed that way if my father hadn't stolen me away.

It was as I awoke on the morning of the winter Solstice, not long before my fortieth birthday, that I heard Gangan's voice in my head after an absence of many years.

"Magic happens, Fable dear," she said. "Be ready."

The voice was thread-like and silvery but it carried a hint of her laughter. I had no idea if she was alive or dead. When our daughter Cara was born, Tony persuaded me to stop trying to trace Gangan and my mother, Jasmine.

"It's best to draw a line under that episode of your life," he'd said. "After all, people like that would only be a bad influence on her."

"You've never met them," I'd said. "You don't know what they're like."

"They may not still be alive," he'd said bluntly, his mouth pulling tight at the corners. "And where your mother's concerned – once an alcoholic, always an alcoholic. I want Cara to grow up with more chances than you've had. I don't want her to have any problems – there's enough in life as it is without introducing alcoholics and gypsies into the equation."

Tony knew nothing about my childhood – other than what he'd gleaned from my father just after our marriage. He hadn't been interested when I'd tried to tell him some of the magical stories that had shaped my world.

"Best to draw a line under the past and move on," was his motto. I'd also discovered that he was good at re-writing history. A few weeks ago I'd overheard him on the phone telling someone he worked with about how he'd grown up in Epsom and had tennis lessons every Saturday. When I challenged him about it, he denied that he'd said it.

"You must be imagining things again," he said coldly.

Since his mother died last year, and he stopped speaking to his brother, I must be the only person who knows he grew up in a terraced house with no bathroom in the backstreets of Croydon. Whatever he says about my childhood, we had an indoor bathroom at 'Starlight' so why has he always imagined that I grew up in a primitive environment?

The problems with our marriage began to show before Cara was born. For over sixteen years I've tried to pretend everything's fine, now I know it's time to move on. All destructive family situations rely on the characters involved continuing to play the same parts. Change only happens when someone stands up and says 'I want to be the princess, not the goose girl.' I was ready to make that change now – but I didn't know how.

As soon as I heard Gangan's voice the memories began flooding back. When I was a child, we always celebrated the Winter Solstice with a bonfire, roasting chestnuts and potatoes in the ashes. Then we'd have tarot readings and make wishes for the New Year.

After Tony and Cara had left the house, I stood washing the breakfast dishes looking out at the frosted garden to where the first pink streaks that heralded the sunrise showed behind the houses at the bottom of our garden. Plane trails gleamed apricot and crimson across the bleached canvas of the sky. Thoughts and memories felt like tangled wool inside my head and I didn't know how to begin to unravel it.

"Magic happens, Fable dear," said Gangan's voice – a little stronger now, "but you have to help yourself."

I left the washing up in the sink, ignoring the mass of

sticky toast crumbs on the breakfast table, and went outside, gathering the things I needed as I went. From our back garden, I knew I'd be able to see the sun rise behind the rectangular gap between two houses in the road behind us.

I wrapped myself in an old car rug, sat cross-legged on a scrap of carpet on the lawn and waited. The air was sharp and clear, smelling faintly of apples, and my breath hung in white clouds.

The sky above the horizon intensified from coral pink to crimson, yellow and gold as the orange ball of the sun rose into the sky. As it did so, I made my wishes feeling a champagne bubble of excitement in my stomach.

"What the hell do you think you're doing?"

Tony was white with anger, his voice barely rising above a whisper. He grabbed my wrist, dragging me indoors, banging my head against the kitchen door-frame in his haste to get me indoors before the neighbours saw.

"How long's this sort of thing been going on?" he demanded.

"What d'you mean?"

I caught sight of myself in the hall mirror. My auburn hair looked wild, my face pale with shock. A bruise was starting to show above my right eyebrow which would no doubt be passed off as another of 'Mum's accidents' when Cara came home from school.

"What d'you mean?" he mimicked, his pin-stripe suited body poised to strike at me. "What am I supposed to think? I come home because I've forgotten some papers for court to find you doing some weird ritual in my back garden."

"I was watching the sunrise," I said, my lips feeling stiff and dry. "I'm sorry if you think that's weird."

The phone rang. Tony answered it, slamming down the

receiver when he'd finished speaking.

"You've made me late now," he said accusingly. "And get this place cleaned up before I get back. The kitchen's a disgrace."

He left and I spent a few minutes finishing the breakfast dishes and cleaning the kitchen table. The fizzy excited feeling was still inside me, despite Tony's reaction - a renewal of the earth's energy that matched the need for change inside me.

I felt too fidgety to stay in the house. I needed to do something to mark the occasion. I pulled on my purple woollen jacket and gloves and walked into Enderbury town centre – going via the footpaths so that I could look at the frost-rimed leaves and rosehips, walking slowly looking for clues in nature like Gangan always told me to.

Her voice was silent now and I almost wondered if I'd imagined it this morning – after all I'd been sleeping badly for sometime. Then near the old market hall I discovered a new shop. The name in black gothic lettering above the fuchsia pink door said "Synchronicity."

"There are no coincidences, Fable," Gangan used to say. "Synchronicity – that's what makes the world go round. Magic happens, and all stories are true."

It was Gangan who'd told me that fairytales were the original counselling tools. "Very useful things, fairytales," she'd chuckle, wiping a dribble of saliva from her whiskery chin, "and completely wasted on children. They're problem solving tools really."

She wore twin sets in sugared almond colours – cream, pink, lilac and purple – and a silver pendant with a large pink crystal in it.

"Rose quartz – for love," she'd said when I'd once tried

to bite it, thinking it was coconut ice. "It was given to me by Reuben the Healer when I was a young woman." I remember how her eyes went misty behind her round glasses when she spoke about him.

On this Solstice morning, I threaded my way through the Christmas shoppers with their collections of brightly coloured bags, pushing open the door of 'Synchronicity.' The door gave a sharp 'ping' as it closed and I was enveloped in an atmosphere I'd almost forgotten existed – a magical combination of citrus, spices and a faint music in the air that was unnoticed by most people.

A blonde woman in sleek black velvet with wide lace sleeves welcomed me and I inhaled the almost-forgotten smell of joss sticks.

"You've come for a reading", she said. "My name is Celeste."

It was a statement, not a question. Her voice had a slight foreign intonation.

I sat opposite her on a maroon upholstered chair. The walls of the shop were painted black so that she almost merged into the background. Her eyes were clear and silvery. As I shuffled the pack of cards she offered me, I gazed around at the collection of wood-framed gothic mirrors, silver jewellery, crystals and pendulums. There were clothes too, made of satin and velvet, the sort of things that reminded me forcefully of my mother.

The gold edged cards felt smooth in my cold hands as I chose three cards and laid them on the carved wooden table between us.

I could immediately see myself in the Eight of Swords – a blindfolded woman on a seashore surrounded by a fence of swords. Next came the Ace of Cups – an overflowing chalice with a dove of peace hovering above it. Then, lastly, the Queen of Wands – a serene-looking woman sitting on a golden throne decorated with lion's heads. There was a sunflower in her hand and a black cat at her feet.

Celeste smiled softly.

"I don't need to tell you what they mean," she said. "You have not achieved your full power yet but you will – and you should know that although you may feel trapped at the moment, you have the means to walk free. Your legs are not tied and you may go whenever you choose. Soon – very soon – there will be a new creative project that will change your life. You will already know what to do. Follow your heart, it will lead you the right way."

Before I left the shop I bought myself a silver ring with a blue topaz stone – clear and glittery like a winter sky – and walked home still feeling the bubble of excitement, wondering what Tony would say if he knew I'd been in a shop like that.

*

It wasn't until one of those 'marking time' days between Christmas and New Year that I found out what my new creative project was.

We'd limped through Christmas Day and Boxing Day when eating turkey and mince pies was punctuated by opening presents and visiting the neighbours for drinks. So far, Tony hadn't mentioned the Solstice incident again, but I knew that he was picking his moment before he said something to Cara.

It was the day before New Year's Eve and Tony was lying on the sofa cracking walnuts and leafing through one of the television magazines looking for a sports programme. Cara was sitting sullenly listening to one of her new CDs on her Walkman. I was staring out at the snowflakes spiralling past the window, looking at the pattern of faces hidden there and trying to imagine a new life for myself.

I knew I didn't dare leave the room unless it was to start the dinner – and it was far too early for that. Tony had this idea that in order for us to be a family we all had to be sat in the same room. I'd never particularly liked television. We'd certainly never had one when I lived with Gangan - she'd have said it interfered with her psychic work.

My father had also rejected television as a waste of prayer time, so it had never been part of my life as a child.

Tony, however, was addicted to it. He'd watch football every night of the week but the only problem was he expected me to sit by him.

"Where d'you think you're going?" he'd ask silkily if I tried to leave the room. "What sort of example d'you think we're setting for Cara if we sit in separate rooms?"

The snow was beginning to settle on the path outside, blurring the shapes of bushes and trees, making the stationary cars look as if they were shrouded in dust- sheets. The light was fading and the sky was yellowish like a faded bruise. There'd be more snow by morning.

"Stop staring out of that window – it makes you look weird," said Tony irritably. He was nursing a tumbler of whisky but hadn't thought to offer me a drink. Mostly, if he poured me one at all, it would be a white wine and soda, which I hated. Even after all these years, he had a horror of me becoming an alcoholic like my mother.

I sat down in the armchair on the far side of the room, which Cara had recently vacated. I could hear her chatting to one of her friends on the phone in the hall.

"Sit here," said Tony, patting the space beside him.

I moved slowly across the room towards the full colour glare of the television, feeling resentful inside, but not wanting to disturb the fragile peace between us.

A new programme was starting – an American chat show of some sort. Tony sighed and reached for the remote control to change channels. Then Cara finished her phone call.

"See ya," I heard her say as she slammed the receiver down.

It rang again immediately.

"Someone for you, Dad," she called, long legs and blonde hair flying as she sank back into her armchair again and replaced the headphones in her ears.

Tony went to answer it, leaving the channel unchanged. By the time I'd heard the first few words that the glamorous dark haired woman was saying on the television, I knew what my creative project was.

I felt my scalp tingle with excitement as I listened, praying that Tony wouldn't come back too soon.

"Write it down – make it happen," she said, her voluptuous figure spilling out of plum coloured velvet and her mouth curving into a generous smile. "Ten years ago I was an abused wife. Now I'm a singer in a rock and roll band. Let me tell you how I did it…"

She talked about how she'd found a way of disappearing into the space inside her head and creating her own world there.

"It's nothing new," she'd said. "Victims of torture speak of doing the same thing. Remember, there's no restriction on dreams. You can order whatever you like."

Tony came back then and switched channels, immediately absorbed in a downhill ski-ing competition.

I didn't care. I sat – to all intents and purposes watching the screen like he was – but in reality remembering those times when I was a child when I wrote stories on scraps of paper sitting at one end of Gangan's scarred kitchen table while she kneaded bread at the other or sat in her rocking chair by the hissing, spitting log fire knitting socks.

"Achieve whatever dream you want, whether you're eighteen or eighty," the lady on the telly had said. "Don't get stuck in someone else's negative viewpoint. Write it down. Make it happen."

I decided what I'd do was go back to the earliest time in my life that I could remember and unravel the memories locked inside my head, pulling the threads until they came loose. Maybe as I rewrote my own story, I'd find the place where the pattern had gone wrong and recreate my life.

I thought about this as I peeled potatoes for tea and tried to think of some combination of left-overs that Tony and Cara would both eat. Tony hated pasta and Cara wouldn't eat anything with mashed potato on it. I settled on layers of mince and potato slices cooked in cheese sauce, which in the end both of them moaned about and picked at grudgingly.

"Call this a dinner?" moaned Cara, jabbing at a lump of potato with her fork as if it was a dangerous animal.

"Just be thankful it isn't left-over turkey again," said Tony, with a heavy attempt at humour.

They looked at each other conspiratorially.

"Yeah," sighed Cara. "Just when you think it's all gone, she finds more of it – like the bloody thing's cloning itself in the fridge."

I picked at my own dinner, feeling the familiar tightness in my chest and the ache in my throat that almost felt like unshed tears.

I felt like screaming at Tony that he should try managing on the budget he gave me, but somehow when the words did find their way out, he always managed to turn it back on me and make it sound like I was complaining.

Later on that night, while Tony was watching a football match, I thought back to the readings Gangan did for people all those years ago.

"It's only a guide," she'd say. "You can pick the best cards in the world and still not work them to your advantage."

She'd cover the little card table between the rose patterned fireside chairs with a purple velvet cloth. Then she lit a candle – 'to get rid of negative energy.' She kept the cards in a wooden box wrapped in black silk and she always took off her glasses when she read for someone.

"Specs is all very well for seeing what's here an' now," she'd mumble (she rarely put her teeth in), "but you need to see the soul's light."

That night I looked out of the bedroom window at the January sky. A new moon hung like a blade above the houses opposite. Gangan said a new moon was the ideal time to begin projects. She planted her seeds by the light of a new moon and harvested them under a full one.

"Gets the neighbours talking," she'd say, wiping crumbly brown earth from her hands.

While Tony snored, looking smug and self satisfied even in sleep, I scribbled the first of my memories. This is how my story began.

CHAPTER TWO

My father, Derek, left my mother Jasmine three months before I was born. She never expected to see him again – but as Gangan always said – fate had a habit of playing nasty tricks sometimes.

Even she had no way of knowing that his return would disrupt all our lives.

Jasmine was a gypsy and never liked being indoors. I often wondered with her restless nature why she hung around somewhere as dull as Foxfield Junction when she could be treading the white dusty roads of Spain or riding a camel along the Great Silk Road.

"One day I'll surprise you all," she'd say, flouncing out of the house dressed in colours so bright they'd be likely to startle most of the local people.

"One day you'll meet your Waterloo," Peggy would mutter under her breath. "I wish you would go. After all, this is my house, not yours."

"Until I die, this house is mine," Gangan said. "And if I say Jasmine can stay, then you've no right to say otherwise, Peggy."

It was like a game where nobody wanted to lose face by moving on, played out in a three storey Victorian villa in a cul de sac near the railway viaduct where trains going from London to the south coast thundered across day and night.

Our street was called Railway Approach, but as Jasmine said, you'd need climbing gear to get anywhere near a train. It was the sort of place where someone was always watching you either from behind white net curtains or under the auspices of doing something in the front garden, sweeping the path one inch at a time.

"Just like a load of rats," Jasmine said. "All whiskers, furtiveness and gossip, but they've not got the courage on their own to say anything to your face."

She made up a song about them – something about 'one had a hoover and one had a broom and the other had a mouth you heard all over town.'

"Who cares what they think," she'd say – her pink lipsticked mouth curved into a lazy smile. "All the time they're gossiping about us they're leaving some other poor devil alone"

"I thought Mrs Cameron was going to fall out of her window when I was planting them herbs," chuckled Gangan as she siphoned tea through her whiskery jaws.

"I don't see why you have to do them at night anyway." Peggy's voice was clipped. "And if you two don't care what people say about this household – I do. Because when it comes down to it, it's my house, whatever you two think."

"Ooh," Gangan and Jasmine chorused as Peggy waddled off. She lacked Jasmine's style and grace where walking away from a situation was concerned.

You'll notice Peggy didn't say 'family.' After all, none of us were related to her. Come to that, Jasmine and I weren't related to Gangan, but she always felt like a proper grandmother.

There was a shop at the corner of our street that sold everything from cough candy to sand paper. From the corner, you did a left turn and ended up at the old fashioned station with its hanging baskets full of pansies and one black taxi outside. A newspaper seller's stall was giving the latest news on the Suez crisis on the day of my birth.

A right turn from the corner of the street took you towards the town where the shops went round two sides of a triangular green where there were swings and a seesaw. Next to the Victorian school building was a church with a square tower like a castle and another one made of red brick that looked more like the modern office blocks we saw when we went somewhere like London or Brighton. It had a statue of a woman in a blue cloak outside that Peggy told me was Mary, the mother of Jesus.

A cluster of houses hugged the other side of the green with a newer estate behind it of what Gangan and Jasmine called 'rabbit hutches' and Peggy thought were wonderful – 'so much easier to keep clean and no garden to worry about.'

"Spoken by the woman who never bothers with either," said Jasmine with a lazy smile.

She and Gangan spent hours in the garden planting vegetables, feeding the hens and managing the beehives.

"Let's face it," she said to Gangan, "Peggy'd be lost without either of us – but we'd manage fine without her."

She and Peggy would face each other like the stray cats that fought in the shadows at the end of the garden until Gangan called a halt to the ongoing quarrel.

"Birds in their nests must agree. Devil knows why fate's put the three of us together, but there's a reason for everything in this world."

Mine wasn't the only birth on that special day in July. I was Jasmine's first child, but Mrs O'Hagan who lived opposite was about to have her fifth. Mrs Cameron, who lived next door to her, was heard to mutter that some people didn't know when to stop.

"Of course they're Irish Catholics," she'd said. "Best left alone."

The word 'Catholic' tasted to me like hot milk that was cooling down and starting to form a skin on top of it.

Patrick O'Hagan, soon to be father of five, was the only

man in our street who owned a car. It was a black Jaguar with real leopard skin seats and he polished it lovingly every Saturday. Patrick himself wore winklepicker boots, tight black trousers and his dark hair was Brylcreemed Teddy boy style. He walked with a swagger, as if he owned the street, looking far too young to be a father of so many children. His wife, Dorothy, by contrast, wore clothes that looked as if they'd been made for a much bigger woman. Her skin was so pale it made you think of bone china and she had permanent violet shadows under her large grey eyes.

Dorothy was booked into the local cottage hospital to have her baby.

"Doctor Smith thinks she may have problems," Peggy said as she came home from her job at the surgery one lunchtime.

She looked up at Jasmine who was standing on the stepladder hanging green gingham curtains at the kitchen window.

"You should be more careful in your condition."

"Well, who's going to do jobs like this?" Jasmine retorted, arms folded at the top of the steps. "You won't do it – and Lily can't. What choice is there?"

Jasmine was working on a cot cover that was a mixture of silks and velvets from her ragbag – jewel colours of purple, crimson, blue and gold that Peggy said was most unsuitable for a baby.

"Give it nightmares most likely," she sniffed.

She was knitting plain white vests and bootees.

"White's the proper colour for a new born babe," she said. "A fine example you and Lily are setting it. The least you could do, Jasmine, is ask your husband to come back and stop messing about with someone else's."

The day I was born, Peggy was still talking about getting in touch with Derek.

"What use would he be?" Jasmine asked lazily, eating cold baked beans from a can. The day was hot – almost thundery – and she'd been prowling restlessly. Dorothy O'Hagan had been taken away in an ambulance that morning. There was no news as yet.

"Ugh. You've got some disgusting habits, Jasmine." Peggy fastidiously flicked her end of the kitchen table with a tea towel before sitting down with her grated cheese sandwich.

Gangan, whose real name was Lily, was out in the garden, picking the herbs Jasmine may need for the birth – motherwort, feverfew and raspberry leaves to make her special infusion.

"You've been up to something, Peggy, what've you done?" Jasmine's dark eyes glinted dangerously under her coal-black unruly fringe.

"He ought to be here for the birth. People will talk. You know how things are." Peggy took exaggeratedly tiny bites of bread, her face prim.

"Got the hots for him have you? Never forgave me for taking your blind date, did you?" Jasmine gave a ripple of laughter, levering her bulky body off the wooden chair and tossing the empty bean can into the bin. She filled the kettle, set it on the stove and lit the gas. Her red sandals pattered on the lino and she hummed a tune under her breath.

"I'm not going to respond to your filth." Peggy put her empty plate in the sink. "I won't bother with tea. I'll wait and have one when I get back to work."

"Worried I might spit in it are you?" Jasmine's laughter pealed after Peggy's large bottom and waddling walk. "I wouldn't of thought his Beatnik style would appeal to you."

"I really fail to see why you married him at all," said Peggy as she picked up her brown leather handbag and prepared to return to work at the doctor's surgery.

"I married him because I thought he was dangerous," said Jasmine moodily. "Then discovered that all he really wanted for all his talk was a little woman stuck at home washing his socks while he went off and conquered the world. If he hadn't of gone all guilty about visiting that prostitute in Paris last year, then we'd still be an item. It was all his talk about God and repentance that finished things if you really want to know."

"That's exactly why I would have loved him," sniffed Peggy.

The curtains at the O'Hagans' house were drawn early that night and a candle was lit. Dorothy was in hospital. She'd given birth to a baby girl. The priest had already baptised the child and given Dorothy the last rites. Neither were expected to survive.

"And what's a man like Patrick going to do with all those children and not a pennyworth of sense?" Peggy whispered to Lily in the scullery. "What he does for a job I'd like to know."

If asked such a delicate question, Patrick would place a nicotine stained finger to the side of his nose and give a silly answer.

"I'm looking after the horses for the Shah of Persia," he'd say with a wink. Or: "I'm cooking dinner for the Queen of Sheba."

"Don't keep on so Peg. You give my bum a headache. And don't go saying nothing to Jasmine neither. It's unlucky for her to hear news like that so close to the birth of her own babe," said Lily firmly.

During the hours before my birth, Jasmine wandered restlessly in the heat haze of the orchard at the bottom of the garden. The scent of ripe fruit was intoxicating and the plums were bursting their skins showing glossy yellow fruit underneath like a slashed Elizabethan silk doublet. The branches were so heavy with fruit they were splitting from the trunk. Butterflies and wasps reeled drunkenly from tree to tree.

That was where Gangan found Jasmine when her pains began – and she knew from the start it would be an easier birth than Dorothy's. Leaving Jasmine lying in the cool grass in the shade of a tree, she scuttled up the garden like a hedgehog, gathering sheets, candles, herbal tinctures and shouting for Peggy to boil water.

When Peggy staggered down the garden with two kettles full of hot water, she was scandalised to see that Jasmine had taken off most of her clothes. Her red satin knickers were hanging like a flag on a blackcurrant bush.

"Well really!"

"I don't know how you think the baby'll get out if I don't take them off. And there's no way I want clothes on. Let the dog see the rabbit eh Lily?"

Gangan chuckled and passed Jasmine a small cup of foul-smelling liquid.

"Jesus, are you trying to kill me? I'd rather have the pains."

Jasmine was on all fours, her large belly hanging down, brushing the cool grass.

"She should be in bed or she'll be the next one to go down with fever. And what if someone sees her from a train?"

"They'd need bloody good eyesight to see me from a train going that speed." Jasmine's last words ended in a scream.

Peggy hurried away with her hands over her ears.

Jasmine crouched, sweat pouring from her, unable to escape the pain ripping at her insides. Gangan held her hand chanting a rhyme over and over like a drum beat:

"We are the flow, we are the ebb
we are the goddess raised from the dead.
Life is here, life is now
we are the goddess raised from the dead."

"More by luck than anything else she was safely born," sniffed Peggy. "Although how you could give her such a heathen name I don't know."

"Probably because I am a heathen," said Jasmine with a lazy smile as she sat on her red velvet bedspread nursing me in her attic room the day she'd finally decided on a name. "And if the sight of me feeding my baby makes you feel ill, Peggy, then just get out of my bedroom."

It was late evening and Jasmine's room was lit by candles in jamjars. There was no electricity in the attic – only little pink gaslights – but anyway Jasmine preferred candlelight.

Peggy didn't leave, she hovered by Jasmine's dusty dressing table looking at the necklace of silver beads and seed pearls that Patrick O'Hagan had delivered with great ceremony earlier that day.

"An odd thing to do for just a neighbour's child," Peggy sniffed. "You'll have people talk."

"And who's going to tell them?" asked Jasmine.

"Pearls bring tears," sniffed Peggy.

"They also mean wisdom," said Gangan who'd been sitting quietly on a purple satin cushioned chair with her eyes closed – meditating as she called it.

Behind Gangan was a clothes rail where several half-finished cocktail dresses hung. The expensive fabrics shimmered in the candlelight - silk, satin, sequinned taffeta and black lace casting a seductive spell – in sharp contrast to Peggy's bedroom on the floor below facing the front of the house that was as neatly arranged as a nun's cell. The walls were painted cream, the surfaces clear with no ornaments or pictures, apart from a photograph of her parents taken on their wedding day. The bed was covered in a white candlewick bedspread with pink roses on it. The room smelled of lavender water and eau de cologne.

Peggy wrinkled her nose at the rose musk perfume Jasmine had just sprayed on herself.

"Let's hope the child's wise enough not to get mixed up with anyone like Patrick O'Hagan when she's older," said Peggy with a nasty look at Jasmine. "Dorothy's still very poorly. The priest's been in to see her and baby Teresa again today. You'd think that man would be at his wife's bedside, not bringing trinkets to a neighbour's child."

Jasmine wrapped me in a pink woollen shawl and handed me to Gangan to nurse. She put the necklace carefully in its black velvet box and then in the top drawer where she kept her own jewellery and silk scarves. She blew away a patch of face powder, causing Peggy to fuss again.

"That baby could breathe that in – get a bad chest."

"She's not "that baby" – her name's Fable."

"You can't call her that."

"I can and I will."

Peggy flounced out. "You'll be sorry," she hissed.

CHAPTER THREE

Our house – Starlight - had a tiny front garden with a gate that opened with a sharp click. When I was little, I liked to swing on the gate – more often than not watched from a distance by Mrs Cameron under some pretext of pruning her rose bush or polishing the privet hedge.

Within a few weeks of my birth, my eyes changed from blue to amber and my wispy black hair was replaced by a riot of copper curls. People often stopped Jasmine to ask how the hairdresser managed to perm such a young child's hair.

Jasmine created little dresses for me from the cocktail dress scraps – red, shocking pink and yellow, causing Mrs Cameron to say loudly to Mrs Fisher next door to her that with hair like mine I should be dressed more soberly.

"She's only being spiteful because she'd love to find out what goes on in this house," said Jasmine loudly.

I swung happily on the gate in the summer sunshine amongst the riot of flowers crammed into the tiny front garden. Gangan certainly didn't believe in orderly rows – nasturtiums, petunias, marigolds, pinks and sweet peas created a riot of colour and scent.

Nasturtium leaves and flowers decorated our summer salads and there would be jamjars full of sweet peas decorating the weathered outside table.

The back garden was just as colourful. Gangan's herb garden, close enough to the scullery door to be reached in bad weather, was edged with lavender and marigolds. The vegetable patch sprouted feathery carrot tops, wigwams of beans, tomato plants and onions. Morning glories, a purple clematis and a passion flower rioted over a rickety trellis and the plum and apple trees at the bottom of the garden were heavy with fruit.

There was an outside toilet where I once thought the Devil lived. Teresa had come to play and she was full of the story their priest had just told her about the Garden of Eden and Eve being tempted to eat the fruit of the tree of knowledge.

She didn't really know what sort of fruit that was but her dark eyes were serious as she looked around our garden. Teresa's garden was just a large square of grass with a derelict vegetable patch at the bottom containing some withered sprout stems and a few rusty bikes. For all his talk about "growing tobacco for the King of Siam," Patrick O'Hagan didn't seem to know a weed from a flower.

"Everyone knows the only thing he makes grow is babies," sniffed Peggy.

Jasmine glared at Peggy and shooed Teresa and I out into the garden. We wandered around the paths shaded by a plane tree looking at the flowers – crimson hollyhocks higher than our heads that looked as if they were made out of crepe paper, foxgloves that Gangan had warned me never to touch. Bees droned in and out of each speckled flower, the sun was warm on our bare arms and peacock butterflies danced in the shimmering light.

Teresa wore a washed out pink dress that had once belonged to her sister Cathy.

We picked tiny bunches of wild flowers – daisies, buttercups, speedwells and forget-me-nots from the orchard and were just walking back up the mossy path towards the scullery door when we heard it. A voice from the outside toilet that said:

"Deliver me from the evil of this house if you can hear me, Lord."

Teresa's face went pale and her eyes filled with tears.

"It's only Peggy," I said. "She does that when she's upset."

But Teresa wasn't convinced and raced inside, burying her head in her mother's navy blue lap.

Dorothy O'Hagan never looked entirely at ease in our kitchen, perched on the edge of a wooden chair, sipping at a cup of milky tea.

"She's a difficult woman to heal," Gangan used to say, shaking her head as she walked back down the long hallway having let Dorothy and Teresa out. "And she may not survive another pregnancy…"

"Don't you go meddling. People won't thank you for it." Peggy glared at her. "Look what it did for my mother. Without your interference …"

Peggy's tirade was interrupted by the familiar sound of the mermaid-shaped brass door knocker.

Gan-gan. Gan-gan.

"Gangan," I said, tugging her long black skirt and pointing towards the front door. The late afternoon sunlight pouring through the stained glass in the upper part of the door was creating diamonds of colour on the polished wooden floor – wine red, green, yellow, aquamarine.

"Gangan."

Lily smiled at me, her dark eyes mischievous behind her round glasses.

"Yes my sweet. Gangan go and see what the people want."

She'd bring the person in to the kitchen and settle them in her corner by the fire. She'd take their hands and look into their eyes.

"You can tell a lot about a person by the feel of their skin and the look in their eyes," she said.

"Every gypsy fortune teller knows that," Jasmine would chuckle.

"And how would you know? They got rid of you soon enough." There was a sharp edge to Peggy's voice.

"I just know, that's all." Jasmine's mouth curved in her usual pink-lipsticked smile.

Gangan's healing sessions began with her settling the person into a comfortable chair by the fire. She'd give them tea in a bone china cup poured from the large black pot with pink roses on it. When they'd drunk the tea, she'd take the cup from them and swish the dregs around until they created a pattern on the inside of the cup. Then she'd read the leaves, giving them a positive message before she produced the tarot cards with their purple and silver pattern on the backs and invited the person to shuffle them and choose ten cards. By then, the person would usually have mentioned the things that worried them.

"I talk to them for longer than that Doctor Smith does – and more often than not that's all they want. Someone to listen to them." Gangan dribbled slightly as she talked, a fleck of spittle landing on her dark purple jumper.

"I can only see it leading to trouble." Peggy pursed her thin lips and turned away.

Looking at the three women – Gangan, Peggy and Jasmine – you couldn't help noticing their shapes. Gangan was like the figures of eight I tried to draw on scraps of paper with a large pencil – the top circle slightly smaller than the bottom one. Peggy was like a cottage loaf. Her bottom stuck out almost like a shelf and she needed Gangan's help to wedge her into her heavy white corset every morning.

Jasmine had slim hips and a large bust which she showed off to perfection in figure hugging tops which Peggy said "left nothing to the imagination." She liked bright colours too – red, purple and orange – which looked dramatic with her long dark curly hair. She clipped her hair up on top of her head when she was working so that it was out of the way. Usually it cascaded down her back like a dark waterfall. Even in the kitchen you could faintly hear her record player belting out a blues or jazz tune as she worked.

Gangan sang old music hall songs as she worked at the scrubbed pine table in the kitchen.

"Oh my Antonio, he's gone away. Left me at home-e-o all on my own-io…"

Her voice sounded like a cracked record and she had trouble keeping in tune.

When she had time she'd let me roll out bits of pastry at one end of the table. When Teresa came and she was allowed to join in, we'd make tiny jam tarts and biscuits and then take them outside and have a tea party with our dolls.

On wet days, Gangan would take all her pots, pans and cake tins out of the bottom of the dresser, put in a blanket and some cushions and let us play in there. Inspired by the trains that were part of our daily life, we'd snuggle in the coconut and vanilla scented darkness and pretend we were on the night train to Edinburgh, imagining we were following the rails stretching into the darkness, pretending we could smell the coal and steam of the engine and feel the rough texture of the seats.

We were never allowed to play in the front parlour. This was only used on Sundays and at Christmas.

"Or when somebody dies," said Peggy, ignoring the stricken look Teresa gave her from under her straight dark fringe.

"Peggy!" said Gangan sharply.

"My father was laid out there for a week in his coffin."

Peggy was like a terrier with a bone now she'd got an audience. "His skin looked as waxy as the lilies – I'll never forget the smell…"

Teresa's hand crept into mine, cold as a little mouse left out in the snow, and I squeezed it wishing Peggy would be quiet. I'd heard this story several times before – the one where she thought she heard her father speak – and hearing the story again always gave me nightmares.

As soon as we could, we escaped and raced upstairs to Jasmine's room, going more quietly when we reached the last flight of stairs so that she didn't hear us creep in and hide in her wardrobe, snuggling against the soft furs and satins, inhaling the smell of Chanel No. 5.

Jasmine was creating party dresses for Teresa and I for our birthdays. Teresa's was pink and mine was white. They had net petticoats and a scattering of sequin stars and they looked as delicate as the sugary meringues in the bakery window in town.

On the day of the party a trestle table was set out in our garden at the edge of the orchard, decorated with pink and white ribbons. Gangan made a cake with pink flowers and white icing and she wrote our names on it in gold.

Our only guests were Teresa's brothers Micky, Joe and Danny and her sister Cathy. You could tell the boys didn't want to play games. "Sissy" they called it, but they made massive inroads on the sausage rolls before the party even started. Patrick arrived, hair freshly slicked into a quiff and the boys became more subdued.

Patrick carried Gangan's wind up gramophone out into the garden – the one that slowed down when it wasn't meant to so that the voice suddenly went very deep and growly.

He danced with Teresa and I and then with Jasmine.

"It's my turn again, Daddy," said Teresa, her face flushed with excitement for once.

"Poor child doesn't get much fun," mumbled Gangan, struggling with her false teeth. She only put them in for special occasions.

Patrick produced a neatly wrapped package for 'the nearly sisters' as he called us that he said he found behind a fairy fountain in the woods.

"More likely someone in the Nag's Head," muttered Peggy as she carried plates back to the kitchen.

They each contained a silver bracelet.

That evening Jasmine went out. Peggy's lips folded like crimped pastry as she watched her coming down the stairs. She was wearing a red silk dress and matching high heeled shoes and handbag. She'd put silver glittery combs in her rippling dark hair and a black shawl embroidered with silver stars round her shoulders.

"You look like you're going out to tell fortunes. I suppose you're meeting him. Don't either of you think of his wife? Or those children?"

"We're both entitled to some fun," snapped Jasmine as she marched down the hall, heels clacking on the polished wood floor, the strong smell of her perfume following her.

That evening, Gangan wasn't feeling well so Peggy put me to bed.

"You're lucky you've got me to step in and look after you," she said sourly.

I didn't like Peggy supervising my bath. She never ran it as deep as Gangan did or put as much hot water in as Jasmine. I liked to imagine I was diving for pearls in the South China sea or pretend to be a mermaid exploring a mysterious underwater kingdom.

Peggy didn't hold with playing in the bath – and it was difficult to do anything with the amount of water she allowed.

As soon as she turned her back, I sucked water from the bath sponge. She must've had eyes in her bottom, because she turned suddenly.

"Fable, that's dirty. That water will have germs in it. Germs are what kill people."

I remembered a group of older boys I saw playing 'Hunt the Germans' in the park the last time Gangan took me to the swings.

"Are Germans called that because they've got germs?"

"Don't be silly, Fable. I think you're over-excited tonight. Come on, it's time you were out of that bath."

She rubbed me hard with a towel that felt more like a sheet of sandpaper instead of snuggling me in the fluffy blue bath-sheet like Gangan did.

I got into bed, feeling as if my white cotton nightie was sticking to me as soon as I did so. My hair was hot on the back of my neck and I could hear older children still out playing and smell freshly mown grass. The air felt hot and prickly as if it was waiting for something to happen.

"It was a night like this when my father died," said Peggy drawing the thin white leaf-patterned summer curtains making flickering patterns on the pale pink carpet.

I tried to shut my ears or think about something else, but Peggy's voice wouldn't be silenced.

"It was her fault of course."

I'd heard bits of the story before and I know she blamed Gangan for the accident. I shut my eyes, hoping I'd be asleep before she reached the horrible bit of the story. My throat was dry and I wanted a drink of water.

"He died of a stroke while he was driving the train

across the viaduct. The fireman had to take over and stop the train just before it went tumbling over the edge."

Curiosity got the better of me. My eyes snapped open.

"What's a stroke? Could Magpie die if I stroked her too hard?

"A stroke is when your brain explodes. The doctor said, if my father'd lived, he'd have been a vegetable for the rest of his life."

The thought was scary and I felt my throat go tight with anxiety. I tugged the sleeve of Peggy's white blouse as my imagination spiralled out of control.

"What if I woke up tomorrow and I'd turned into a cabbage or carrot. Would people know who I really was or would I just get – eaten?"

Peggy glared at me. "It's pointless trying to say anything sensible to you, Fable. You're just like your mother in that way. My poor father would be spinning in his grave if he had any idea of the situation I'm living in now."

She went downstairs, leaving me with the nightmare images circling round inside my head – Peggy's father's head exploding, the green metal snake-like train nearly sliding down the embankment, the smell of steam and hot metal, the sound of screams, giant vegetables with grinning faces leering at me from the shadows at the edges of my room.

I fell into a fitful sleep where the same dream kept replaying and I felt as if I was trapped in a box and couldn't get out.

I screamed until Gangan came in, wearing her purple nightdress and dressing gown. She took me downstairs for hot milk with brandy and sugar in it and massaged my wrists and forehead with lavender oil.

"Tomorrow, I'll make you a dream catcher," she

promised. "That way only nice dreams will come to you."

She took me back to bed and tucked me in and I felt totally safe as I drifted into a dreamless velvet soft sleep.

The next morning I awoke to the sound of Jasmine screaming hysterically. I peered through the banisters on the first landing and saw she was lying on the rag rug at the bottom of the stairs, a letter crushed in her hand, jagged black letters on stiff white paper.

"He says he'll go through the courts if that's what it takes to get Fable away from me. He can't do it, can he Lily? He can't take her away from me…"

"Hush now." Gangan rocked her like a child.

I crouched at the top of the stairs in the little gap where they turned to go up to Jasmine's room, not sure whether to go downstairs or not. From my vantage point I saw Peggy come out of her room and peer over the rail to the hall below. As she turned to go back to her own room, she was smiling. I'd never seen her smile before and I was afraid without knowing why.

CHAPTER FOUR

"It was an ill day for me when the wind blew you here," snapped Peggy to Gangan as she searched through the wicker ironing basket for her corset.

I was sitting in Gangan's rocking chair by the window with Magpie the black and white cat on my lap. Outside the window, the early morning was misty grey and the September leaves were beginning to change colour.

"Stop rocking that chair for Pete's sake, Fable. That endless creaking's getting on my nerves," she added as she pushed past me. The stale smell of her breath reminded me of old flower water.

I wanted to ask, did the wind really blow Gangan here but I could tell by Peggy's snappiness and the way that Gangan's lips were tightly pressed together until they showed white at the edges that it was better to keep quiet.

Magpie purred loudly, arching her back and digging her needle-sharp claws into my leg through the thick fabric of my red velvet dressing gown.

"And why your mother persists in putting you in a colour like that with hair like yours, I don't know," said Peggy as she found the missing corset.

By now I was sitting at the table drizzling patterns on the surface of my porridge with cream and golden honey. Peggy's bowlful was growing a leathery skin as she fussed with trying to put on her corset in the cold scullery. I kept catching glimpses of rolls of white fat escaping from ice white elastic, knowing that if Teresa had been here we'd have been in fits of giggles. I saved up the story to tell her later.

Gangan sat by me, sipping her tea and eating her usual breakfast – a slice of thin white bread and butter spread with orange marmalade - which she always ate before she put her teeth in.

"Tastes better without them things," she said smacking her lips.

"This roll-on's shrunk again," grumbled Peggy, her voice sounding muffled.

Gangan got slowly to her feet and went to the scullery to help her.

"It's a cold morning, Peg. Why don't you dress by the fire?"

"If my father'd had any sense he'd have sent you packing before you got your feet under his table," grumbled Peggy.

Gangan struggled with the zip, forcing Peggy's fat body into an hourglass shape. "Breathe in, Peg," she said.

Peggy breathed in, her usually pale face going puce with effort.

"A fine mess you'd have been in without me – you and your Dad," Gangan said quietly.

"You killed my mother." Peggy put her powder blue candlewick dressing gown back on over her roll-on and sat at the table poking moodily at her porridge.

Gangan sipped her cooling tea, pulling a face.

I concentrated on eating the last of my porridge. This was an argument I'd heard many times without really knowing the story that provoked it.

"I didn't kill your mother," Gangan said quietly. "She'd left it too late for any surgery. I did what I could with my herbal remedies…"

"You fed her home made soup and she died. I saw what happened. Then you got your evil claws into my father and killed him too. You thought you could steal my house – but you can't. I'll get even with all of you." Peggy pushed her porridge aside and rushed out of the room, feet thumping up the stairs towards her bedroom.

Gangan got slowly up from the table and headed towards the scullery door. I left her a few minutes before going to find her. I knew exactly where she'd be – sitting on the wooden seat by her herb garden amid the damp early morning scents of sage, mint and rosemary.

From upstairs I could hear Peggy singing "The Old Rugged Cross" – the hymn she'd told me they sang at her mother's funeral. Usually, Jasmine retaliated by putting her transistor radio on loud but today she remained quiet. I imagined her lying in her big bed ('French Empire darling') with her dark hair spread across the white linen sheets and wine red velvet bedspread.

Gangan's eyes looked as soft as pansies behind her round glasses – as if she'd been crying but didn't want anyone to see.

"I was meant to come here," she said. "Peggy may not think so but we all have our special pathways. And they all lead back to the same place."

"Where do they go?" I already knew the answer but I liked hearing the story.

"All the pathways lead to the garden of the heart – the Garden of Eden if you like. When the souls arrive after their journey they are replanted in the light so that they can grow and travel again."

"Have you been on a long journey, Gangan?"

I couldn't imagine Gangan with her rounded figure and flat feet walking very far.

"Walking here was my pilgrimage. I walked for many

months, sleeping in hedgerows or barns, working for my food."

"Did Reuben the Healer go with you?"

I really wished Gangan would tell me about Reuben. There were loads of times when I thought she was going to, but something always stopped her.

"He was dead by then," said Gangan.

She crushed her lace edged hanky between her fingers, her eyes going dreamy.

"I had only the memory of one special night and then he was gone. I started walking and one day I reached the end of my journey – here."

She paused for so long I didn't think she was going to say any more.

"I stopped at a café in the town to ask for work. The year was turning from autumn to winter. I was cold and tired and my boots were wearing into holes that I'd patched from inside with old pieces of carpet. They leaked and squelched with every step and my feet felt like blocks of ice.

In the café I drank tea and ate a slice of Bovril toast. The woman who served me had a nasty cut on her arm. I dressed it for her with some of my lavender salve and that's when she told me about Peggy's mother."

"Can you help her," she asked.

I sat silent, not knowing what to do. A white dove flew past the steamy window by my table and I knew this was a sign I'd reached the end of my journey.

"Where do I find them?" I asked., picking up my travelling bag.

The clouds were a dirty yellow and heavy with snow as I took the road out of town towards Railway Approach. The ground felt hard as iron and my chilblains chafed in my worn boots.

Snow began to fall as I walked and the sky darkened, leaving me feeling disorientated and unsure. The spiralling flakes formed patterns as they fell and I thought I saw Reuben's face.

I turned into Railway Approach and knocked on the door of number four. Paint was peeling from the front door and the garden looked neglected.

A thin man with sandy hair and a smell of coal dust and tobacco about him opened the door.

"Thank God the hospital sent you in time," he said. "She's worse today."

I didn't have the heart to tell him that whoever had sent me it wasn't the hospital. He pulled me into the gas-lit kitchen, poured me a mug of black tea from a large iron pot and gabbled something about needing to get to work.

"I can't stay off no longer. The gaffer won't stand it. Says there's other men'll do the job, see." He grabbed a greasy-looking black canvas bag and went out into the snowy night. I heard the drop of the latch and knew there was no going back now I'd arrived.

I stood in the doorway between kitchen and scullery, unsure of what to do next. I was just about to shut the scullery door when I heard a scuffling noise. I hoped it wasn't a rat. I'd always hated rats – something about them long hairless tails…

I peered into the darkness not seeing anything at first. Then I noticed a small girl crouching white-faced by the washing copper. She was wearing a thin cotton dress and her bare feet were mottled bluish purple with cold.

The expression on her face was hostile. "God says if I stay here all night then Mummy won't die." Her lips were white with cold and she could barely talk for shivering.

"God will be very disappointed if you don't come out."

She looked at me warily.

"If you don't come out you'll miss the special story about the snowflakes and God would really like you to be a good girl and come and get warm."

She came out reluctantly and I wrapped her in a piece of blanket I found in the untidy kitchen. I boiled some milk for her and added sugar and a sprinkling of cinnamon. I sat her on my lap and held the cup while she drank – she was shivering so much that she'd have spilled the hot liquid.

The sky was black against the uncurtained windows as we sat by the coal fire that I'd coaxed back into life, watching the snowflakes perform their wild ballet.

"Snow's dangerous. Dad says so." The little girl's sharp face looked wary again.

"There's also an ancient story that says the snowflakes are really an old woman who's plucking the feathers from her geese. As the feathers fall all who see them are blessed with good fortune. This is how the rhyme goes:

'Here comes the old woman a picking her geese
selling the feathers a penny a piece.'

By the time I finished the story, the little girl had fallen asleep, her fair curls gleaming yellow in the firelight.

I busied myself tidying the kitchen until I was startled by a creak and a soft moan from upstairs. I'd been so busy with the little girl, I'd forgotten the real reason for being here.

I went quietly up the wooden stairs from the hall. A woman lay in the rumpled bed in the front bedroom. An unemptied chamber pot was beside the bed and there was dried vomit on the wooden floor.

I carried the chamber pot downstairs and emptied it

down the drain outside the scullery door, rinsing it with water and bleach. I aired sheets from a wooden chest in front of the fire and then changed the bed. The woman moaned softly, her lips cracked and dry, her face whiter than the sheets, dark circles round her blue eyes.

"Peggy?" Her lips framed the word.

"I'm not Peggy."

"My little girl…"

"She's fine." I tucked the patched eiderdown round her thin shoulders.

Later I tried to feed her sips of milk and brandy with a spoon. She swallowed a few mouthfuls before sinking wearily back on the pillow and closing her eyes.

Peggy's father returned in the early hours of the morning carrying the smell of snow and coal dust into the kitchen. His face was etched with weary lines.

"Some of the railway lines are blocked," he said.

I swung the heavy iron kettle onto the stove and made tea for him as he unlaced his boots.

"Thanks for all you've done," he said. "You'll stay until Molly's better?"

Gangan took a deep breath and it was a while before she spoke again. The sun appeared from behind a cloud, streaking the garden with watery sunlight.

"She died, of course…"

An angry yell echoed from inside the house.

Gangan and I raced indoors.

Peggy and Jasmine were hissing and spitting at each other in the kitchen. Jasmine was still wearing the clothes she'd gone out in last night. She had a garland of wilting moon daisies in her hair and reeked of gin and stale perfume.

"What sort of example are you setting your daughter

behaving like that?" Peggy was wearing a pleated skirt the colour of pond water and sounded self-righteous.

"What bloody business is it of yours how I live my life. And how dare you meddle with things. Give me that letter." Jasmine snatched the white envelope Peggy had been holding just out of reach.

I recognised the spiky black handwriting from that last letter that had sparked all the fuss.

"What do you want it for? You wouldn't understand it," taunted Peggy.

Jasmine flushed angrily. "I know you're meddling. And I'm going to put that on the fire where it belongs."

"Derek's very upset at the way you're bringing up his daughter."

"What've you said to him?"

"We had a little chat when we met in London last week. Over a nice lunch. Very nice indeed." Peggy moved towards the kitchen door, picking up her brown leather handbag ready to make her way to work.

Jasmine lunged at her, snatching the letter and rushing up the stairs with it. Her garland of moon daisies fell off, the crushed flowers losing their petals on the polished wooden floor of the hall. Her bedroom door slammed.

Peggy left the house, a smug look hovering on her thin lips

When she'd gone Gangan climbed the stairs slowly and tapped on Jasmine's door.

I followed at a distance.

Jasmine hurled herself into Gangan's arms, sobbing pitifully. She'd ripped up the letter and Gangan picked up the pieces, putting them together carefully on Jasmine's wine red velvet bedspread.

I sat and watched, inhaling the familiar smells of face powder, Chanel perfume and gin.

"There's nothing here that can't be fixed," said Gangan. "All wind and knickers as far as I can see. And nobody's taking Fable away from here while I've got breath in my body. Don't know what's got into that Derek. Always was a funny one – can't see him as a man of the cloth can you Jas?"

"None of this would've happened if he hadn't visited some tart in Paris. He came back full of some tale about a vision he'd had in the middle of the night and how it was his mission in life to rescue fallen women.

Jasmine's pink lipsticked mouth stretched in a wide smile.

"Can you see me as a vicar's wife, Lily? Who's he kidding? What I know about him'd get him thrown out – and he knows it. Well – he can think again if he thinks I'm letting him anywhere near Fable."

Out of the corner of my eye I noticed a look of sadness cross Gangan's face and I felt shivery - as if a shadow had gone across the sun.

CHAPTER FIVE

On my first day at school, Gangan brushed my hair and tied it in two plaits with red ribbons at the ends.

"We can't have you looking wild like you usually do," Peggy said before she left for work. "And you can't send her with red hair ribbons Lily – they look common. The child should have white for school."

I was nearly always 'the child' to her – never Fable.

Last week Gangan and I went shopping at Miss Wright's shop in the town. She had a sign up saying she was the 'school outfitter,' which sounded really exciting. I bounced along beside Gangan who walked as though she had hot coals under her feet. She was wearing her rusty black coat and carrying her scuffed black leather bag that usually held her spare set of tarot cards.

The shop bell pinged and Miss Wright (whose face looked as wrinkly as a well-baked apple) appeared as if by magic from behind a curtain. The shop smelled of peppermints and mothballs and was gloomy. Miss Wright made a great show of measuring me and said I was 'only a little scrap.' She looked disapprovingly at my red gingham home made knickers (made to match my dress) and produced some navy blue serge ones from a drawer, putting them on the polished wooden counter next to a dull grey pinafore dress.

I felt my earlier excitement disappear like air escaping from a leaking balloon.

"Haven't you got any pretty colours," I asked.

Miss Wright looked at me as if I was mad.

"You all have to wear the same when you go to school dear. And bright colours wouldn't do. Wouldn't do at all."

Gangan winked at me. "Schools have their silly rules,

Fable."

"Oh it's not silly," said Miss Wright shaking her head. "It's discipline. Not silly at all."

"I don't want to go to school," I wailed as Gangan peeled my red gingham dress off me and buttoned me into the already hated grey pinafore dress and jumper.

"It's nasty and it smells funny," I said as I looked at my new reflection in the cheval mirror.

"A lot of little girls and boys worry about starting school," said Miss Wright, "but they all love it when they get there."

I had a feeling I wasn't going to like it any more than I liked the clothes. Knowing how I felt, Gangan had bought me red hair ribbons, despite Miss Wright complaining that red was the last colour a child with my hair colour should wear.

"I'd be hard put to know what colour to suggest for her apart from white," was her parting shot.

"We're lucky not to need your advice then," said Gangan as she fumbled in her purse for the money.

Miss Wright put the money in a little tube above the counter and sent it whizzing up to the room above where an even older lady called Miss Bartram wrote out a receipt in spidery handwriting and sent it back with the change.

Then we were out in the autumn sunshine, carrying the hated pinafore dress in a paper carrier bag.

"We deserve an ice cream," said Gangan leading me towards the kiosk in the park. "Look, them leaves are like duck's feet."

She smiled and I wondered why she hadn't really looked herself today. Then I realised it was because she rarely bothered to put her teeth in – except for when she went out. She'd told me once that she'd ended up with false teeth at a very early age because she'd never brushed them properly.

"Thash better," she said, fishing them out and putting them in her handkerchief inside her handbag.

She licked her strawberry ice cream.

"Antonio's used to be better. He was one of them Eye-ties. Never trusted Eye-ties after that business with Mussolini in the war…"

"Sing me the song," I said, knowing that she could go on about the war for the rest of the day.

So she did.

"Everyone was looking at us," I told Teresa when she called round that evening to tell us about her first day at school.

She'd started at the Catholic school and had to leave early to get the special bus to Blackfen. Her uniform was navy blue and she didn't like looking the same as everyone else either.

"That navy blue makes that poor child look washed out," said Gangan. "Look at them shadows under her eyes."

Teresa's eyes were like dark pools in her white face.

"All the nuns wear black and you can't see their hair," said Teresa. "We said prayers three times and the teacher told us we should colour our pictures in lightly. God doesn't like it if you use strong colours or go outside the lines."

We were sitting on the stone seat by Gangan's herb garden listening to the bees droning amongst the blue flowers on the rosemary bush. Gangan had just brought us glasses of milk and some of her coconut biscuits.

"It'll put some colour in your cheeks," she said, laying a gentle hand on Teresa's smooth dark hair.

*

Teresa had said her school was dark inside and smelled

of beeswax polish. My school was in what Peggy called a Victorian building.

"They put the windows high up so children couldn't waste time looking out," she said.

The playground was scary – more children than I'd ever seen in one place before were racing round playing games. They all seemed to belong and they all looked as if they knew what they were doing, even the ones who were new like me.

A teacher with grey hair that looked as if it was made out of corrugated iron dragged me away from Gangan. Her name was Miss Forrest.

I watched through a mist of tears as Gangan walked slowly away from me across the playground. Before she'd got half way across, Miss Forrest had shut the arched wooden door and the latch fell with a loud click making me feel like a fairytale princess who'd been locked away in a castle dungeon.

There were an alarming number of rows of coat pegs that all looked the same and a smell of stale cabbage and old gym shoes.

Miss Forrest led her class into assembly. The word 'assembly' tasted to me of crumbly ginger biscuits. We sat on the hard wooden floor with our legs crossed and our arms folded while another teacher told us a Bible story about a man called Noah who built an ark to get away from a flood. We sang a song, which that teacher was said was called a 'him'.

"Do we sing one that's called 'her'? I whispered to Miss Forrest.

She glared at me and I was too scared to ask any more questions.

We filed along a grey linoleum corridor that was damp at the edges and smelled of bleach into a classroom that was full of little desks and chairs.

It seemed that all morning we sat chanting letters of the alphabet over and over. I already knew them because Gangan had made up stories about them. The time dragged.

"Is it time to go home yet?" I kept asking until Miss Forrest threatened to put me in the corner if I asked again.

I hugged the edge of the playground at playtime, not knowing what to do. Gangan had put me an apple in my coat pocket, but I didn't know where to find it and I was suddenly shy of asking anyone in case they put me in the corner.

The toilets were on the far side of the playground – a long thin building with no roof on it with a door labelled boys at one end and girls the other and a dividing wall between the two. There was a large white wash basin and a damp towel hanging on the wall.

I soon discovered that the boys took great delight in seeing if they could wee over the wall and into the girls' section. There was always a queue of them round by the toilets waiting to have a go – several of them keeping a wary eye in case a teacher came by.

I walked across the playground, dodging several games of football and girls having skipping races and went in nervously. The toilets had a raw sewage smell despite the amount of fresh air there was. It was raining now and the stone floor was slippery. Two older girls followed me in as I shut myself in one of the cubicles. The toilet seat was wet and so was the paper – that thin Izal stuff that Peggy liked but Gangan said was only fit for tracing paper.

"Scratches yer bum something cruel," she used to chuckle.

"Ooh – look at 'er."

I looked up. Two faces were staring down at me from the cubicle on either side.

"Look at 'er. She's got lace edged knickers on. That'll make the boys laugh when she does P.E."

Gangan had refused to buy the navy blue knickers from Miss Wright.

"Why waste good money on stuff like that," she'd said.

I fled from the toilets in tears and was thankful when the bell rang for the end of playtime.

The day seemed to be getting better. Miss Forrest said we were going to do painting. I already knew I was an artist – after all weren't my mother's cocktail dresses the talk of the town? She was even getting orders from people in London. The only trouble was, Jasmine wasn't one to be told what to do.

"If they want it badly enough, they'll wait," she'd say lazily, settling down on the bed and reaching for her gin bottle.

"Wicked waste," Gangan muttered as she failed once more to get Jasmine out of bed in time to take me to school. "You could really make something of your life, Jas. Look at them cards you got the other day – The Empress, The Ten of Coins, The Ace of Cups. You'll learn one day. I hope I live long enough to see it."

Miss Forrest was getting the paints out when I got back into the classroom – big pots of red, blue and yellow. I already knew you had to mix blue and yellow to make green. Each child was given a large sheet of sugar paper. I wasn't listening to what Miss Forrest said any more. I heard her say something about painting a sky. I knew exactly what sort of sky I wanted to paint. A few days ago, we'd had a storm and the sky above our orchard had turned purple like a bruised plum. I set to work mixing red and blue until I'd created the right colour, smearing it all over the paper.

"Cor, you'll be for it," said one of the boys. "You're not supposed to do it like that." There was a look swinging between admiration and fear on his freckled face.

"Miss Forrest, look what Fable's done."

Miss Forrest shot across the classroom as if she was on roller-skates. "Were you not listening to me, Fable? I said we were going to paint a sky and that it had to be a strip of blue across the top of your paper – with no nasty drips. We've already had one silly boy who's got his paper the wrong way round. Now it seems we've got a disobedient little girl who thinks she can do what she likes."

The whole class sat in frozen silence as Miss Forrest snatched up my painting and threw it in the bin. "Now – go and stand in the corner and in future, do as you are told." Her voice whined like the sawmill we passed on our way to school.

I stood in the corner feeling close to tears, knowing the other children were looking at me and laughing. All I wanted to do was go home.

The bell went. Miss Forrest clapped her hands and told the children to put their paintings carefully on the big table on the far side of the room. Out of the corner of my eye I could see that they'd all painted a lollipop tree balanced on a cat's lick strip of green grass under the slice of uniform blue sky. The space between grass and sky was blank like an untold story.

She made me wash up the paint pots in the Belfast sink in the corner of the room behind her desk so I was one of the last to join the queue for dinner.

The school hall had been transformed since assembly. Tables and chairs had been set out and at the far end, below the stage, were a line of plump ladies standing behind a row of steaming cauldrons. The ladies were dressed in shapeless green overalls and hats, making them look like variations of Mrs Tiggywinkle in my Beatrix Potter books at home.

An overpowering smell of stew battled with the existing

smells of old gym shoes and bleach, making me feel sick. I carried my plate to the first lady who dolloped on a large spoonful of lumpy mashed potato. Gangan's mashed potato was always smooth and buttery. I didn't like the look of this. The carrots looked even more unappetising and the peas looked grey – and as for the stew – it looked gristly and scummy on the surface.

I watched helplessly as the dinner ladies loaded up my plate. A teacher I hadn't seen before pushed me towards a table where several other children were sitting. I picked at my food, not tasting anything, feeling homesick and close to tears.

The freckle faced boy who'd told Miss Forrest about my painting was staring at me. "Don't you want that?"

I shook my head.

He snatched my plate, pushing his empty one towards me, and gobbled up my untouched food.

The bell rang for the end of dinner and we went back into the classroom.

*

That night I was awoken by Jasmine and Peggy arguing in the kitchen. My bedroom was above the kitchen and if I lifted the carpet away from the corner of the room I could see into the kitchen through a crack in the ceiling.

"It was an ill day for me when that gypsy woman brought you here. I didn't want you. Lily should've done what my father said and put you in an orphanage."

"Well here I am and here I'm staying. And so is Fable – whatever nasty meddling you try to do." Jasmine's voice had a belligerent edge to it. "Nobody's going to take my baby away from me."

I felt scared. The shadows in my bedroom looked witch-like and strange as if something nasty was about to come and carry me away. I wanted to run downstairs to the security of Jasmine and the fire, but I didn't want to leave the safety of my bed and cross the wide ocean of my bedroom.

As if by magic, Gangan appeared – quietly pushing open my door until a triangle of light from the landing showed.

"Take no notice of them, love," she said. She was wearing her purple dressing gown and fluffy slippers and her wispy grey hair hung in a long plait down her back. "Silly women both of them at times." Her face took on a far away expression. "Jasmine will learn but it'll be a hard road. A hard road."

"How did she get here?" I asked.

I knew the story already, but never got tired of hearing it.

Gangan settled herself on my bed, snuggling herself under my eiderdown and cuddling me against her shoulder.

"It was a dark, wet night," she began, "the sort of night just before Hallowe'en when no human soul wants to be out. There was a knock at the door. Peggy's father was just off to work on the railway. I'd pleaded with him not to go – I had a bad feeling – a premonition. But he took no notice, just carried on getting his bag ready as if I hadn't spoken.

I answered the door. An old gypsy woman was standing there with a large basket in her arms and a small child walking by her side.

"Princess Lily," she said when I opened the door.

It was a statement, not a question."

"What does she want?" asked Peggy's father. "We've no money for clothes pegs or fortunes or whatever else she's selling."

"This is Reuben's child," said the woman, pushing Jasmine forward. "She's yours now." She thrust the basket into my arms and before I had time to collect my thoughts, she was gone. There was a note attached to the basket written in pencil on a grubby piece of paper.

"TAKE CARE OF JASMINE. I'M DYING. SHE SHOULD HAVE BEEN YOUR CHILD. HE NEVER LOVED ME LIKE HE LOVED YOU. LUCY."

"She can't stay here," Peggy's father said.

I'd taken the child to warm by the fire and was drawing water to wash her dirty face.

"D'ye hear me. I want her gone before I get back."

"She's Reuben's," I said, stroking the child's matted dark curls.

"Then he can have her back."

"He can't. He's dead," I whispered sadly.

"Either way, she's not staying here." He stormed out without saying goodbye and I spent the next few hours praying for a way to be able to bring Jasmine up as my own child. That night there was an accident on the viaduct. Peggy's father was killed."

CHAPTER SIX

It's two o'clock in the morning and I woke with ideas and memories churning inside me. We're only two weeks into the New Year and already my life has begun to change. I've filled two notebooks with stories from my childhood, hiding them in my handbag during the day or in the drawer where I keep my Tampax knowing that Tony would never go there. As far as I know, he's not noticed what I've been doing.

Sometimes writing about the memories makes me ache to be back there in the kitchen at Starlight safe and warm by the fire listening to one of Gangan's stories.

I'd been lying awake thinking when I heard a noise downstairs. Tony was lying flat on his back snoring, looking as self-satisfied in sleep as he does when he's awake. He snores loudly – stopping immediately my bedside light goes on and beginning again as soon as I'm about to fall asleep.

I got out of bed to investigate the noise, tucking my notebook in the pocket of my dressing gown.

Cara was downstairs in the kitchen making tea and a chocolate spread sandwich – a sure sign that she was worried about something.

"What's up Cara?"

She looked at me coldly. "I'm not at Playgroup now, Mother."

She'd always been a prickly child to get close to, something I've always blamed on her traumatic birth and the post-natal depression I suffered afterwards, but at one time she'd have cuddled up with me on the sofa and told me what the problem was.

That was until about a year ago when she's been taking sides with Tony against me and criticising everything I do.

According to Cara I don't walk the same as other mothers or wear the same sort of clothes and nobody else, apparently, makes home made biscuits or bread. Most other mothers have professional careers.

The only reason I've been a 'stay at home Mum' is that Tony never wanted her to be a latch-key kid.

"I had enough of that when I was a child," he'd said. "My mother being off doing some job or other. And where did it get us? Nowhere."

I know lately that Tony's been getting at Cara and nagging at her to get the best possible grades at school.

"You don't want to end up like your mother with no qualifications and no prospects," he said.

As I've always said to him, I've no idea if I have any qualifications or not. With the traumatic events of my sixteenth year, it never seemed important to go back to school and find out how I'd done.

I know that Cara despises me, and I blame Tony for turning her against me. Over the last year, every time I've tried to be myself and Tony's disapproved, he and Cara have gone upstairs for one of their special meetings.

Tony has then come down and said something like: "Cara and I aren't happy about…"

Since New Year, the latest thing to upset him has been my friend Jan's return to college to do crystal healing – something that Tony thinks is mumbo jumbo and not to be touched with a barge pole.

Jan asked me if I'd be a guinea pig and I agreed.

Tony hit the roof when he found out.

"What's all this costing?"

I wondered how he thought I'd finance anything, since he never gives me any money.

"Nothing. I'm just helping her with her course-work."

"You should be helping Cara – not some woman who doesn't need to build a career."

"Cara doesn't need my help," I said softly. "And Jan's a single parent. She's starting her own business."

"She's probably a lesbian," said Tony, "gets her kicks from looking at your body."

"You don't need to undress," I said patiently. "All it involves is lying on a couch with crystals positioned on certain parts of the body."

"What does she do then?"

Tony had the sort of face on that he'd have if he were cross-examining a witness in court.

"She walks around me swinging a crystal pendulum, clearing the energy."

"And then?"

"I feel better."

"Rubbish. All that stuff is in the mind."

"Exactly."

"It's just like I've said before, Fable. You're naïve, stupid and gullible."

"I would be if I was paying for it. Don't you realise people pay over £30 an hour for treatment like that – and I'm getting it for nothing. I'm a guinea pig. I told you."

Tony took Cara upstairs again and they came down after a long conversation in her bedroom.

Later that night, Tony said: "Cara and I think you've been behaving most oddly lately. She agrees with me that you shouldn't have anything more to do with this – Jan person."

As I sat with a monosyllabic Cara in the kitchen in the early hours of this morning, I remembered how people used to visit Gangan and tell her about their problems.

There'd be the familiar knock on the door – 'gan-gan gan-gan' followed by the click clack of footsteps along the hall to the kitchen. Then there'd be the person's story teased out over tea and the reading of the cards.

"They have to find their own way through," Gangan used to say, " but it don't hurt to give them a bit of help."

For those who thought they needed pills, there were Gangan's special ones – bright red in a sparkling glass bottle decorated with a star – to be swallowed at bedtime with a glass of water.

"'Course," said Gangan one day, "they'm only Smarties really, but it don't do to tell them. If they think they'll work, then they will. Cured people of cancer and all sorts they have – because the mind changes and heals the body."

I nursed my mug of tea while Cara ate another slice of bread and chocolate spread staring moodily at the wall. After she'd stomped off to bed, I sat scribbling for another hour until I heard Tony stirring restlessly upstairs. I went back to bed with Gangan's voice in my head saying "stories are magic and all stories are true."

CHAPTER SEVEN

I remember the day Gangan told me about Reuben the Healer –
and how Peggy threw a tantrum and stormed out of the house.
It was a January afternoon when the snow outside had turned
to brown slush and the weather was dark and dismal.

Tempers were getting frayed after several days enforced
togetherness over Christmas and New Year and the familiar
irritations rose to the surface.

Jasmine was in her room – I'd seen her lying on the bed
swigging what looked like water from a sticky glass and
smoking one cigarette after another. Several half-finished
cocktail dresses in sugared almond colours hung limply on
hangers but she didn't seem to have the inclination to finish
them.

I'd got bored with playing with my doll's house and,
hearing Gangan and Peggy's raised voices from the kitchen, I'd
wandered downstairs to see what was going on.

"Reuben the Healer once said…"

"For the last time, Lily, there was no such person. And
don't go filling the child's head with nonsense. She's too highly
strung as it is." Peggy buttoned herself into her brown woollen
coat and went out of the kitchen, down the hall and out of the
front door, slamming the door after her so that the stained glass
panels rattled.

"She don't know what she's talking about," said Gangan
winking at me and picking up her earthenware mixing bowl.
"It's queer how you know some folks for years and never really
know them, and others you know for a few hours and they
change your life."

I watched as she measured soft butter and crumbly
brown sugar into the bowl and added raisins, cinnamon and

lemon juice. The fire spat and crackled and the spicy lemon smell filled the kitchen as Gangan mixed the ingredients with a wooden spoon and began her story.

"It was autumn when I first met Reuben the Healer. The days were cooler with that hint of frost and smell of ripe apples in the air. The gypsies had been camped in the gravel pits for several months – they came every year for the fruit picking. Strawberries at first, then peas …

Someone was knocking at the front door. Gan-gan, gan-gan, gan-gan.

Gangan put down her wooden spoon and wiped her hands on her apron. I felt frustrated, wondering if I'd ever get to hear the story.

Two sets of footsteps came back along the hall – Gangan's slow and steady, the others quick and sharp, tapping on the wooden floor. I recognised those footsteps – it was a woman called Marge Henderson who was a friend of Mrs Cameron. I'd often seen them gossiping together outside the corner shop. They'd watch you as you walked past and you'd hear them make some comment – as if they didn't realise you could hear them.

Marge always smelled of chip fat and mothballs and her voice grated like razor blades.

"She 'ad a miscarriage yesterday. They could get the police after you for this…

A few days ago, Marge had been round here whining that her Lisa had got herself in the family way and what could be done about it.

"All I gave her was raspberry leaf tea," said Gangan firmly. "I'm not one of them back street women with knitting needles."

"Just when I was coming round to the idea of a little

one about the place," whined Marge.

"Folks like you wants to make up your mind."

"Like I said, we could get the police."

I raced upstairs.

Jasmine had roused herself and was working on a cocktail dress in an acid yellow colour that reminded me of some cough mixture Peggy tried to give me once.

Despite the cold, her window was wide open. Jasmine was wearing a bright red angora wool v-necked sweater with matching lipstick. The edge of her velvet curtains were rimed with frost.

"Mrs Henderson says she's going to get the police."

Jasmine leapt up. Her eyes were bright and glittery. She held me fiercely and I could feel the warmth of her body and smell the jasmine oil she put on her dark hair.

"She said something about Lisa and a mis … mis…"

"And I suppose she's trying to bribe us again. Well it won't work – not now or ever. I'm Jasmine, daughter of a Gypsy Queen and people like Marge or any of the old tabbies round here won't get the better of me."

She raced down the stairs. I heard raised voices and the sound of Marge's shoes tapping along the hall – a lot faster than they came in.

When I got down to the kitchen the first thing I noticed was a smell of burning. One tray of spicy lemon biscuits she'd made earlier was ruined. Gangan was sitting in her chair by the fire. She looked deathly pale and her lips were blue. Jasmine had found the medicinal brandy and had poured a small glass for Gangan.

"Swallow it down," she said.

Gangan swallowed, pulling a face. "Mucky stuff," she said. "How you can drink that gin, Jas, beats me. Smells like cheap perfume."

Jasmine was looking out of the window at the wintry garden.

"Why can't those old tabbies leave us alone? If I had my way I'd leave here. We could buy a caravan and a horse and go travelling. We'd keep chickens and rabbits and nobody'd bother us again…"

"And the band'll play 'Believe It If You Like,'" said Gangan. "There's no such thing as a life without trouble."

I wished she'd go back to her story about Reuben the Healer, but it wasn't the right time to ask.

*

That night, in spite of the dream catcher Gangan made me from coloured string and feathers, I had a nightmare. There was a spooky shadow by my wardrobe followed by a shaft of light that zigzagged across my bed and onto the floor, making a shape like a trap-door.

As I watched, the trap-door opened and I found myself pulled down a dark tunnel that dripped with water. The walls were made of stone – clammy and icy cold. There was a smell of mothballs and bleach and my legs felt heavy.

I called Gangan but a harsh voice answered that she'd gone away. Gone away forever.

"This tunnel is your home now," it said. "It's the place where stories are stolen away…"

I woke in the darkness of my own bedroom. The shadow by the wardrobe had changed. Now it looked like a man in a black cloak. When I sat up it disappeared. I went to find Gangan.

She was still in the kitchen with Jasmine. They'd been eating cheese on toast and a cooling pot of tea stood on the kitchen table between the debris of dirty plates and cups.

When Gangan saw me, she wrapped me in a purple shawl and heated some milk, adding a teaspoon of sugar and one of brandy.

"There's things I should tell you," she said.

I wasn't sure if she meant me or Jasmine, but neither of them said anything about going back to bed, so I sat on my chair, wrapped in the soft woollen shawl, wondering if I dared ask for a biscuit.

As if reading my mind, Gangan cut me a slice of bread and jam and then went on with her story.

"Peggy might scoff," she said softly, "but what happened between me and Reuben changed my life. It was like we went on a journey – I really thought we were flying – and the colours... You should've seen the colours. And the trees. Such tall trees and all the colours of the rainbow. It was the first time I really knew who I was.

I often wonder if I'd stayed at home and not gone for that walk in the woods, what would've happened to me. Would I have just married the man who'd been chosen for me and lived an ordinary life – or was there a third pathway I could've taken?

Those were strange times. My mother'd died in the influenza epidemic after the Great War and I missed her so much. My father spent most of his time alone in his study – drinking whisky, not working like he used to. I didn't like the way someone who worked for him – Edgar his name was –all boiled gooseberry eyes and clammy hands – was worming his way into our house. I didn't like the way he looked at me or the creepy things he said.

I knew there was some funny business going on – that's why I decided to get out of the house and walk to the nearby farm to buy butter and cheese.

As I walked up through the October woods I gazed at the way the leaves were turning from green to yellow, orange and russet. I breathed in the rich damp smell of them and in my head I recited that skipping rhyme my mother taught me:

"My mother said I never should
play with the gypsies in the wood.
If I did, she would say
'Naughty little girl to disobey.'"

Strange tales were told about the gypsies. They came every year to the chalk pits nearby and worked on the farms picking first strawberries, then peas – staying until the potatoes were gathered.

I heard a story from the village woman who attended births and deaths that she was called there to a woman in labour. It was a difficult confinement and when the child was born it was clear there was something amiss.

"Never see a disabled gypsy do you?" Gangan didn't wait for us to answer. "No – because, as with this one, he was left outside in the cold, uncovered an all. The gypsy law said if he survived then he earned the right to be part of the group – if he didn't, well that was the law of nature."

I finished my bread and jam and sipped my milk slowly to make it last. I wanted to ask whether the baby lived or died, but didn't want to break the mood of the story.

Gangan took a deep breath and carried on.

"There was a group of them in a woodland clearing. I could smell woodsmoke and hear someone singing in a language I didn't recognise. A couple of ragged black eyed children stared at me as I passed by and I remembered tales of children being stolen.

I didn't notice him at first – a tall man dressed in faded black with hair the colour of the russet leaves – just like yours, Fable. He stared at me as I walked past. I stared back. His eyes were liquid amber and his body looked as if it had a halo of light round it.

I don't know how long we stood there looking at each other.

A young gypsy woman with rippling dark curls shouted something at me. She pushed herself into the man's arms and kissed him full on the mouth and then stared defiantly back at me, flouncing her rainbow coloured skirts.

The man was waiting for me when I left the farm. I don't remember what we talked about but I knew I'd see him again - I could tell that by the way our fingers touched when we said goodbye at the end of the woodland path.

When I got home, I could tell my father had drunk enough to make him belligerent.

"Where've you been?" he asked.

"Out walking."

"And what sort of answer's that, girl. You've made me look a complete fool."

"You're more than able to do that for yourself, father."

"Edgar's been here."

I swallowed nervously.

My father's face crumpled like a crushed napkin.

"It's all gone, Lily. The business, everything."

"That's hardly my fault, father. You'd never let me help, any more than you would Ma."

His voice grew thick with tears. "Leave your Ma out of this."

"What've you done?" Something bad had happened, I could tell. The house had a strange smell about it like rancid fat.

"Edgar'll let us stay here if you marry him. I said you would. Well, you weren't here to ask were you?"

"You did what? Said I'd marry – him. A man that Ma would never give house room to? You gave him MY word?

"Lily I had to do something." He had hold of my sleeve and was tearing at it like a mad dog. "He'll turn us out else – and where'd we go?"

"Something will turn up." I turned away from him and went upstairs to my own room, wishing I felt as confident as I sounded.

*

"You can't marry him." Reuben said as we walked in the woods a few days later.

"I don't know what else to do."

He looked steadily at me before he took me in his arms. I'd told him how Lucy had come to the house earlier. She'd glared at me as she shook her fist in my face. I didn't step back.

"Leave Reuben alone," she'd said. "He's mine. If you don't, you'll both die."

"Just get out," I'd yelled at her. It was only after she'd gone that I remembered my mother always said it was unlucky to cross a gypsy.

I didn't mean to go any further with Reuben that night– it just happened. All I can say is I gave myself to him completely under the canopy of leaves and it was as if we flew together, seeing magical landscapes and rainbow colours. I lay in a trance-like state for a long time afterwards and it was as if I'd been given the key to the secrets of the universe.

He walked me back to our house and I was thankful to find it in darkness. My father and Edgar had gone out somewhere together – they'd left a note. I sat up all night praying for a miracle – watching the round face of the moon –

praying that I didn't have to see Edgar ever again.

At six o'clock that morning, the local constable was knocking on the door. There'd been an accident. Something had caused my father's horse to shy as he'd travelled home from a drinking bout at a local club and the pony and trap had overturned, killing my father and Edgar instantly.

"Do you need anyone with you, Miss?"

I'd been silent for so long that the constable thought I'd not heard him properly.

"No – there's nobody…"

They weren't the only deaths that day.

Lucy stabbed Reuben through the heart just as she'd threatened to do. The gypsies disappeared later that day – leaving no trace but a few burnt out fires. I wish she'd ended my life too, but I'd made a promise to Reuben that whatever happened, I'd spend the rest of my life as a healer.

I sorted my father's affairs, paid off his debts and began my pilgrimage."

CHAPTER EIGHT

We hadn't heard the last of Marge Henderson. She was back before we'd had breakfast the following day. Her voice sounded like a rusty key in a lock.

"Have you thought about what I said?" The familiar smell of mothballs and bleach wafted from her crumpled grey clothes.

I looked past Gangan, down the small front garden and across the road. Mrs Cameron was out there already, sensing something to gossip about. She was polishing her door-knocker one slow inch at a time.

"I'll swear that woman never sleeps. You better come in Marge, but you know the answer'll be the same."

We were late getting up but there was no need to rush. There had been a sudden thaw and the water pipes at school burst, and the building was closed. We didn't have to go back until tomorrow. I felt relieved when I woke up this morning and didn't see my school uniform hanging ready – I'd never got used to the scratchy texture of the pinafore dress or the starchy tapioca smell of it.

Marge followed Gangan along the hall. She had no stockings on and her legs looked red and mottled. They had lumps on them like Brussels sprout stems.

The kitchen had a strange musty smell this morning – as if all the secrets told last night had settled into a fog.

I remembered how Jasmine had reacted last night when Gangan finished her story.

"I hadn't realised," she said putting her head in her hands. "In all this time, I never thought about how it was for them."

When she looked up again, her face was so pale, I

thought she'd faint. Then she'd put her head down on the table amongst the remains of the supper dishes and sobbed.

Gangan got out of her chair and went to her, cradling her in her arms as if she was a little girl.

"I never realised…" was all Jasmine kept saying over and over again.

"They're at peace now dear," Gangan said soothingly. She looked at me and nodded towards the door.

I didn't want to go to bed, but I was tired, and if the truth was known a bit disappointed with the story of Reuben. It was all silly grown up stuff that I didn't really understand.

Jasmine went out just after I'd got into bed. Gangan came to me then, looking sadder than I'd ever seen her look before - pinched and white about the mouth as if she'd been out in the cold too long. She plumped herself down on my bed.

"I'd no idea Reuben's story'd affect her this bad," she said.

"I don't want you to die," I said, holding her tightly round the neck. Her wispy hair smelled of cake mixture and Devon violets.

"We all have to go sometime, Fable. But we're all linked somehow, remember that. Whether we're blood relations or not I'm part of you and you're part of me. Like Reuben once said – we're part of the same web and we all come from the same garden and we all go back to it when we pass on."

"Where's Jasmine gone?" I was used to her nocturnal adventures, but she didn't usually go out after midnight on a night that was so bitterly cold.

"She'll be back, love. She always comes back, you know that."

Now, this morning, Marge looked furtively round our untidy kitchen. The fire had gone out and Magpie the cat had left grey ashy footprints all over the hearth as she went to seek a warmer space. I knew Marge'd be savouring every detail of unwashed crockery, sticky gin bottle and dirty floor to tell Mrs Cameron when she got outside.

Gangan didn't ask her to sit down or offer her a cup of tea.

"So what do you want Marge?" Her voice was soft.

"I know a thing or two about your family that you may want kept quiet, if you get my drift." Marge's bloodshot eyes looked shifty under her nicotine-yellowed fringe. Her claw-like fingers clutched Gangan's arm.

"Your Peggy's on our side. We've had some interesting chats with her, Mrs Cameron and I."

"Peggy should know better than stoop to pick up rubbish." Gangan shook off the bony fingers impatiently.

Marge goggled at her.

"Just go," said Gangan. "And take your bad energy with you." She ushered Marge out and shut the front door with a bang, leaning against it as if she expected Marge to try and get back in through the keyhole.

"You'll be sorry you didn't listen…" we heard Marge say.

I wondered what it was that Peggy had been telling them. Why would she talk to people like Marge or Mrs Cameron? None of it made sense.

Gangan was sweeping the kitchen with a small brush made of blackberry twigs, going round the four walls and then down the hall. Then she sprinkled the kitchen, hall and front doorstep with water from a blue glass bottle.

"Rose water – it clears the negative energy," she said, drying her hands on her apron.

I wondered where Peggy was. I'd noticed her room was empty this morning – the door standing wide open. Peggy herself had been behaving oddly. She'd taken time off work – something she never did and then two days ago she'd left the house early, dressed in the navy suit she kept for special occasions.

Something had changed. There was a prickly atmosphere in the house like you get before a thunderstorm. Another of those letters had arrived, together with one in a brown envelope that said 'solicitor' on it. I didn't know what a solicitor was, but I didn't like the taste of the word like those nasty rubbery tablets I'd had once when Peggy took me to the doctors with a throat infection. I remember how annoyed Gangan was that Peggy had gone behind her back – she'd been treating my sore throat with a mixture of crushed garlic and honey.

"You don't want that mucky stuff," she'd said, throwing the tablets on the fire where they'd burned with a greenish light.

Jasmine was back but she hadn't seen the letters yet.

That was another odd thing. Jasmine's door was tightly shut – I'd been up to check because sometimes if she was still in bed, she'd hold back the red velvet bedspread so I could get under it and snuggle up with her for a while, inhaling the comforting smells of Chanel perfume, Floris soap and gin.

Today there was no sound of any music playing, but Jasmine was awake and out of bed. I could hear her scrabbling through drawers and cupboards like a pet rabbit sorting through its bedding.

"Got to get away, got to get away," I heard her whisper over and over as I put my ear to a crack in the door.

I wondered how she'd react when she saw the letters

and if she meant what she said about buying a gypsy caravan.

Gangan called me back to the kitchen and I went slowly down the stairs. The kitchen windows were running with condensation and the room smelled of hot toast and bubbling porridge. Gangan put a bowl of porridge in front of me sprinkled with brown sugar and sat with me while I ate it, sipping a mug of tea.

There was another knock at the door – more of a gentle tap – gan   gan .

"If it's that Marge again…" I didn't hear the rest of what Gangan said as she was walking towards the front door. She was followed back by two sets of footsteps – one delicate and clip-cloppy that I recognised as Dorothy, Teresa's mother – and the other light and skippy.

"… so if it's not too much trouble…" Dorothy was saying.

"Easier to look after two than one, dear," said Gangan comfortably. "And you know how pleased Fable will be."

Dorothy smiled her tight smile.

"Like she's got the wind," Gangan used to say.

"Be a good girl, now, Teresa," said Dorothy primly. She didn't kiss her goodbye.

I hugged Teresa, full of excitement that we had the whole day to play together. I had no idea it would be the last time I'd see her.

We played an elaborate game of weddings and funerals – creating wedding veils from an old piece of net curtain Gangan gave us and cutting up small pieces of coloured paper for confetti. We got out my tea set and created a wedding breakfast from all the play food in the doll's house.

"What if the bride died at the wedding," said Teresa.

So we laid the doll bride in a box lined with Gangan's

black velvet shawl and sang hymns.

"The nuns at school say we should lie like this in bed," said Teresa. She laid down and crossed her hands on her chest. "It's so that if we die during the night, the Lord knows we've confessed our sins and we'll go to Heaven and not Hell."

"Gangan doesn't believe in Hell," I said.

"That's because you're heathens," said Teresa comfortingly. "Never mind, you can't help it."

"Do you two girls want to make some little cakes?" Gangan shouted up the stairs – so we spent a happy hour or so making cakes and squeezing names and patterns on them in pink icing.

While we were busy with this, I heard Gangan in the hall talking to Jasmine about the letters. She'd reacted violently when she'd seen them, stabbing at them with the embroidery scissors she had in her hand.

"He can't just take Fable away, dear. Now come and eat something – just a bit of toast, that's a good girl."

Jasmine had come into the kitchen, but she hadn't eaten the toast Gangan made for her. She sat huddled in Gangan's purple shawl by the crackling fire, cuddling Magpie on her lap, staring vacantly at the flames as if she could see another world there.

I wondered why people I didn't know were writing letters about me. Something scary was happening and it felt as if the threads of my life were unravelling as easily as my hair got loose from its plaits on school days.

Something was out of place – like that time Teresa's Dad had taken us both to the park to play on the swings a few months ago.

He'd left us for a few moments to go and buy cigarettes, leaving us in the small play area surrounded by horse chestnuts

– their creamy candles blazing. Teresa and I swung to and fro on the red painted swings and then hopped off, deciding to have a go at the see-saw.

A man in a white greasy raincoat had come to talk to us.

"Sisters are yer?"

He had bad breath and his few remaining teeth were stained brown.

We ignored him.

"Yer Dad said you was to go and meet him over by the wood. I'll take yer – we'll find some conkers on the way."

Teresa and I looked at each other. We both knew it wasn't time for conkers. Earlier, Teresa had picked up one of the creamy horse chestnut flowers. When you looked at them, they weren't white or cream, but a mixture of cream, bright pink, orange and yellow.

The man stood there, holding out his hands to us. We'd run out of the play area separately – racing across to where Patrick stood chatting outside the cigarette kiosk.

Patrick had reacted angrily, swearing he'd separate the man from his breath if he got hold of him – but by the time we got back to the play area he was nowhere to be seen. I never felt the same about the swings after that – there was always that nasty feeling of being watched.

I had that feeling the day after Teresa's visit when I was back at school. Teresa had gone home after tea and we'd kissed each other and said we'd be friends forever. After all – we were nearly sisters weren't we?

I didn't want to be back at school after such a magical day, but Gangan said it was for the best.

"You could get in trouble for not sending her," she told Jasmine. "At least they can't say you've neglected her schooling."

I sat in school in the cold classroom, feeling as if I had cotton wool inside my head instead of a brain. We were learning the nine times multiplication table and I was the only one in the class who got it wrong. The word 'wrong' tasted like tinned peaches which I liked – so why was wrong a bad word?

I joined the queue of children in the hall for school dinner, but I didn't feel like eating beef stew, carrots and mashed potato. I was like Jasmine when I felt anxious – it was as if there was a steel doorway in my throat making swallowing difficult.

"Very small please," I said holding my thick white plate out to the dinner lady.

She dolloped a large helping of stew onto my plate followed by a huge spoonful of lumpy mashed potato.

I sat at a table by myself picking at my dinner– most of the other children had finished theirs and gone out to play. The stew had gone cold, forming a skin as it did so. I hated lukewarm food.

"You won't grow if you don't eat your dinner." A large overall-clad dinner lady tried the jovial approach first.

I tried and failed to swallow a small forkful.

"Eat it." She stood over me as I did so.

The room had grown suddenly hot and had the feeling as if I was on a fairground ride that was slowing down, spinning in slow motion.

I was violently sick all over her big feet.

"I don't know why I bother doing this job," she chuntered as she cleared up the mess and took me to sit outside the head teacher's office with a few other kids who weren't feeling well. "Why didn't you say you felt sick?"

I didn't bother to answer and in the end she went away.

I watched as the children in the playground lined up when the bell went, ready to go into afternoon school. I knew I wasn't ill – I just needed to get home. When the last child had filed in and the teacher turned away, brass bell in hand, I saw my chance and ran out of the door, across the playground and out through the gate.

As soon as I'd left the shelter of the school building I realised how cold it was outside – there was no chance of getting my duffle coat with its nice snug hood. I'd have had to go to the coat pegs for that and someone would be bound to ask what I was doing.

The frost had melted from the pavements leaving them looking glazed on the top like Gangan's special lemon sponge. Icy drops of water dripped from the bushes and the air nipped sharply at my face and hands as I walked as quickly as I could without slipping over.

It was only when I was halfway home that I remembered what Gangan once said about waiting for someone to collect me. It was only then that it dawned on me that she wasn't worried about me getting run over by a car. She'd had the same dream as me about the man in the dripping darkness of that tunnel where stories were stolen away. I looked warily at every parked car, thinking again about that man in the greasy raincoat in the play area – and the shadowy image of the man who wrote those letters about me to Jasmine; the man who called himself my father who wanted to steal me away.

I played a version of that game where you don't tread on the lines on the way home – except that this time I approached each corner warily, making sure that nobody was lying in wait. I walked in the middle of the path so I couldn't be snatched by a passing car or leapt on from an alleyway.

I felt a sense of relief when I got to the corner of our

road with the familiar corner shop exuding the combined smells of floor polish, bacon, freshly-baked bread and aniseed balls. If I'd had some money in my pocket, I'd have gone in and bought some sweets. Like Jasmine, relief had made me feel hungry. I felt I could eat anything that was put in front of me now.

The sense of relief soon faded as I saw the gaggle of women gathered opposite our house – Mrs Cameron in the lead.

For once, the attention wasn't focused on our house. The women were staring at Teresa's house. It had been occupied this morning when I left with Gangan to go to school – Cathy had waved to me from the front doorstep as she put the milk bottles out. Now it was empty – the curtainless windows like sightless eyes. Even Dorothy's small wooden angel that stood in the hall window was gone. The only trace left behind to show the family had ever lived there was an old pair of red Wellingtons that used to belong to Teresa. Everything else was gone. The black patch of road where Patrick's car used to stand was already frosting over.

I ran the last few yards on legs that felt like jelly, banging on the door as hard as I could.

I heard Gangan's voice. "Come on now, Jasmine dear. There's nothing broken that can't be fixed."

She looked surprised to see me. "Fable, lamb, how did you get here?"

She looked up and down the street as she let me in. "I'd go and look for your mother if I knew where she'd be."

"Teresa…"

"Teresa's gone, dear. They had to. And I dare say Jasmine's trying to find him. It's a bad business, a bad business." She pulled me indoors and into the kitchen, holding

- 79 -

me close, warming my frozen hands and feet as she rubbed them with her work-roughened hands.

"Teresa left this for you," she said when I'd warmed up a little and was sipping a cup of warm milk.

I couldn't eat anything now– not even a slice of Gangan's best chocolate cake.

I put my hand into the crumpled white paper bag she gave me and pulled out the silver St Christopher Teresa had worn ever since her first communion. As Gangan put it round my neck I thought how odd Teresa would feel without it.

"She said you could give it back when she saw you again."

My stiff muscles relaxed a little as I tried to believe we would see each other again.

"They had debts up to their eyeballs and some of the people were getting difficult. So much for all the fancy jobs he was supposed to have… it was all a web of deceit…"

I sat staring into the fire as Jasmine had a couple of nights ago – trying to see pictures in the flames as she had, feeling I was in the middle of a nasty dream. I had no idea then that things were going to get much worse.

CHAPTER NINE

I remember that last night at Gangan's house as a series of black and white photos, the sound muffled as if the action was taking place under water.

Just after it got dark, there was a loud thumping on the front door..

Gangan was as calm as ever. "That'll be Jasmine," she said. "Grief does funny things to people."

She shuffled along the hallway in her slippers, calling out: "Come on in, love. There's nothing that can't be put right."

I followed behind. My only experience of grief had been when Magpie's brother Clarence had died and I'd come down that morning to find him stiff and cold in his basket by the fire. At first I'd thought he was asleep, but then I realised I'd never see him wake up and stretch his sleek black body ever again or jump up on my lap to have the white flash under his chin tickled.

I remembered having a prickling sensation at the back of my nose, and trying to swallow what felt like a huge lump in my throat just before it spilled over into tears, but I couldn't remember throwing anything. Gangan had sat me on her lap and told me to have a good cry if that's what helped me and she told me that Clarence's spirit – the best part of him – had gone on to live somewhere else.

"You'll see him again one day, Fable," she'd said, "and everyone else you grow to love in this life. You'll see them again."

I couldn't understand what Jasmine had to be upset about. As I saw it, I'd got more reason to be upset because I'd just lost my best friend but I followed Gangan along the hall, carrying Alicia, the rag doll Jasmine had made for me. As Gangan reached the front door and opened it, I expected to see Jasmine there, black hair wild and lipsticked mouth stretched in a yell like it was sometimes when she'd drunk too much gin.

Gangan opened the front door letting in a chilly blast of frosty air and a skitter of dry leaves. Jasmine wasn't there.

A brick struck the corner of the house and ricocheted off into a blackened clump of dahlias in the garden next door. I peered into the darkness, suddenly noticing the semi circle of women standing in the road outside our house. Mrs Cameron was the first in line with Marge Henderson next to her. None of them were dressed for a fight and must've been frozen in their pinafores and thin shoes.

Gangan took no notice of the women. She peered into the gloom shouting for Jasmine.

"Murderer," shouted Marge Henderson, throwing a half brick that fell short of our gate, skidding along the icy road.

The women stepped forward, moving unsteadily on the ice before being scattered like skittles as a black Morris Oxford turned into our street, headlights blazing.

Peggy stepped out of the shadows near the gate looking unlike herself in the unfamiliar pancake make-up she was wearing, her red lipsticked mouth looking like a gash in the middle of her pinched face.

Nothing today was making sense. I'd never seen Peggy wear make-up before.

"Yes, Lily, it's me," she hissed. "And today is Judgement Day. I told you I'd get revenge on you for the way you stole my house."

"Peggy, I didn't steal it. Your father left it to me, provided I still gave you a home."

Peggy's face twisted with malice. "I still say you killed

him and you stole what was rightfully mine. I always said you'd rue the day – and I meant it." She turned as a tall man dressed in black stepped out of the car and came towards the house.

The semi circle of women edged backwards, watching from the safety of a low brick wall opposite, eager for gossip.

"Our bags are in the hall," Peggy told the man.

Gangan stepped back into the house, holding me close. "Peg, what've you done? You can't uproot this child from her life here. Think what it'll do to Jasmine."

"I'm thinking," said Peggy with an evil grin. "And I can't wait."

The man loaded two brown suitcases into the car.

Then he came and spoke to me, crouching down so his face was at the same level as mine. He had brown eyes that looked hard as bullets with flecks of blood in the whites of them. He smelled of peppermints and stale tobacco.

"I'm your father, Fable. I've come to take you home."

I turned my face away, clinging onto Gangan. "I don't want to go with you. I don't like you."

"You don't know me yet." His smile didn't reach his eyes.

He and Peggy dragged me away from Gangan. My father picked me up, carrying me under one arm, like I carried Alicia. My head was hanging downwards like those ducks and chickens that hung outside butchers' shops. I could see the patterns of ice on the pavement and feel the sweat on my father's hands as he held me. He opened the car door and pushed me onto the back seat, locking the door. I beat on the windows as Gangan hobbled down the path towards me.

"Don't fret, lamb," she shouted. "We'll see each other again in this life."

"Don't forget my bags," shouted Peggy as Derek walked

away from her. "You promised to take me with you."

"I did no such thing," he said as he got into the driver's seat and started the engine.

I was screaming and trying to get out. The doors were locked.

Peggy ran after the car yelling 'stop Derek' at the top of her voice.

She slipped on the pavement and didn't get up. I couldn't see Gangan.

We turned left at the corner of the road towards the railway station. Jasmine was coming towards us, black hair wild flinging her arms wide in an effort to make my father stop the car.

"Bastard," she screamed. "Don't take my baby away."

He didn't stop – just drove on into the black night.

*

On the journey I remember the smell of the leather seats, mixed with the mildewed smell of old books. We stopped at an all night café where leather clad bikers and lorry drivers ate bacon sandwiches and drank coffee as they fed coins into a juke box.

A Beatles song floated on the greasy air, reminding me poignantly of Jasmine. My father held tightly to my hand and I held on tightly to my rag doll, Alicia.

"I'll get you a glass of milk, hmm?"

I shook my head.

"You'll feel better if you eat something."

He drank a coffee, his hand shaking. I noticed how he'd put three paper packs of sugar into it and how some of the leather-clad bikers looked at us oddly.

I didn't even try to eat the cheese sandwich he bought me. I made a break for freedom, running without knowing where I was going, having a near miss with a car as I ran across a busy road - the headlights, like the eyes of a wild animal dangerously close. My father caught me easily and tossed me into the back of his car. If anybody noticed they didn't say anything. They almost seemed frightened of him because of the funny white back-to-front collar he wore.

It wasn't until we were on our way again, I realised I'd let go of Alicia's hand when I'd tried to escape. I imagined her lost in the darkness, feeling scared without me to look after her, not knowing where I'd gone or why I'd abandoned her.

I cried until my throat ached and my eyes felt stiff and sore. I shouted that I didn't want to go with him. I wanted to be with Gangan and Jasmine not a nasty old man like him. I wanted him to go back to that café for my dolly.

He didn't answer me, although his long fingers turned white on the black steering wheel – and he didn't turn back.

Eventually we arrived at a cold, dark house. He carried me up to a bedroom with walls painted dull beige. The blankets on the bed were damp. He brought up my suitcases – obviously packed by Peggy because she'd put in my least favourite clothes and none of my toys.

I began crying again because I missed Alicia desperately and knew I'd never see her again, just as I might never see Gangan or Jasmine again.

"I can buy you another dolly."

I knew then that he'd never understand me and that I'd never truly think of him as my father.

*

The vicarage was old – Victorian gothic my father said - with funny pointy windows like a house I saw on a cinema billboard for a horror film. Lying in my damp bed at night I heard strange creaks and groans and there was a place along the mildewed corridor that led to the bathroom that grew unnaturally cold sometimes. Gangan had told me about cold spots in houses and I knew what they meant.

"It means it's haunted," I said.

"There's no such thing as ghosts," Derek said with a superior smile, but I could tell he'd seen and heard things just as I had. The graveyard with its lichened headstones went almost down to the river Avon.

I knew Derek had nightmares because I heard him shouting about perishing by fire or flood.

"… the dead will be washed from their graves", I heard him shout over and over, like a record that had got stuck night after night.

The old people in the parish were full of stories about the floods of 1947 – when the Avon rose at the rate of six inches in every half hour and those living in cottages nearest the water carried their most treasured possessions upstairs before the river got in and destroyed or carried away the rest. Some had escaped in boats and others had waited several days before the flood levels fell, managing as best they could.

"Why are you frightened of drowning?" I asked.

Derek glared and said he had no concerns about it at all.

"Why do you shout things in your sleep?"

"I never have nightmares," he said. "You must've imagined it."

I wondered why he bothered to lie about his feelings.

If one colour described the vicarage it would be brown. Scratched brown furniture stood on cheap nylon carpets or brown lino. Faded brown curtains hung at the dirty windows and in the kitchen there was no lampshade – just a dim bulb hanging from the worn flex.

There were snowdrops growing amongst the graves when I first moved to Isbourne and I was reminded of a story Gangan once told about a woman who had her identity stolen by the Duchess of Ice.

That was how I felt the first time Derek took me into the clammy, musty smelling church. This wasn't really me – Fable Rose – this was happening to someone else. Soon I'd wake up in my bedroom at Starlight and be my true self again.

I remember some of the conversations I had with Derek that went round in frustrating circles and got nowhere.

"I want to go home."

"This is your home now. Soon there'll be other boys and girls to share it with – children with backgrounds like yours who need to learn about the love of the Lord Jesus and the Christian faith. If your mother had been sensible, she could've shared this with me – guiding other women back to the true faith."

I'd overheard him talking to someone about his plans for the Vicarage – and I knew what people were saying about it.

"I hear the vicar's trying to save fallen women," one old man said to another as they talked at the end of the service.

"That's a good 'un," said the other. "Ask him to save me one if he finds any. There's life in the old dog yet."

My response to my father was always the same. "I want to go back to Gangan and Jasmine."

"Your mother is in hospital," he said patiently, not quite looking me in the eye. "She can't cope with you. She's ill in her mind."

"I'll stay with Gangan, then."

"She's not a blood relative. I am. I love you, Fable and you must learn not to be so stubborn."

"I don't love you." I swore a special oath, using a pinprick of blood (Teresa and I had done this once when we swore to be friends forever) that I would never ever love him because of what he'd done to me.

I had to start a new school. This time the uniform was navy blue – reminding me of the suit Peggy wore for special occasions. I hated this uniform worse than the last one. It felt itchy and smelled of sick. I still hated school, but I hated being at the vicarage more.

The other children tried to be friendly and several of them invited me home for tea – but I didn't want to go. The only friend I wanted was Teresa. I wore her St Christopher under my school blouse and wished we could be together again.

I overheard Derek talking to someone about me. "She's settling in well but things are bound to be strange for her with the sort of dysfunctional situation she was in."

I tasted the word dysfunctional – and it conjured up the taste of liver and onions – with the onions soft and caramelised like Gangan cooked them.

I decided I'd rather be dysfunctional than how Derek wanted me to be.

The headmistress at school was concerned because I was so quiet – introverted she called it – and arranged for me to see an educational psychologist.

The psychologist looked like the giraffe on the wall-hanging in my bedroom at Starlight – the one Jasmine made me when I was a baby. One bedtime, Gangan and I made up voices for all the animals and decided on the songs they'd sing. We thought the lion would have a deep growly voice and sing 'Old Man River', the monkey would sound chattery and sing 'She'll Be Coming Round The Mountain' and the giraffe would sing 'One Potato, Two Potato, Three Potato, Four' in a cracked falsetto voice.

He sat behind his desk, with his fingers steepled like Derek did sometimes when he was thinking about a sermon, looking seriously at me through silver rimmed glasses. I was surprised when he eventually spoke that his voice was low pitched and smooth as melted chocolate.

"Are you under any pressure at school, Fable? Are you happy there?"

"Of course she's not under any pressure. How could she be?" Derek ran his finger round the inside of his clerical collar. He'd insisted on coming into the room with me. "She's highly strung and has a vivid imagination which should be curbed."

The educational psychologist scribbled something on a piece of paper. I never saw him again.

Shortly after this, Derek advertised for a housekeeper. The avalanche of fallen women he expected to flock to his Rescue Centre had failed to show up. A woman called Sheila and her son, Nathan, moved in. Things went from bad to worse. Previously, an old woman from one of the cottages in Isbourne had come in every day to clean. She'd run a greasy mop over the floors, leaving lumps of grey fluff in the corners, scrubbed the toilet with bleach and left us something for dinner – a pasty from the local bakers or a bit of bacon which Derek cooked in a blackened frying pan.

When Sheila moved in, even the food got nastier. Worst of all, Nathan was at the same school as me and he tried to get into Derek's good books by telling tales on me.

"She never talks to anyone," he said. "Just stands all break time by herself, staring into space."

Then I'd get a telling off for not being friendlier or for being awkward and not fitting in with other people. I didn't want to fit in here. I wanted to go home to Gangan.

I decided to run away.

Derek had given me pocket money every week since I'd been in Isbourne. He'd also bought me a dolly with golden hair.

"Better than that other thing you had," he'd said.

I hated the dolly – she wasn't real like Alicia was – and I didn't even bother to take her out of the box, shoving it face down under my bed. Derek got the hint eventually and gave her to the local hospital.

I planned my escape carefully, emptying out my school bag and putting in clean socks and knickers and a thick jumper. I'd planned my route in easy stages, looking at a rail map in Derek's study, hoping I'd have enough money. I walked on shaking legs to Isbourne station, hoping nobody would see me and wonder why I wasn't at school. I knew I'd be happier once I got to London. I wasn't sure what I'd do when I got to Paddington, but at least I'd be free and there'd be someone to ask.

I sat on a bench in the waiting room, watching the slow tick of the clock, hoping the train would come soon. I watched it snake into the station and stop, heard the doors fling open before I hurried out of the waiting room towards the nearest carriage.

As I stepped up, I was grabbed from behind and swung off my feet. My school bag skidded across the platform, making an old lady pushing a loaded trolley swerve.

"It's no use running away, Fable," said my father. "You've nowhere to go."

*

We went home in silence. He never discussed my escape attempt or bothered to ask why I was unhappy.

"You ought to be ashamed of yourself," said Sheila as

she minced cold gristly beef for cottage pie. "Your father has enough worries with the parish without you being inconsiderate."

I took no notice of her.

She had bleached blonde hair with black roots showing and something about her uneven teeth and whining voice reminded me of Marge Henderson. I hadn't stopped thinking about Marge or the lies she'd told about Gangan.

The only good thing was, Derek didn't stop giving me pocket money – and I never gave up the idea of escaping.

I hid my piggy bank under the jumpers at the bottom of my wardrobe. Nathan was always snooping around the place and I didn't trust him. He was fat and blond with bulging blue eyes, smelled of sweaty socks and reminded me of the picture of George IV in my school history book.

My only consolation was the money I was saving to be able to get out of here. Then one terrible day I reached for my piggy bank and discovered it was empty. I knew there was two pounds fifteen shillings and sixpence in it because I'd only counted it two days ago.

Sheila was dusting the landing windowsills and Nathan was watching her with a smirk on his face, lounging insolently against a bookcase.

"Did you take my money, Nathan?" I asked.

I knew by the look on his face that he had.

I shoved him out of the way and pushed open the door to his room – Sheila never made him tidy it, although she never stopped nagging me to tidy mine. His room smelled of unwashed P E kit and old plimsolls. The drawers were untidily packed and overflowing and there were torn comics and dirty cups all over the floor. Sheila never let me have drinks in my bedroom.

Nathan came storming after me as I opened the door of his tallboy. I pulled open the top drawer. It was full of money. I counted it feverishly, knowing it was mine because it was the exact amount that I'd lost. Only two days ago, Nathan had been complaining he had no money left – so how had he come by this other than by taking mine?

I flew at him, scratching and pulling at his hair.

"Thief! Bastard."

Sheila screamed. Derek raced up the stairs.

"We can't prove this either way. It's your word against Nathan's, Fable. You can't put your name on coins. And I won't have you swearing like that."

Nathan looked smug as Derek divided the coins between us.

"No more arguments now," he said. "You've both got the same."

It was yet another thing I wouldn't forgive him for.

*

Derek lied to me about Jasmine. He told me she was in hospital and that she'd never come out. I knew he was lying because I saw her in church. I'd crept in there one day to get away from Nathan. The only lesson at school that I liked was painting and drawing and I had a project to finish. Nathan never bothered much about his schoolwork but he took great delight in wrecking mine. On several occasions he'd ripped up essays I'd written – Sheila saw him do it once, but wouldn't admit that she had when Derek asked her.

I didn't like the church any better than I liked the vicarage, but it was cool after the September heat outside and it was safe because Nathan would never come in here. He said churches gave him the creeps.

It took a few moments for my eyes to adjust to the

faded light.

Jasmine was by the altar, ripping petals from the red chrysanthemums and yellow dahlias in a large pedestal arrangement and placing them in patterns to make her name. She'd written her name in red chalk above the altar. She was wearing a long white dress and her dark hair was loose, falling across her face as she worked.

She'd just finished when the church door was flung open with a loud creak, letting in a wide slice of golden light.

My father raced in, followed by two policemen.

Jasmine stood up, scattering the remaining petals around her bare feet. "I want Fable back, Derek. You stole her."

"You're not fit to look after her. The courts agreed."

"You didn't give me a chance to fight back."

She caught sight of me and we ran towards each other. I was smothered by her warm arms and hot kisses as she said over and over again about how much she loved me and how one day we'd be together and nothing would split us apart.

"I love you Jasmine," I said.

The policemen came and took her, their pudgy fingers biting into the brown flesh of her arms.

I heard a voice screaming at them to let go of her – she was my mother and I loved her. Everything went black and when I woke up I was lying in my bed in the vicarage.

Derek was trying to give me water from a cracked pink mug. The white sheets felt cold and clammy on my sweating skin.

"Where's Jasmine?"

He looked sadly at me. "As I've said before, you have a vivid imagination, Fable. Your mother wasn't here."

A few days later, I went into the church. I could still faintly see tiny patches of red chalk above the altar. The altar flowers had been changed to a yellow and white arrangement, but under one of the pews, a handful of red petals still remained to confirm the story.

I didn't care what Derek said. I knew what I'd seen. My mother was there and she still loved me.

CHAPTER TEN

Something Cara said one day after school conjured up the smell of hawthorn blossom, drawing me back to the summer I was sixteen – a time I wanted to re-live and erase from my memory in equal measure.

Cara had come home from school, tossing her red canvas school bag down in the hall and hooking her black ski jacket over the newel post at the bottom of the stairs in a way that drove Tony mad.

"It makes the place look like a junk shop," he complained. "You're as bad, Fable, the way you leave all your stuff about."

What he classed as 'my stuff' was things like mending (mainly buttons off his shirts) and ironing, both of which I hated and so left as long as possible.

"You're absolutely no good at housework," he said. I wish I had a pound for every time he'd said it since we'd been married. It hadn't seemed to matter at first. The balls of fluff that gathered under the sideboard had been a joke at one time, although he'd never offered to help with housework or cooking. He'd only gone food shopping once since Cara was born and he'd come back, reaching for the aspirins saying it had been the most stressful event of his day.

A defiant streak inside me that's been gaining strength since the Winter Solstice demanded to know why not being good at housework was a crime.

I remembered hearing a radio interview with Agony Aunt Claire Rayner where she said that she'd told her children early on in their lives that she hadn't been born with a mop in one hand and a broom in the other and they were to keep their own rooms tidy.

Even so, I still didn't feel brave enough to answer Tony back. I had a feeling that my new reserves of strength would crumble under his ice-cold glare. Thankfully, he was still at work. In one hour he'd be home and I'd need to tread carefully until I knew what sort of mood he was in. I'd just done the weekly shop, trying to keep the cost as low as I could. Sometimes he'd record the bill without comment in his account book. Other times he'd scrutinise every item and I'd have to justify why I'd needed to buy rice or flour or Tampax, feeling like a naughty schoolgirl who'd forgotten her homework as I stood there beside him. He constantly questioned why I needed to get a taxi home, feeling that I should make two trips and carry the bags home myself rather than waste five pounds a week.

Cara was rooting through the newly stocked fridge – her black-trousered bum sticking out. She emerged with two cream cheese triangles, which she proceeded to spread on a bread roll, followed by a thick layer of chocolate spread.

"Cara – that's disgusting."

"You kidding, Mum – it's great."

She shook her head when I offered her tea and I noticed she'd already opened a can of Coke. At this rate the fridge would be empty by the weekend and Tony would whinge about there never being anything interesting to eat.

I reflected that it was funny how Cara called me Mum when we were alone together, but it was always 'Ma' when Tony or her friends were around. I also wondered whether it was the notebook that was making me more sensitive to things.

"Good day?" I asked.

She shrugged and tossed back her curtain of blonde hair. "Okay, I s'pose. History was boring. The only thing I can remember is Miss Watts saying how her mother said white flowers were unlucky. And how red and white flowers shouldn't be given to brides 'cos it was like blood on bandages and that was unlucky too…"

*

I didn't listen to the rest of what Cara was saying. In my mind I was walking out of the vicarage and along the path that led to the river. Sheila had just thrown a tantrum because someone had put a spray of hawthorn blossom in a vase on the hall table.

"White flowers are unlucky," she screamed as soon as she clapped eyes on me. "Especially May blossom. How could you have been so stupid as to bring it indoors, Fable?"

"I didn't do it."

"It must've been you. Nathan wouldn't do anything like that and I'm sure your father wouldn't."

"I didn't do it. I've only just got home from school." I went up to my bedroom that overlooked the graveyard. The river looked smooth as olive oil in the May sunshine. I needed to get out of the musty-smelling, stifling atmosphere of the Vicarage. I changed into my black cotton caftan with the pink and gold embroidery and the leather sandals a friend had passed on to me that laced up around my ankles, brushing my hair out of the single plait I usually wore for school so that it hung loose over my shoulders, glinting copper in the sun. As I went downstairs I heard Derek come home.

"Did you find that blossom I picked for you?" I heard him ask Sheila as he went into his study.

She didn't answer him.

She glowered at me when I came downstairs but didn't apologise for what she'd said. A few minutes later I heard her banging pots and pans around in the kitchen.

I left the vicarage by the back door and headed towards

the path that led to the river. I had a project to do for art and had the idea of using leaf shapes to create an abstract painting. At the bottom of the garden I could smell cut grass and rosemary, which made me think of Gangan and the herbs she used to grow.

"A sprig of rosemary under your pillow stops bad dreams," she used to say.

Gangan had also travelled to Isbourne to try to get me back, but she'd failed just as Jasmine had.

As before, Derek had denied she'd ever been here.

"I'm afraid to tell you that she died," he said solemnly. "She hasn't answered your letters, has she?"

I'd written to her every week since I'd been here, but as Derek said, there'd been no reply. I knew that all the time she had breath in her body, she'd have written back. Despite what Derek said, I didn't believe that Gangan was dead. The bond between us was so strong that I knew I'd feel it somehow if she'd moved on to the Garden of Souls. I also knew I had to keep her memory alive and that, if I continued to believe, I'd see her again in this life like she'd promised I would.

On this May afternoon, I walked slowly along the narrow pathway bordered by woodland and edged with Queen Anne's lace, breathing in the scent of elderflower and hawthorn blossom, remembering Gangan's elderflower champagne. She'd scour the local lanes, collecting the creamy blossoms in a large canvas bag. When we got home, the next part of the process involved a large plastic bucket, hot water, ginger, sugar and a lot of stirring and wish-making.

A week or so later, with great ceremony, the mixture was siphoned into a glass jar - a "bellyjohn" Gangan called it with a chuckle, waiting for Peggy to say in her prim, precise way: "Demijohn, Lily, I've told you before. It's a demijohn."

Gangan kept her fermenting wine in the airing cupboard on the landing, where it bubbled and spat, usually with no ill effects. However, one night there was a loud explosion and Peggy rushed out of her room shouting that the bomb had gone off.

I smiled at the memory of seeing Peggy in hairnet and nightgown squawking like a headless chicken, all set to evacuate the house while Gangan clicked her tongue at the waste of good champagne as she mopped out the bottom of the airing cupboard and cleared up the broken glass.

Gangan wouldn't have May blossom in the house either.

"Very unlucky," she'd say.

I was just wondering whether to do something childish like pick some and smuggle a sprig under Sheila's pillow – just to pay her back for not apologising to me – when I was aware of someone watching me.

A boy dressed in jeans and leather jacket was staring at me from the shelter of a coppice of trees a bit further along the path. It reminded me of the time when I was a child, walking in woodland with Gangan and Jasmine, and coming face to face with a deer. The deer had stood and stared at us, but as soon as I turned away, he was gone.

The same thing happened this time. I dropped my gaze to the cracked mud of the footpath and when I looked back at the clump of trees, the boy had gone.

I picked a few field maple leaves, just so that Sheila couldn't dispute why I'd been wandering by the river.

Just lately she'd been picking on everything I did – from the little bell I wore round my neck that I'd bought from a market stall in Isbourne to my friendship with a girl called Kirsty who'd been the only person since Teresa that I'd really counted as a best friend.

Sheila didn't like the music I played – although she never complained about Nathan's. I'd bought a second hand record player from a boy at school – the arm was dodgy so it had a penny glued onto it to weight it – and I played songs like Scott Mackenzie's 'San Francisco' and my 'Woodstock' single, dreaming one day of breaking free and going to these places, imagining myself in bikini and sunglasses strolling along a sunlit boulevard in California.

The boy was waiting for me a bit further along the path, watching me through narrowed eyes so that I felt myself going hot. Beyond him I could see a shiny black motorbike hidden amongst the bushes and I remembered something the verger said the other day about 'undesirables' hanging around by the river. I wished I hadn't come down here. I was trapped in a narrow green and white corridor surrounded by the intoxicating soapy smell of hawthorn blossom.

As I walked slowly, focusing on the dappled patterns made by the sun through the trees that bordered the path, I wondered what Kirsty would do. She was a lot more sophisticated than me. She said she'd kissed seven boys. One of them felt her breasts and another had put his hand down her knickers and touched her.

"It's a great feeling," she'd said, tossing her hair and squinting in the mirror in the school toilets as she applied grey eye-liner before we walked home. She wore pale lipstick and had a figure like Twiggy even though she was always eating.

"What was it like?"

"I didn't want him to stop, but he hadn't got anything and I don't want a baby so he had to. Come on – me Mum'll be mad if I'm not there to look after the other kids."

We'd left the toilets and hurried home. A hundred

unanswered questions burned inside my head.

Now, I glanced quickly at the boy. Our eyes met and I felt myself growing hot as he smiled at me. I felt my heart race. His light brown hair curled over the collar of his jacket and was ruffled by a light breeze coming off the river. There were grass stains on his faded denim jeans.

He looked at the handful of leaves I was carrying.

"What're you doing?" His voice was deep and musical.

"Just something for school." As soon as the words were out of my mouth I realised how stupid they sounded. Kirsty would've made up something that sounded really cool.

"Nature table do you mean?"

"I'm not a kid."

His eyes swept over the fullness of my breasts and I felt stupid again.

"No, I can see that." His voice was full of laughter.

"I'm doing a painting – an abstract. I wanted the leaves for inspiration." That sounded better.

He looked interested, sweeping another look over me as if seeing me differently.

We were down by the river now – I could feel the cool grass against my bare legs. He hadn't gone away – but then neither had I. He was wearing a pale blue shirt under his leather jacket, open at the throat where I could see a silver St Christopher as large as a half-crown. His eyes were green flecked with hazel, reminding me of a William pear.

Further away I could hear the sound of heavy boots tripping over tree roots. I had a sudden panic that Nathan might turn up, smirking nastily at all the tales he could tell about me to Derek.

"Tobias, where the fuck are you?" shouted a rough voice a short distance away. "We've finished now."

"Christ…" He turned in the direction of the voice. "Give us a few minutes to get clear. Sorry – can't explain…"

As he handed me a few hawthorn leaves he'd picked, our fingers touched. His felt warm and rough against mine.

He raced away from me back up the path. I heard the rub of motorbike tyres on mud and then the sound of him kick-starting the shiny black Norton 650 and the revving of the engine in the distance as it took off along the road towards Pershore.

The leaves he'd given me were still warm from his touch. He hadn't said anything about seeing me again but somehow I knew he would.

CHAPTER ELEVEN

At breakfast the next morning, Derek looked at Nathan and I over the top of his reading glasses and gave us a lecture about danger lurking near the river. Nathan was busy digging trenches in his porridge with his spoon and pouring in milk, just like a three year old would. He did the most disgusting things with his food but neither Sheila nor Derek ever said anything.

I took another spoonful of grey lumpy porridge the colour and texture of wallpaper paste.

"There's evidence of people dealing in drugs," Derek said. "The verger found a syringe when he was walking his dog. We must all be wary and vigilant."

I thought of the leaves Tobias had given me that I hadn't used for my painting, pressed carefully in the back of the Bible Derek had given me when I first came to live here.

While Derek went on about the danger of drugs, my thoughts drifted to the abstract painting I'd begun based on leaf shapes. Art was the only subject at school that I cared about. I liked the way a paint-loaded brush became the vehicle that took me to another place. I couldn't paint at the Vicarage of course. Despite the fact that the furniture and flooring was old and threadbare, Derek and Sheila wouldn't have paint in the bedrooms. In any case, any work that I did at home was likely to be damaged by Nathan. It was safer to stay at school late and do extra work there.

Miss Hetherington, the art teacher, was impressed with the work I put in.

"You've got a real flair for design and colour," she said, "and I'd really like to speak to your parents about you going on to Art College, Fable. I'll have a word at Parents' Evening."

"It won't do any good, Miss," I'd said softly.

"We'll see about that," she'd said grimly. "Some people make sweeping judgements about art simply because they don't know what's involved."

I knew it wouldn't do any good – Derek had already told me he expected me to do a secretarial course when I left school and forget any ideas about doing something airy fairy.

"You need to keep your feet firmly on the ground, Fable," he'd said one day when he'd found me sitting in the church and drawing a cartoon strip, not reading my Bible like he'd told me to. "Art and the imagination can be a dangerous thing. If it hadn't been for the grace of God I could've been swept away by it all. That weekend in Paris when I fell into the pit of temptation was a blessing in disguise. Your mother, alas, wasn't so lucky."

A vague memory stirred in my head of when I first heard the story of how Jasmine and Derek met.

I'd been about three or four at the time – digging in my little patch of garden that was next to Gangan's herb patch. She and Jasmine were sitting outside watching me, drinking tea and talking surrounded by the smell of bruised mint and the sound of bees droning lazily amongst starry blue borage flowers.

I'd planted orange marigolds, carrots and beetroot in rows surrounded by white alyssum and blue lobelia.

"That looks a real picture, Fable," Gangan said, sipping her tea.

"Better than anything her father did, that's for sure," said Jasmine with a harsh laugh.

"You loved him once," said Gangan gently, "and he's still Fable's father, You'll never change that, either of you, however much you fight."

"Love!"

Jasmine said nothing for a few minutes. Even the bees stopped droning as if they were waiting for what she had to say next.

"He could've been someone. The next artistic sensation – that's why I fell for him, because he was different – dangerous. Then we had that stupid argument and he took off on that trip to Paris. When he came back, I knew as soon as I saw him that everything had changed. He started going on about God and seeing the light and making amends for the way he'd behaved in the past."

Jasmine paused to take a swig of tea.

"I'd have gone along with whatever he wanted to do, so long as he let me be myself. But he couldn't let things rest, had this bee in his bonnet about starting a home for fallen women – and was insisting that I went through some sort of repentance and started going to church."

She laughed harshly, throwing back her head so that her cascade of hair almost touched the ground and her mouth became a wide pink gash in the middle of her face.

"Can you honestly see me in a tweed skirt and lace up shoes like Peggy ladling out soup to the poor and needy?"

She set down her mug so hard on the ground next to her that it almost cracked.

"He couldn't see that I had a right to be myself. That's why I told him to go."

*

A few afternoons later, I was down by the river again, ignoring what Derek had said about drug dealing and the like. We'd finished tea – sausage, lumpy mash and watery baked beans. Nathan was staying the night with a friend, Sheila had gone to her sister's and Derek was in his study writing a sermon. I should've been doing revision for my maths exam the following week, but a warm breeze was blowing through the flimsy purple curtains I'd found in a junk shop carrying with it the smell of hawthorn blossom, bringing back memories of a few nights ago and the touch of Tobias's fingers as he passed me the leaves.

I changed into my white cheesecloth dress with blue embroidery and brushed my hair until it crackled.

He was sitting on the riverbank throwing bits of his cheese sandwich to a family of ducklings. He'd taken off his leather jacket and was wearing jeans and a black t-shirt. He got to his feet when I reached him. I'd already noticed his black motorbike hidden in the bushes.

"Why d'you do that?" I asked.

"What?"

"Hide your bike. It makes it look as if you're up to no good."

He laughed, making his green-hazel eyes sparkle. "That bloke with the dog – did someone say he's a virgin – has got orders to shoot us on sight." He made machine gun noises as he pointed his hand at me.

I blushed at the word 'virgin'. In fact I blushed at a lot of things, which as Kirsty sometimes pointed out, made my face clash with my coppery hair. Kirsty never blushed at anything.

Nathan was always coming out with comments like:

"What do virgins have for breakfast?"

If you ignored him he'd say:

"So you're not one, then," and snort with laughter in that horrible way of his.

If you answered:

"Porridge and toast," which was what we usually had, then he'd say:

"Why are you eating that if you're not one?"

"I don't even know your name," the boy said softly.

I brought my attention back to the riverbank, knowing I'd probably been staring into space for the last few minutes.

"It's Fable."

He whistled. "No kidding? I thought I was the only one with the weird name. I mean – how many other blokes do you know called 'Tobias'?"

"I like it."

"I like yours too." There was that smile again that made my heart flip over like a pancake. "It's kinda weird, but I like it."

We walked on along the riverbank in silence for a few minutes. The river was jade green under the early evening sunlight, moving slowly, its texture as smooth as glass.

"So how come you live over there?" He jerked his thumb in the direction of the vicarage. "And how come that bloke with the dog's a virgin?"

I laughed.

"I live over there because that's where my father lives. He's the vicar. And Mr Pennington isn't a virgin – he's got grandchildren. He's the Verger – he works for the church…"

"So you're religious?"

I shook my head.

"No. And as soon as I'm able to, I'm going to get away from here."

Tobias gazed into my eyes.

"They look like pieces of amber."

Nobody had ever looked at me that intently before and I could feel myself getting hot again.

"Where are your friends?" I asked.

"I came to see you. I've come every night – hoping…"

His arm brushed against my shoulder and I could feel the warmth of his skin and smell the spicy scent of his aftershave.

"I knew you'd come back."

We walked further along the riverbank and in the shadow of a willow he put his arm round me. The top of my head reached to just below his collarbone. I could feel the heat of his body through the black t-shirt. A warm breeze stirred the reeds at the water's edge and I heard the call of a green woodpecker.

"What were you doing here – the other night, I mean?"

He went quiet and a small scar he had by his mouth whitened. I could feel the thud of his heart close to my ear.

"Nothing important."

There was an awkward silence.

"I'm saving money so I can travel the world. It's my ambition to ride Black Angel to India – see the Taj Mahal."

"Black Angel?"

"My bike. I'll take you for a ride one day – if you'd like?"

I nodded, feeling a thrill of excitement. What would Sheila say if she knew what I was up to now? I could just imagine the things she'd say:

"You're turning out just like your mother – and you're a bad influence on my Nathan…"

Tobias would be my secret. I didn't know if I'd even tell Kirsty. After all, I told myself, there probably won't be anything to tell.

"Jasmine – my mother – always talked about travelling," I said as we started walking slowly back along the riverbank. Sheila would be home from her sister's soon –and Derek never agonised over his sermons for long. I'd be missed and then awkward questions would be asked.

"She was a gypsy and she was always talking about

going miles away from Foxfield Junction and travelling the Great Silk Road in a painted caravan."

My voice wobbled slightly and I realised I was shaking. I'd not told anyone except Kirsty about my mother before.

"I'm hoping to go in July - if I've enough money by then." Tobias's voice cut across my thoughts.

My heart clenched. "I'll be sixteen then."

We'd reached the junction of the path where his motorbike was hidden. Tobias let go of me and pushed his arms into his black leather jacket, zipping it up.

"Christ – I forgot you're so young." He took my hand, kissed the palm and folded my fingers over the kiss.

I walked away from him, wishing I'd not said something so stupid.

He hadn't said anything about seeing me again.

*

I didn't see him for two weeks. By then, my exams were nearly finished and I was feeling certain he wouldn't come back. I wasn't sure how old he was, but from what he'd said about the places he'd travelled on Black Angel, he must be at least twenty-one. I could just imagine what Derek would say about me having a boyfriend who was so much older – something along the lines of him 'only being after one thing' and that I'd end up like the women he was trying to help.

When I did see Tobias again, it was on a Wednesday in the middle of June and I was doing the weekly fruit and veg shopping with Sheila. It wasn't that she wanted my company – she just needed someone to help carry the bags. Derek was doing a funeral and Nathan was 'busy.'

We headed along the Pershore Road, walking along the dusty grass verge until we reached the shop that looked more like an elaborate garden shed. Baskets of scarlet geraniums hung around the sides of it and inside and out were wooden crates of every kind of fruit and vegetable you could think of – new potatoes like polished marble, ripe tomatoes, aubergines, courgettes, peppers, ropes of onions, bleached white mushrooms jostling for space next to fresh raspberries and crimson cherries.

"Mind your backs. 'Scuse me madam."

Tobias passed as close to me as he could without it looking odd.

He was carrying a crate of spring onions.

"Where d'you want this, love?" he asked the woman behind the counter.

His hair had blond highlights from being out in the sun and his bare arms were brown.

"Tonight," he whispered as he dumped the first crate of spring onions and went back for the second.

"Fable, stop dawdling and staring into space," squawked Sheila from the far end. "You're supposed to be helping."

I was aware of Tobias staring at me as Sheila and I left the shop. He was standing by a small white pick-up truck. Sheila didn't notice – she was too busy carrying on about the price of new potatoes. I didn't look back, but inside my heart was buzzing with excitement. Tonight. He'd said tonight.

It was only later that afternoon I realised he hadn't said what time.

I escaped from the vicarage as soon as I could.

The hawthorn blossom had finished now – giving way to wild roses and poppies. The red silky texture of poppies and the black inside at the heart of the flower always reminded me of Jasmine and I wondered if what I'd said about her had put Tobias off.

He was there waiting for me in the usual place by the river.

"Who was the old trout you were with earlier?" he asked as we walked slowly along the riverbank. He was holding his leather jacket by its loop in one hand. He hadn't kissed me or put his arm round me and I felt a twinge of disappointment.

"That's Sheila – my father's housekeeper. What were you doing today? And where've you been. I've missed you." I hadn't meant to say that – the words just slipped out.

Kirsty said boys didn't like it if you were too clingy. 'Better to play hard to get' was her motto.

"I had to go away for a bit – work – nothing you need to know about." His face gave nothing away.

I felt a trace of fear, as if a cloud had gone across the sun, remembering what my father had said about Mr Pennington finding used syringes in the woods. What if Tobias was mixed up in that? If it wasn't that – why couldn't he tell me where he'd been?"

"I've moved to a new place," he said. "Just over there. Got some work on a farm – strawberry picking, that sort of stuff. I was deliverin' when you saw me the other day." He pointed to the opposite bank of the river. "It's not much of a place but it'll do till I'm ready to leave – July time maybe. Who knows?"

"I'll miss you when you go."

I looked away so he wouldn't see the tears in my eyes.

He took my face in his hands and turned me gently to face him. "As I said, who knows?"

He kissed me gently on the lips and my legs went weak and my stomach felt as if it was a lift that had gone down too fast.

"Wow," he said when he released me.

We walked along the riverbank and found a place that was like a little den under the curtains of a willow. Tobias laid his jacket down for me to lie on. I was glad I'd put on my black caftan tonight. At least the grass stains wouldn't show.

His breath was warm on my face and smelled of a mixture of strawberries and fresh mint. "I'd like to take you out for the night," he said. "Can you get away?"

"I'll find a way." I knew what he was asking – would I sleep with him. I was scared of getting pregnant – it had happened to a girl at school. But then Kirsty had done it lots of times with her latest boyfriend and nothing had happened to her.

"I'll find a way," I repeated.

I knew if I confided in Kirsty, she'd help me.

*

"What you so keen to get to school for?" asked Kirsty the next morning, rolling over the top of her already short skirt and scowling at the result in her wardrobe mirror. "It's only a bleedin' maths exam. You don't even like maths."

I sat on her bed watching her back-comb her short dark hair. Kirsty's house always smelled friendly – a mixture of hot toast, cheap perfume and washing powder.

"Don't say 'bleedin',", I said. "If Nathan hears you, then Derek won't let me out with you ever again."

"Bugger Nathan," said Kirsty, who didn't like him either. "What you bothered about them lot for? You're sixteen soon – you can do what you like."

She looked thoughtful.

"Mind you, sex was more fun when it wasn't legal – but 'course I'll help yer. Don't worry about that."

*

The hidden space under the willow became our special

place. There were times when things didn't go to plan – like the time when there was more than one motorbike hidden in the shrubbery.

On the day the exams finished we got another warning from Derek about the dangers of what he called 'undesirables' hanging around the woods and graveyard.

I'd been on my way to meet Tobias as usual, carrying some almond cakes wrapped in greaseproof that I'd bought from the bakery earlier and a bottle of lemonade. The weather was hot and sultry, humidity rising from the enclosed path, making my red t-shirt stick to me.

My path was blocked by a leather-clad biker with a shaved head and scarred cheek.

"What 'ave we 'ere?" he asked, leering at me. "Little Red Riding Hood on her way to her grandmother's? Run home little girl. Didn't your Mummy tell you woods is dangerous places?"

I went home, wondering where Tobias was. Black Angel was left in the bushes next to two others.

As I fled back along the way I'd come, I turned to look at the biker with the shaved head. His leather-clad back was turned to me and bore the words 'Devil's Advocate.'

"Tobias, where the fuck are you?" he was shouting.

I knew I was on dangerous ground, but there was no way I could walk away from Tobias now. I loved him too much.

CHAPTER TWELVE

After that meeting with Devil's Advocate, Nathan followed me everywhere. I'd even noticed him watching me with binoculars from his bedroom window as I walked up the front path towards the main road. I wondered where he got the binoculars. They were expensive, in a leather case, and must've cost a lot more than he earned from his paper round.

A few days ago he'd asked me some weird questions.

I was in the kitchen making tea and toast at lunchtime and he stood lolling against the sticky worktop watching me, making me feel uncomfortable.

"Was that you I saw walking by the river yesterday?"

I shrugged. "Maybe. It's not a crime is it?"

"What do you do there?"

I shrugged, trying not to show how uncomfortable I felt. "Look for leaves and flowers for my art project – that sort of thing."

"That sort of thing," he mimicked. "You trying to be top of the class or something?" He gave me a nasty look. "I could tell Derek you're mixed up in something dodgy. What's it worth not to drop you right in it?"

"What d'you mean, what's it worth?"

"Money, stupid."

"I'm not paying you anything," I flashed back at him defiantly. "If you like we can both go and see Derek and I'll tell him you've been trying to blackmail me. Come on. And you can tell him that you've been spying on me with your new binoculars." My heart felt as if it was hammering in my throat and I pushed my hands into the pockets of my jeans to stop them shaking.

"Fuck off, you stupid bitch, you'll be sorry you ever said

that," growled Nathan pushing past me and going upstairs. I heard his bedroom door slam.

*

I told Tobias about the two incidents when I next saw him. He didn't seem surprised.

"Do you know that 'Devil's Advocate' bloke?" I asked.

"Danny?" Tobias pulled a face. "Yeah, we had some unfinished business."

"I didn't like him."

"Not many people do."

"Are you a drug addict?"

Tobias looked at me steadily. "No."

I looked away first. "Sorry."

"What're you sorry for?" He lifted my hair away from my face and looked into my eyes.

"I should trust you, shouldn't I?"

"Yeah, specially if we're gonna be travelling partners."

We lay in each others' arms in our special den and I felt a starburst of happiness when he said that. I remembered a line of a poem – John Donne I think – that we'd done at school last year. Something like 'Oh that this too solid flesh would melt.' I hadn't understood it then, but I did now, lying in Tobias's arms, bathed in sultry greenish light, our bodies pressed together, his hands caressing me under the thin cotton skirt and top I was wearing.

*

Kirsty and I spent ages working out how we could go out with our boyfriends without either her Mum or Derek finding out.

"It's like my Mum says," said Kirsty, sniffing at a bottle of perfume in Boots after school one day "if you're gonna tell lies, you need a bloody good memory. Phew, that Gingham stuff smells like cat's wee. I prefer this one over here – Rain Flower."

It took some working out, but in the end, Kirsty's Mum thought she was going out somewhere with me and Derek and Sheila believed I was doing a sleep-over at Kirsty's for her sister's birthday. It suited them, because they'd been invited to a diocesan something-or-other and wouldn't be back that night, Nathan was staying at a mate's house for the night and they didn't trust me to be there on my own.

Kirsty's Mum believed we were going to a disco at The Cross Keys in Isbourne. She'd cooked us fish fingers and chips and then we'd spent ages getting ready in Kirsty's bedroom, trying not to giggle too much. Kirsty lent me some of her lilac eyeshadow and white lipstick and I spent ages helping her get her hair right. I felt guilty as Kirsty's Mum watched us from the door as we went off down the road together –Kirsty tottering in her high heels.

"'Bye girls. See you later. I'll leave the door on the catch."

"Thank God she didn't shout out what she usually does," said Kirsty as we reached the alleyway where we'd arranged to meet Kirsty's boyfriend and Tobias.

"What does she usually say?"

"The last time I went out with my sister, Julie, she came to the door and shouted out 'Kirsty, Julie, are you clean underneath?' I was so embarrassed I could've died."

In the alleyway we sorted out a meeting time so that we got back to Kirsty's together. Tobias helped me put on the spare crash helmet.

"You needn't have spent all that time doing your hair," joked Kirsty. "You'll look like Wurzel Gummidge by the time you get there."

"Funny!" I said, punching her arm playfully, but I was too happy to care.

I felt a tremor of excitement as Tobias kick-started Black Angel. I got on the back putting my arms round him and we roared off into the warm sunlit evening towards Martlebury fair.

"Less chance of seeing anyone you know there," said Tobias when he'd suggested it, "and if you are unlucky to meet anyone they'll think you're there with your family."

I laughed. "Yeah, I can really imagine Derek somewhere like that. It's the dog collar that does it."

I could hear and smell the fair long before we arrived. The sound vibrated through the ground as Tobias eased Black Angel into the motorbike end of the makeshift car park. The smell of fried onions from the hot dog stand made my mouth water and I felt a surge of excitement.

I could feel the heat rising from the ground and beating down on my head and shoulders as we moved towards the entrance. Within minutes, my jeans felt as if they were sticking to me. Tobias had insisted I wear jeans –"not that I'm expecting to crash the bike, but it's best to be prepared."

"Hey, Tobias." I recognised the voice of the 'Devil's Advocate' biker and felt sick.

Tobias didn't turn round but I could feel his arm tighten around my shoulders.

"I told him I'd finished with all that," he muttered.

He paid our entrance fees and pulled me towards the ghost train.

"You're the one true, good thing in my life," he whispered. "And don't you forget it." He kissed me in the eerie darkness and I wished we could sit there all night, just going round and round.

On the shooting gallery he won a small pink teddy for me. He'd taken off his jacket and there were dark patches of sweat on his red shirt that made me think of blood. I flicked my fingers to rid myself of the thought – something I could remember Gangan doing when someone had upset her.

A girl with long blonde hair called to Tobias from the shadows near the hoop-la stall. He waved back and she wiggled her hips provocatively, ignoring me. She had a mouth like a rubber tyre.

"Who's that?" My voice sounded acid with jealousy.

"Someone I used to know when I worked the fairgrounds for a while. She's a good sort ..."

I pulled away from him, wishing I hadn't come after all.

"Hey, Fable, what's up? That was before – right? You're with me now. End of story. OK?"

I took a deep breath, swallowing my unease. "OK."

"Hot dog or candyfloss?"

"Candyfloss first – and ferris wheel."

He laughed, hugging me close. "Don't blame me if you're sick."

I bit into the soft pink sugar – 'angel hair' Gangan used to call it – as I relaxed in his arms, looking down on the dazzling lights below and the ebb and flow of people. It was getting dark now and the first stars were beginning to show.

The wheel slowed and as I looked down I noticed Danny – the Devil's Advocate – was staring up at us.

"You owe me, Tobias," he shouted.

"Shall we go somewhere else?" I asked.

Tobias shook his head stubbornly. "I promised my girl a night at the fair and no jerk like him's gonna stop that."

We got off the ferris wheel and I shivered suddenly.

"You cold?" Tobias put his jacket round my shoulders.

"No – just someone walked over my grave."

"Weird expression."

"One of Gangan's – can't you tell."

He understood. He'd told me once that one of his grandmas said funny things.

We saw a sign for 'Madame Zara – Fortune Teller and I felt a sudden nostalgia for Gangan and her tarot cards.

"Count me out on that one," Tobias said. "I'd rather not know what's coming. I'll wait for you."

I paid my money and pushed open the thick velvet curtains at the entrance to the gypsy caravan. Madame Zara had a face that looked as if it had been carved from mahogany. She had chocolate dark eyes and gold hoops in her ears.

I sat down on a wooden chair and she took my hand, tracing the lines with a nicotined forefinger.

"Welcome, daughter," she said.

I watched her face change as she carried on tracing the lines. She was silent for a few minutes.

"What can you tell me?" I asked, my tongue feeling as if it was sticking to the roof of my mouth with anxiety.

"You have some years of sorrow but joy will come to you in the end when you learn to follow your own pathway."

I pulled my hand away from her.

"What about love? What about Tobias?"

She looked at me steadily and shook her head.

I heard shouting outside the caravan and pushed back my chair, ignoring Madame Zara's insistence that I should come back and let her tell me the full story.

Tobias was in trouble.

He and Danny the Devil's Advocate were scuffling on the dusty ground near the shooting gallery. The girl with long fair hair we'd seen earlier was watching. Danny got up, brushing the dust from his leather jacket. Tobias was lying still on the ground.

"No Amsterdam trip, no money. You know the deal we agreed. And you know how we treat people who don't fit in." Danny aimed a last kick at Tobias's inert body before he draped his arm round the girl and they went off towards one of the caravans.

I dropped to my knees next to Tobias. He sat up slowly, wiping a dribble of blood from his nose, lighting a cigarette with shaking hands. The chain on the silver St Christopher he always wore had snapped and it lay glinting on the dusty ground. He picked it up and put it in his pocket. My fingers strayed to the one Teresa had given me all those years ago that I always wore on a long chain. I knew how bad I'd feel if I lost it and I knew Tobias'd be the same with this one. He'd once told me it had been his brother's.

"What's going on?"

My lips felt stiff and sore. I wished I'd asked Madame Zara why it was bad news about Tobias but I was too scared.

"How was your fortune?" Tobias managed a weak grin.

"OK." I didn't want to talk about it. I just wanted to keep him with me, keep him safe.

"Do you have to go to Amsterdam?"

He grimaced. "Wish I didn't, but there's an old score to settle. Wipe the slate clean once and for all. I can't say any more till I come back."

"I wish we were going travelling now, tonight."

"Me too," he said.

We left the fairground and found a field of ripe wheat edged with cornflowers and poppies. Tobias propped Black Angel near the hedge and we sat on his jacket at the edge of the field. Wrapped in Tobias's arms looking up at the stars, I felt my fears subside. Everything would be fine. He'd go to Amsterdam and return safely, then we'd make plans for our own journey.

"Is it all right for me to do this?"

Tobias unzipped my jeans, feathered gently inside my pants, his fingers creating an ever-widening whirlpool of desire that I felt myself being drawn deeper into with each caress.

I touched him, feeling his hardness through his denim jeans, unzipping them, sliding my hand in through the gap, feeling him, hearing him groan with desire.

He pushed me gently away in the end.

"Fable, I want your first time to be good. Here isn't right. I want there to be champagne and all that stuff – a proper celebration. Something you'll remember forever. When I come back from Amsterdam…"

I touched his lips gently with my fingers. "Before then. Wednesday. My birthday. You won't go before then, will you?"

He shook his head.

"Promise?"

"We better go," he said, "it's nearly midnight – Kirsty'll be waiting." He got to his feet, pulling me up after him, put on his jacket, kick-started the bike and we took off into the night.

Kirsty was frantic when we met up back in the alleyway. "Christ, I thought you'd had an accident or something. I was just thinking what I could say to my Mum."

I gave Tobias a last hug before he left me, standing there in the darkness listening to the sound of Black Angel's engine fading away.

"Come on, Fable," said Kirsty. "Mum'll have locked the doors if we don't hurry."

It was only when I was lying on my camp bed at Kirsty's, cuddling the small pink teddy Tobias had won for me that I realised he hadn't made any promises about my birthday. I felt sick with fear that I'd never see him again.

CHAPTER THIRTEEN

After the night at Martlebury Fair, we had three days of torrential rain 'just like a monsoon' one of the old men in the parish said. It was humid and the nights were hot and sticky.

Derek's nightmares returned. He woke yelling and shouting and then I'd hear him pacing the floor, up and down, like a caged animal. Sheila was away visiting her sister and Nathan was staying with a friend. I got out of bed, not sure whether I should go to him or not. Through a crack in his bedroom door, I could see him on his knees by the bed, praying.

"She comes to me on the scent of hyacinths, O Lord. Deliver me from having to relive my downfall, I beseech thee. Let me sleep O Lord, in order that I may serve thee better. Let me not perish from fire or flood."

On and on he prayed through the long humid nights. During the day he hardly left his study and he barely touched the trays of food I left for him.

The Avon rose until it lapped over the edges of the bank, trying to escape its lush green boundaries, heading towards the lower edge of the graveyard. The sky looked bleached out with rain still to come, and the distant hills – Bredon, Malverns, Cotswolds – were painted out as if by a giant's brush.

Derek's anxiety was contagious.

I also slept badly, worrying about Tobias, hoping he was keeping safe. The word 'Amsterdam' kept beating on my tired brain to the rhythm of the ceaseless rain.

"What happens, Lord, when the dead rise? Who will save us then…"

The darkness echoed with Derek's voice and I

remembered how this scared me when I first came to live here.

I knew that if I mentioned what I'd heard, I'd get the same defensive response as before. Derek would be just as likely to claim I was over-wrought because of my exams (if only he knew the real reason) and drag me off to the doctors for medication, especially as Sheila and Nathan always said they'd heard nothing when he'd had nightmares in the past.

I stood at the window, fretting at the ceaseless torrent, wondering if Tobias was safe, wondering how I could get a message to him. There was no logical reason for prowling the riverbank in this weather, even if it wasn't flooded. I didn't know where Tobias lived.

Just as I was giving up hope of ever seeing him again, he bumped into me at the school gates on Friday afternoon. He was wearing an unfamiliar brown leather bomber jacket and his hair was plastered to his head, dripping down his face. I was huddled under my umbrella, trying to keep the rain out of my schoolbag, my mind on the history lesson I'd just finished.

"Sorry," he said, winking at me, pausing just long enough to pass me a note saying he'd pick me up from school at lunchtime on my birthday. He moved away quickly, melting into the rain-soaked kids filing out of school. As I looked quickly at the note he'd passed me, written on a tiny piece of white paper, I wondered why he needed to be so secretive.

*

On Tuesday, the day before my birthday, something happened that Derek couldn't say was a figment of my imagination. I was tidying the dining room – Sheila's orders – looking out at the faint glimmer of light in the sky on the other side of the river, hoping for a dry day tomorrow – when there was a frantic hammering on the front door.

I was used to this and carried on dusting the cheap

wood-veneer table and chairs. The hammering continued and I heard Derek open his study door and then his slow footsteps along the hall. I heard the creak of the front door opening and then the sound of Miss Price, one of the flower ladies, leading off with a hysterical tirade about something she'd just seen in the church.

My heart raced with excitement when I heard what she said and I dropped the duster and can of polish and crept out into the hall. Miss Price was holding onto the sleeve of Derek's jacket. I'd never seen her so agitated before. Her white hair was like wet sheep's wool and her beige mac and shoes were leaving wet marks on the hall floor.

"I tell you, vicar, there was a ghost in the church. I saw it with my own eyes and so did Mrs Harris. They've just taken her away in an ambulance, poor soul. The church door was wide open when we got there, the porch soaked where the rain slanted in and when we opened the door I thought at first we'd had vandals in. It wasn't vandals, though Vicar. There was a woman in white…"

"It must've been some kind of prank. Nothing to be concerned about," Derek broke in smoothly, but I noticed how his hand shook as he ran his finger round the inside of his clerical collar.

I'm sure he remembered, as I did, the time just after he brought me here that Jasmine turned up and wrote her name in chrysanthemum petals. She said then that she'd be back.

I hoped she'd come to wish me happy birthday and that I'd see her again soon. Tobias and I would be together and Amsterdam would be just a bad dream. How wrong I was.

*

My sixteenth birthday dawned with weak sunshine and a new-washed look to the sky like a blank canvas. I got out of bed and dressed in my school uniform, feeling a tremor of excitement in my stomach as I stashed my jeans and a pink cheesecloth top into my schoolbag.

When I got downstairs, Derek wished me a happy birthday and Sheila dumped a bowl of lumpy porridge in front of me. I accepted it cheerfully thinking this would be one of the things I'd laugh about when Tobias and I were far away from here.

Derek gave me a card with a mawkish picture of a bloodhound on it and a new Bible. Sheila gave me two pairs of cheap tights the colour of strong tea. There was no sign of Nathan this morning but I didn't expect anything from him anyway.

The tights reminded me of a joke going round at school amongst the boys.

A boy and his girlfriend were having sex.

The boy said: "If I'd known you were a virgin I'd have taken more time."

The girl said: "If I'd known we'd got more time I'd have taken my tights off."

I felt myself going hot, thinking about what I'd be doing later if all went according to plan. Anxious feelings kicked in – what if he didn't turn up – what if he'd already left and hadn't been able to let me know – would losing my virginity hurt and just how careful would he be? "Amsterdam" whispered a nasty little voice in my head as I left the Vicarage.

*

He was waiting for me behind the bike sheds when he said he would be and I felt some of the anxiety melting away when I saw him. He didn't look any older than some of the sixth formers as he leant against the wall eyeing me lazily as I walked towards him. His eyes were the give-away – their hazel-flecked green depths had seen far more than any of the kids carelessly dumping their bikes and jostling their way into school.

The sun was shining and the scent of roses was on the warm breeze and it felt like a good omen.

"It's a long time since I went behind the bike sheds with anyone," said Tobias pulling me into his arms.

I wondered how many girls he'd slept with before me, suddenly realising how little I knew about him – like where he went to school and how old he was.

Black Angel was hidden amongst the laurel bushes at the end of the school drive.

"Happy birthday my angel," said Tobias as he handed me my crash helmet. "Hope it's the best one yet."

He'd made an effort to make things lovely for me at his caravan. The caravan stood at the end of a rough farm track at the edge of a field, looking more as if it had been abandoned. There was a patch of woodland behind it and a hay field in front of it. I could see the gables of the farmhouse where Tobias was working sticking up behind a clump of trees like a cat's ears.

The caravan had once been white but was now green and mildewed on the outside, its windows patterned with generations of cobwebs.

"They were going to scrap it," said Tobias. "It's not much of a place, but I was glad of it."

It smelled damp inside, reminding me of the vicarage when I'd first been taken there. I pushed those images away.

The light inside was dim and greenish – a bit like our place under the willow tree down by the river. Tobias had drawn the thin curtains even though he said hardly anybody ever came near here.

There were clean white sheets on the bed and a red silk bedspread that gleamed like a ruby on a muck-heap.

"Cost a fiver from a second hand shop. Thought you'd like it," said Tobias gruffly. "Sorry about the flowers – I was gonna get you roses."

I looked at the buttercups and red clover in the cracked blue mug and smiled.

"You picked them for me. That's what counts."

He pulled me into his arms. "Soft aren't I?"

He kissed my neck, caressing my back and belly through the thin fabric of my pink top with gentle circular movements with his fingers.

There were more surprises. Chocolate cake. Champagne. A long thin present wrapped in red tissue paper.

I unwrapped it carefully.

It was a silver bracelet with pink stones that looked like pieces of coconut ice.

"Rose quartz for love. So the lady in the shop said."

It felt cool and heavy on my wrist.

I wrapped my arms round him, feeling the beating of his heart through is soft blue cotton shirt. "I wish we could go now. To India."

He turned away. "I didn't want to tell you. I'm off to Amsterdam tonight."

"Take me with you."

"It's too dangerous. You've seen what Danny's like. I need to do this one last thing. If I don't I'll never be free of him."

"I don't trust Danny."

"I'll be back. Nothing'll keep me away from you. I promise."

He opened the champagne – cold from standing in a

bucket of water – and poured some into a tin mug for me.

I drank quickly to swallow back the tears.

"Hey, gently – it's not lemonade! I can't take you back drunk. Anyway you'll fall off the bike." He wiped away my tears with a gentle finger.

He eased off my top, peeled away my bra, until I was wearing nothing on my top half except the St Christopher Teresa had given me, kissing my breasts, tugging gently at the nipples with his lips.

I took off his shirt, noticing a few white scars under the soft golden hairs on his chest.

"Where's your St Christopher?" There was a circular patch of paler skin just below his throat.

He shrugged. "Meant to get it mended. Don't want it getting lost."

I wanted to say that I'd feel happier if he was wearing it, but the words wouldn't come.

We fed each other pieces of cake. There was squidgy chocolate mousse in the middle and we licked each other's fingers.

He unzipped my jeans, sliding his hand inside, touching me through my thin cotton pants.

"You sure about this?"

I kissed him back, feeling his hardness through his denim jeans, unzipping his flies, feeling scared about what happened next.

He sensed my fear. "It'll be wonderful, you'll see. I'll look after you."

I swallowed. "I know."

We drank more champagne and he laid me down on the bedspread, peeling off my jeans and pants. The red silk felt cool on my bare skin. I felt shy now I was naked. Tobias peeled off his own jeans and white cotton pants. His erection looked massive and I wondered how all that would fit inside me.

Through a gap in the curtains I could see the sky was a clear blue with no clouds. A white dove flew across the patch of blue, reminding me of Gangan's story about Reuben.

"What're you thinking about?"

"Gangan. She only made love once in her whole life and it changed her for ever and she never stopped loving Reuben."

"What happened to him?" Tobias's face was close to mine, his breath warm on my cheek.

"He was killed by my grandmother Lucy."

Tobias kissed me gently, his lips going further and further down my body.

"It sounds like a complicated story. God, you're beautiful."

I moaned softly as his tongue reached the place between my legs. He kept going until it felt as if that part of me was melting away, spiralling upwards somehow into a magical spectrum of colours.

I drew back, feeling afraid.

"Let it go, baby," said Tobias softly, holding me close and touching me, making me feel warm and oily, as if there were only me and him and this magical feeling in the whole world.

It felt as if I was on a narrow ledge very high up, looking down on brilliantly coloured trees – bright orange, lime green, yellow, aquamarine. I heard myself shout as I felt myself falling…

"Don't let go, don't drop me."

"I've got you, baby. I've got you."

I felt him move on top of me, felt his hardness between

my legs, drew back slightly as a shaft of pain went through me, but then it was as if a new rhythm took over and we were moving together. This time, it was Tobias who called out before he collapsed against my shoulder.

He mopped gently between my legs with a white cotton handkerchief. The red silk bedspread was patterned with blood.

The magical colours were gone now and I felt shivery and tearful.

Tobias pulled a rough blanket over us both and rocked me like a baby, kissing away my tears.

"It's OK baby. It'll always be OK."

I believed him and let him to rock me to sleep.

*

The next morning I woke in my bed in the vicarage feeling feverish. Riding home on the back of Black Angel yesterday afternoon had been agony. I'd not wanted to leave Tobias, but he insisted, saying he'd be back by the weekend.

I'd gone straight to bed when I got home, not wanting to face Derek, Sheila or Nathan.

"Post exam stress," said Derek, leaving me alone for once.

I lay still, reliving the images inside my head, only getting out of bed when I needed to go to the bathroom. Sheila knocked on the door once to say that there was supper downstairs if I wanted it. I didn't bother to answer her and after a few minutes she went away. I dozed for a while and when I next opened my eyes it was after midnight. The sound of a motorbike had woken me and I felt a surge of hopefulness that Tobias may have come for me.

I got out of bed and peered through the window at the far end of the landing – the one that overlooked the road to

Pershore. There was no sign of a motorbike, but I heard faltering steps going along the front path followed by someone fumbling with a key in the front door.

I went back along the landing, feeling stiff and sore, and looked over the banisters. There was a light on in the hall and I could see a slice of pale orange light under the door of Derek's study. The slice of light widened as the front door opened and Nathan came stumbling in.

What is the meaning of this disgraceful performance?" Derek's voice was the one he used from the pulpit on Sundays – rounded and strong.

Nathan's response was slurred.

"Whose clothes are you wearing, Nathan?"

"None of your bloody business, Vicar," There was a thump as Nathan tried for the bottom step of the staircase and missed.

*

When I next woke up, the sun was streaming in through my purple curtains and there was an argument in full spate on the landing between Derek, Sheila and Nathan. I got out of bed and watched through a crack in the door.

Derek and Sheila were fully dressed. Nathan was wearing crumpled grey boxer shorts and his hair was uncombed. His flabby white body looked like a slab of lard.

"I've kept quiet about a lot of things for too long," said Derek. "Nathan, I want to know what you're up to. How have you acquired the means to buy all these things – binoculars, cameras, watches? Whose clothes did you come home in last night? Who is the Devil's Advocate?"

"You're always getting at him." Sheila sounded edgy and tearful. "You never reprimand your precious Fable."

"For once, she's done nothing to merit a reprimand."

Derek's voice was sharp.

"I know some things about her," growled Nathan. "Ask her where her new bracelet came from."

My blood turned to ice water. I realised I was still wearing the bracelet Tobias had given me for my birthday. I took it off quickly, wrapped it in my t-shirt and hid it under a loose floorboard under my bed.

"What new bracelet?" Derek's voice was dangerously quiet.

Nathan was about to reply when there was the sound of hammering at the front door.

"Police! Open up."

CHAPTER FOURTEEN

"I'll go," said Derek. "There must be a logical explanation for this intrusion."

He turned as he reached the top of the stairs. "But woe betide you Nathan if you've brought trouble on this house."

I got back into bed and pulled the covers over my head. On my bare arms I could still faintly smell Tobias's aftershave. The space between my legs was still tender and last night I'd worn a sanitary towel because there was still a faint trace of blood and Sheila was pathological about any getting on the sheets.

I heard loud voices downstairs and then Sheila's shrill voice cutting across them followed by Nathan yelling 'I didn't do it,' over and over and Derek's voice rising above the tide of sound, pleading for calm.

In the last few minutes, the rain had returned with a vengeance. It sounded as if handfuls of water were being thrown against the windows. I was desperate for the toilet now, so I got out of bed and headed for the bathroom. Sitting on the loo, I dragged a comb through my hair. Then I scraped a damp flannel under my arms, sprayed deodorant and dressed quickly in an old pair of jeans and a blue t-shirt, knowing that Derek hated people coming down to breakfast improperly dressed especially when there were strangers present – not that it sounded like there was much breakfasting going on.

Sheila, Derek and Nathan were sitting round the kitchen table under the dim light of the shade-less bulb that had always reminded me of an interrogation lamp. It had always puzzled me that Sheila was so fastidious in some ways but had never suggested buying a lampshade for the kitchen.

Two policemen – one dark and the other with spiky

ginger hair were leaning against the worktops listening to Nathan's account of what he'd done the previous evening.

Everyone stared at me as I walked uneasily into the room.

"This is my daughter, Fable," said Derek. "She is in no way connected with any of this."

Sheila fussed around, pouring me a mug of strong tea.

"About time you showed your face," she hissed.

I felt queasy and didn't really fancy tea, but I was grateful for something warm to hold. It was cold and clammy in the kitchen and murkier than usual because of the curtains of rain streaming down the window.

"So, Nathan," said the ginger-haired policeman, "tell us again what happened after you left the 'Rising Sun' pub with your friend Danny. Let's see how the story changes this time."

I stiffened at the mention of the name 'Danny', remembering the Devil's Advocate biker who'd set on Tobias at Martlebury Fair. Nathan was casting evil looks at me.

"I think you'll find she does know more than you think," he said pointing at me.

"We're interested in what you can tell us, Nathan," said the policeman. "Let's have it."

"Not without a brief," said Nathan. "You're getting at me. Twisting everything I say. It's always the same, everywhere I go."

"Nobody's getting at you Nathan. We're just making routine enquiries at the moment about a drugs-related incident last night when a young man was stabbed to death."

I held my breath. It couldn't be Tobias. It couldn't. He'd gone to Amsterdam.

It felt as if everything in the kitchen was spiralling round slowly, like a merry-go-round when it gradually comes to a stop. There was a brief moment of silence, broken only by the ticking of the clock, when even the storm outside stopped temporarily.

Nathan sat silent, his head bowed.

"The vicar has already given us a statement saying you didn't come home in the clothes you went out in. What happened to the clothes you were wearing, Nathan?" asked the dark-haired policeman.

My mug of tea was forming a greasy scum on the surface. I put it down on the table, knowing if I drank it I'd throw up. The faint smell of last night's cottage pie was adding to my queasy feeling and I felt stiff and sore sitting on a hard kitchen chair.

"Let me ask you another question, Nathan," said the ginger-haired policeman. "How do you manage to buy expensive items like cameras and binoculars when your only income appears to be from a paper round?"

"He works very hard," said Sheila.

"No doubt, Madam," said the policeman, "but we're talking serious money here for the amount of stuff stashed in his bedroom. Right young entrepreneur aren't you, Nathan?"

Nathan didn't reply.

The policemen looked at each other.

"Nathan William Hawkins," said the dark-haired one, "I am arresting you on suspicion of the murder of Tobias Martin Latimer on the night of Wednesday 26th July. You do not need to say anything until your legal representative arrives."

The sound of someone screaming echoed in my head.

My own voice was frozen.

As Nathan was handcuffed and taken away, all I could think of were two things – both totally irrelevant. I thought that until now I hadn't known what his second name was and I wondered whether or not he was wearing his St Christopher.

The walls of the kitchen spiralled round faster and I remembered someone catching me as everything went black.

CHAPTER FIFTEEN

Cara is the same age as I was when my life was derailed for the second time. As I look at her painting her nails silver looking as if she hadn't a care in the world, I wonder how she'd cope with the same situation.

As far as I knew, she'd never had a serious boyfriend and I wondered just how Tony would cope when she did. When she was a baby, he'd been extremely protective of her. He'd gaze at her when she was in her cot and say things like: "I don't want her to have any problems in her life."

I remembered how my friend Kirsty's Granny used to say: "Setbacks are good for young people," every time Kirsty or one of her sisters complained about something going wrong.

After Tobias was killed I had what the doctor called a 'complete nervous collapse.'

"Most likely connected with exam stress," he said as he signed a prescription for tranquillisers.

"What's she got to be stressed about?" I heard Sheila mutter. "As if I hadn't got anything better to do without having to dance attendance on her."

"If Nathan is totally innocent as he claims he is, then he'll be set free," said Derek soothingly.

I lay in bed with the covers pulled over my head, not bothering to eat, not even bothering to wash myself. After several days of torrential rain, the weather had lapsed into sullen gunmetal skies that threatened thunder and an oppressive humidity.

I constantly re-ran that last perfect day with Tobias – every touch and caress, the spiralling of passion and the wonderful colours and the magical climax – as if it were a film that I could watch over and over again. I remembered how

Tobias had brought me to a deeper and deeper feeling of bliss with each feather-light touch on my clitoris. I'd clung onto him as the waves of ecstasy had flooded over me and I'd writhed and yelled as the colours came like a tidal wave.

Kirsty came to see me, Sheila grudgingly showing her into my room.

"Charming isn't she?" said Kirsty, sitting down on the bed. Her pale blue cheesecloth dress barely covered her knickers.

I didn't say anything.

"So what now?" Kirsty asked.

I burst into tears. She let me cry.

"The thing is," I sniffed, blowing my nose on a crumpled tissue, "they could've made a mistake. Maybe it wasn't Tobias. I don't even know where he came from... The doctor's given me tranquillisers. Said it was exam stress."

I showed her the little white box of tablets.

"I miss him so much Kirst – last night I was tempted to take the lot just so I could be with him."

"Give me that box." Kirsty held out her hand. "We'll have no more of that sort of talk." She sounded just like her Mum. Whatever happens, you have to go on. For Tobias."

I started to cry again. "I can't."

"Could you be pregnant?"

I gulped. "I don't know."

Tobias had asked me if I was on the Pill, seeming surprised when I said no. He'd said he'd use a condom, but somehow in the heat of the moment it got forgotten about. It hadn't seemed important then.

"Either way, we need to get you out of here in case Nathan's released. I don't see him coming back and just settling down nicely with Mummy, do you? So all the more reason not to take these things. Especially if, you know…" She shook the box at me before shoving it in her bag.

*

That night I thought I heard Gangan's voice in my head.

"That one night with Reuben changed me for ever. When I heard he'd gone, I wanted to die too. But you can't just lie down and die to order. Life ain't like that. I had to go on. So must you, Fable. Your journey isn't over yet…"

That morning I got up and washed and dressed for the first time for over a week.

I knocked on the door of Derek's study. He looked surprised to see me. "Those tablets must be helping. You look a little more like yourself."

"I'm not taking them."

He didn't ask me to sit down.

I stood in front of his large brown desk in his gooseshit green painted study. "I want my birth certificate."

"Why?"

"Because I'm leaving."

"Where will you go?"

"That's none of your business."

His cheeks flushed angrily. "How dare you be so insolent at a time like this?"

I willed myself to stay angry. If I'd thought about Tobias I'd have broken down in tears again. I was convinced I was pregnant – and I knew I had to get away from here. There'd be no question of me keeping the child if I stayed.

"You'll stay under my roof, Fable, until you're twenty one – or longer if I deem you incapable of managing your own life."

"If you don't give me my birth certificate I'll get a copy

from Somerset House. Or I'll ask my mother."

He flinched as if I'd slapped him. "Your mother is still in hospital and is likely to remain so for some considerable time. In my opinion she may never be fit to leave."

"So you're a psychiatrist as well as a vicar."

"Don't be cheeky, Fable. It doesn't become you."

"I'll find Gangan then."

"She's dead."

The words, spoken too quickly, hit me like a blast of cold water. Then I thought, if she'd died I'd know. I'd heard her voice in my head only last night, so she couldn't be.

"I don't believe you and I'm leaving here whether you like it or not – and I'm going to find my mother."

Derek remained in his chair, his elbows on his desk, his long fingers steepled together as if he was praying.

I walked out, slamming the study door.

Sheila was in the kitchen, banging about with pots and pans.

I opened the front door, not sure where I was heading. On the way out I collided with the postman.

"Steady on, love," he said. "When did the starting gun go off?"

I didn't answer him.

"These are for you." He thrust a bundle of letters and a small package into my hands.

The letters were all addressed to Derek, but the small brown paper-wrapped package was addressed to 'Fable Latimer.' I felt giddy for a moment, wondering what would've happened if the postman had pushed that through the door like he usually did. The package could only be from Tobias – although I'd never seen what his handwriting was like.

I walked round the perimeter of the vicarage until I

reached the path that led to the river. The memories of walking that path to meet Tobias were too raw – but I needed to be somewhere quiet to open the package.

I walked on towards the rusty gate that led to the graveyard, walking past the rows of headstones until I reached the older part down near the river. The air was hot and sticky, the moody grey clouds pressing down like a heavy blanket. Bees droned lazily on the ivy flowers that were patterned by red admirals.

I sank down in the cool shade of a willow and looked at the package, pulling at the parcel tape, teasing open a corner. Tobias's St Christopher was wrapped in a single sheet of grubby lined paper.

'Look after this and know I'll always love you. T'

The 'T' was like a junction sign. His words reminded me of that First World War poem we'd done at school – the one about 'age shall not weary them nor the years condemn.'

I lay on the cool grass under the willow and cried until I felt empty and exhausted.

*

It was dark when I got back to the vicarage. My birth certificate was on my bed with a brief note from Derek.

'Fable, I am sorry things have ended this way. If you are stupid enough to go in search of your mother, I wash my hands of you.'

"That's it, then," said Kirsty when I went round to see her the next day. All the belongings I cared about were in my new blue rucksack. Tobias's St Christopher was round my neck, keeping Teresa's company.

"Julie and I'll come with you to find your mother or Gangan, like we promised. Bet they're sitting at home wondering where you are. Never thought a vicar'd tell lies."

I stayed at Kirsty's for a couple of days. Then on the second Friday in August, the three of us headed for the station. Julie was nearly nineteen and about to go hitchhiking in France with some friends. She acted like she was in charge of us, but I could tell she was excited as the train to London pulled into the station.

We'd had a thunderstorm a couple of days ago, which had cleared the air. The pink rose bushes on the station looked as if they'd been polished and the air had a fresher feel to it.

"What're you going to do if there's nobody at home?" asked Julie.

"Trust you to think like that." Kirsty shoved her sister playfully. "Like Mum says, you're a real Wednesday's child."

I sank down in my seat. I thought of all the times I'd tried to escape, all the times I'd dreamed of catching this train. Now that I had, especially with the horror of Tobias's death, it seemed like an anticlimax. Julie had voiced the fears that lurked at the back of my mind.

*

The walk from Foxfield Junction station to Gangan's house was both familiar and different. Trains still went across the viaduct and I remembered the stories Gangan told about the day I was born. I remembered some of the journeys that had begun from this station – day trips to London and Brighton, outings to the country, carrying a picnic in a large wicker basket and bags and boxes for blackberries, sloes or nuts.

I led the way from the station.

"Are you sure it's this way?" asked Julie. "Shouldn't we ask someone?"

"I haven't forgotten," I said stiffly.

The corner shop was still there – but run by an Indian lady in a purple and gold sari. I stood in the doorway and inhaled the familiar mixture of smells – dusty potatoes, polish, liquorice and sweaty cheese overlaid by foreign spices and incense.

The Indian lady smiled, her teeth white in her brown face.

Railway Approach looked narrower than I recalled. Most houses had cars parked outside them and I thought back to the time when Patrick O'Hagan was the only person in the road to have a car.

There were new people in their house – people with pink net curtains that Dorothy would've said were 'common.'

I knew before I even knocked on the door of number four that there was nobody at home. The curtains were drawn and hung unevenly at the grimy windows. There was even a hole in one of them, reminding me of my birthday at Tobias's caravan. I felt a piercing ache of longing to be with him.

Gangan wouldn't have let the place get in such a state if she was still alive.

Julie pushed past me, banging on the door – something was wrong with the rhythm. The noise went 'bang-bang-bang' not 'gan-gan gan-gan.'

She peered through the letterbox.

"Anyone at home," she called. "Cor it smells riffy in here."

"Gangan's not there," I said sadly.

A woman had come out of the house opposite. She looked like a younger version of Mrs Cameron. Remembering what had happened on my last day here, I didn't want to talk to her. Kirsty and Julie had no such scruples.

I stood looking at the overgrown front garden. White convolvulus trumpets and black bryony had taken over, their tendrils twining over everything, choking the marigolds and pansies struggling for survival underneath.

The turquoise paint on the front door was flaky and when I looked through the letterbox I could see that unopened post was piled high behind it. I put my hand through the letterbox, feeling for the spare key that always hung on a chain behind it. It was gone.

I walked away from the front door and slumped against the gate.

"They've all gone away," said the woman who looked like Mrs Cameron. "You're not from the council, are you? Or the press?" Her teeth were yellowish and rat-like in her narrow face. "We've had enough bad news round here to last a lifetime." She turned her back on us, going into her house and slamming the door.

"So what now?" asked Kirsty.

"Home again, I suppose," said Julie. "When's the next train?"

I felt like I was sleep-walking. I'd begun this journey expecting to be going home – having burned my bridges in Isbourne.

Now I had nowhere to go.

CHAPTER SIXTEEN

We didn't catch the next train back to London.

"The old bag over the road wasn't much help," said Julie, getting a crumpled pack of cigarettes out of her pocket, tapping one on the box, putting it between her lips and striking a match, leaning into the flame as she lit it.

She blew a smoke ring towards where the Mrs Cameron look-alike was sweeping her path, inch by inch, trying to pretend she wasn't the least bit interested in what we were doing.

"I bet they're born with a broom in one hand round here," Julie said loudly.

The sun baked down, glaring off the car windscreens, highlighting how different the road was now to the way I remembered it as a child.

I looked at the overgrown front garden of 'Starlight' searching for clues as to what had happened to Gangan and Peggy.

"Didn't you say your aunt – Peggy – worked somewhere near here? What if she's still there?"

"Doctor's surgery," I said slowly.

I was holding onto the wooden front gate, remembering how I used to swing on it. I felt light-headed as if I had a fever. My body was heavy and all I wanted to do was lie down, fall into an endless sleep and not wake up again.

"Drink first," said Julie, dragging us towards the corner shop. "Fable looks like she's dead on her feet. And chocolate."

The Indian lady in the shop served us with many smiles.

"No ladies. I know nothing," was all she said to Kirsty and Julie's questions about the people who lived nearby.

"No ladies. I only come here six months."

I drank a can of Coke, feeling just as thirsty as soon as I'd swallowed it. Julie made me eat a few squares of chocolate too.

"Keep you going," she said briskly. "Don't want you passing out on us."

She and Kirsty walked on each side of me, holding my arms as if I was under arrest.

The windows of the doctor's surgery where Peggy used to work were boarded up – the brickwork surrounding them charred and the roof gone.

Kirsty stopped a woman with a shopping basket who pointed us in the direction of the new health centre.

"It's been there a long time," she said, looking at us as if we'd just landed from Mars.

She peered curiously at me. "Is she all right?"

The new health centre was a single storey brick building with chrome and glass automatic doors. Inside it smelled of spray polish and antiseptic. The receptionist had dyed blonde hair and a sickly smile. She looked at Julie as if she was mad when she asked the usual questions.

"I'll go and ask someone," she said.

We could see her through a glass door at the back of the reception area talking to a man sitting at a large desk, jerking her head occasionally towards the three of us standing at the reception desk with its huge green leather-bound diary and brass bell.

"The old doctors retired a few years ago – just after the fire. I'm not able to tell you what happened to the people who worked there. The fire was started by an employee."

"Where would a person be sent if they were put in a mental hospital?" asked Julie.

The receptionist swept us a look that said she thought we should all be locked up in one.

She flashed her sickly smile again. "We don't send people to those places any more, dear," she said. "It's Care in the Community now."

"All of which means we got nowhere," said Julie kicking viciously at a tuft of grass by the edge of the path. I wondered how she and Kirsty could feel so passionately about things when I just felt numb.

"Last stop – Library," said Julie. "Then we head for the train."

I sat on a hard chair by a wooden table, meant for people studying, slumped forward resting my head on my arms and fell into a deep sleep. I don't know how long I was there but as I climbed painfully out of the pit of oblivion I could hear two librarians discussing whether or not they should send for the police.

"She looks too young to be drunk," said one.

"Don't you believe it! Take it from me the young ones are the worst," said the other.

I pushed myself upright, shaking my tangled hair out of my eyes wishing I felt less giddy. At that point, Kirsty and Julie came back looking down in the mouth.

"Thought we were on to something there," they said, ignoring the librarians. "We actually spoke to someone who'd heard of your mother – Jasmine – yeah? Only thing is, she's not there any more. She left the hospital a few months ago – some new government initiative they said – but they wouldn't say where she'd gone."

CHAPTER SEVENTEEN

I don't remember the journey back or what happened in the few weeks following our failed expedition. After I got back, Derek came to see me at Kirsty's house, his appeal to come back to him hovering between threat and cajole.

I lay in my camp bed in Kirsty's room surrounded by her Rolling Stones posters and discarded clothing while Derek sat awkwardly on the edge of Kirsty's bed promising that things would be different if I came back to live with him. I didn't see how they could ever be.

"I'm disappointed in you, Fable," he said. "Very disappointed. I thought if I removed you from your mother's influence in time that you'd be saved."

"That was the worst thing you ever did to me." I buried my head under the covers and didn't come out till he'd gone.

I had to get away from Isbourne. My period still hadn't started and I'd begun to count the weeks, feeling hopeful that I still had a part of Tobias inside me. I had no idea how I'd support myself if I was pregnant. The small amount of money I'd saved to go travelling with Tobias was dwindling fast.

Julie and her friend Moira, who lived in Worcester, were still talking about going travelling in the autumn. Moira – a plump girl with short dark hair – offered me a job in the café she worked in 'nothing thrilling, just making sandwiches, clearing tables, washing up.'

I took the job – and the mattress on the floor in Moira's cluttered sitting room where there were endless items of lacy underwear airing on wooden clothes horses.

"When we go, I've got to pay the rent anyway to keep this place. So you may as well stay and make it look lived in. When you've had the baby, we'll think what to do next."

I liked the way she said 'when' not 'if.' It started to make things feel real. I should've known that things in my life never ran that smoothly.

The café wasn't far from the river in Worcester – near the bridge where large numbers of swans clustered. I noticed people – particularly those with children – saving the crusts from their sandwiches to throw to them. I imagined doing that myself with my own toddler – feeling sure that it'd be a girl, imagining her running on unsteady legs along the towpath ahead of me.

In my heart as I worked in the sweltering fried bacon and toast scented kitchen, I still clung to the miracle that Tobias might be alive somewhere. Sometimes when I was wiping the sticky chrome tables or sweeping the red and grey tiled floor, I'd notice someone walking past who looked like him and my heart would stop. Once I even ran out after a man, realising as I got close that any similarity was only a trick of the light, feeling a piercing ache of disappointment.

It was on a Thursday morning in late October when I started getting niggling pains in my stomach. I went to the staff toilet at the back of the café – a chilly dank place decorated with large white tiles. When I noticed the first faint smear of blood on the thin scratchy loo paper I didn't believe it.

Half an hour later I stumbled out of the loo and into the café doubled up in agony. Mick who owned the café was complaining because none of the tables had been wiped and a man who'd been sitting at a table by the window had dropped chips all over the floor.

"About bloody time, Fable, I thought you'd gone on holiday," he roared when I came through the kitchen door.

He took one look at me and called an ambulance.

Moira came with me to the hospital.

After I'd been to theatre, a young Scottish doctor sat by my bed and held my hand.

"Ye'll have lots of other chances to have children," he said.

I turned my face away, knowing my chances of having a child with Tobias were gone forever.

CHAPTER EIGHTEEN

After the miscarriage, I stayed on at Moira's. The journey she and Julie had planned was postponed until the following spring – I can't remember why. I couldn't face going back to work at the cafe – where every visit to the toilet would've reminded me of when the miscarriage started. I got a job in a trendy clothes shop where loud music played all day, blocking out the need to talk to anyone. Moira was concerned about how quiet I was and kept saying she thought I was depressed.

"Go and see the doctor," she'd suggested.

I'd ignored her.

I was better during the winter – I'd only known Tobias in the spring and summer – but the following May, when the cow parsley growing along the green edges of the towpath and the soapy, sexy smell of hawthorn blossom reminded me of that first time I'd seen him, I knew I had to get away.

When Julie and Moira decided to dust off their plans and go hitch-hiking through France and Spain for a couple of months, I went with them. When I reached the white dusty roads of rural Spain, edged by orange groves and olive trees and with the smell of citrus and spices in the hot dry air, so different to the rampant green and white of England, I felt I could walk forever. I'd almost decided to tell Julie and Moira to leave me here where I could live from one day to the next, eating olive bread and oranges and drinking the rough local red wine, moving from one place to another under the hard blue sky, picking up work where I could.

That was until the day when we'd just left Cordoba when we saw some gypsies camped by the side of the road. I immediately thought of Jasmine and how she'd always talked of travelling here. I walked towards their painted caravans, even though

Moira and Julie were hissing nervously at me to come back. "They're probably thieves or murderers, Fable, come back"…

An old woman with a face like carved mahogany dressed all in black whose slow movements reminded me of Gangan was stirring a large bubbling cooking pot over an open fire. An aromatic smell of onions, herbs and garlic came from it. She'd been slicing tomatoes and bread and the black handled knife was still in her hand.

She put the knife down when I crouched in the dust in front of her, covering it with a red cloth. Then she took my hand in hers and turned it over, tracing the lines on my palm, reminding me of the fortune-teller I'd seen at Martlebury Fair. Remembering what happened then, I pulled my hand away, wishing I'd taken notice of what Moira and Julie had said.

The gypsy rubbed her thumb and forefinger together, indicating she wanted money. Her dark eyes sparkled.

Other gypsies had gathered to watch what was going on, the young women dressed in brightly patterned skirts, the men for the most part wearing black. I looked around anxiously for Moira and Julie, noticing that they'd moved further along the road and were sitting in the shade of some orange trees.

I placed some silver coins in the woman's outstretched palm. She spat on them and put them in the pocket of her skirt and snatched my hand back, ignoring my protests.

In a high, imperious voice she called one of the young men over. "He spik England," she said.

A torrent of musical Romany flowed from one to the other as she stared at my hand as if she couldn't believe what she was seeing.

The man had oily blue-black hair that reminded me of a crow's wing and his teeth were very white in his dark face as he smiled at me.

"She say you find answer in England. You go back.

Look for ommens."

"Ommens?"

He wrinkled his forehead. "Zings that bring ze luck."

"Omens," I said.

"Yes – omens." He copied the way I spoke carefully.
"When?"

He questioned the old woman who answered again in
Romany. "She say you know when time come."

That night I heard Gangan's voice in my head saying:
"Didn't I always tell you to trust the universe and believe that
there's a meaning to everything. Our lives are mapped out
before we draw our first breath."

I returned to England, resolving to settle in the first
English place name I saw when we got off the ferry at Dover.
The first place name was on a removals lorry going to Croydon.
I told Julie and Moira that I was hitching a ride with the driver
– a young guy with tattooed fore-arms and a shaved head who
said he knew of a café job that might suit me. I said goodbye to
the two girls, promising I'd travel to Worcester to collect my
stuff as soon as I could.

"You've had some weird ideas since I've know you,
Fable," said Julie, "but this is about the daftest. How d'you
know he won't murder you on the way to Croydon …"

I didn't say anything.

"God, Fable, I'm sorry. I didn't think."

"She's right though," said Moira. "You don't want to
do stuff just because some old gypsy says."

"It feels right," I insisted.

They left me to it when I promised I'd get in touch as
soon as I got there. I noticed as they walked away that Julie had
written down the name of the removal firm and the registration
number.

The removal van driver was as good as his word, taking me to a café-bar near East Croydon station that was advertising for waitresses. It was called 'The Office' - a place where men stopping for an extra drink after work could hire a recording of office noises – typewriters, telephones, muffled voices – and tell their wives or girlfriends "back soon, dear. I'm still at The Office."

One of the girls working there said there was a spare room in the house she shared with two other girls. It felt as if things were working out at last.

Less than a month later, the Spanish gypsy's prediction came true.

I met Tony.

One of the other waitresses had served him with his coffee – strong, black, no sugar - but it was me he was staring at, in a way that reminded me of that first meeting with Tobias.

I stole covert glances at him while I was cleaning the glass-fronted counter where the cakes and doughnuts were. He was wearing a trendy aubergine coloured suit with a lilac shirt. His hair was dark brown and curled over his collar and his eyes were blue.

He was scanning through some paperwork – writing on some of the pages with an expensive-looking fountain pen. I noticed as I cleared a table near him that his handwriting was small and neat and that he used green ink.

Our eyes met as he gathered his papers together and zipped them into his black leather briefcase.

I looked away first, wondering why I felt nervous.

He was back again at lunchtime, sitting in what seemed to be his favourite seat in the corner by the window. I served him this time. His voice held traces of a Croydon accent – I noticed when he told me he worked in a solicitor's office in

Katharine Street, the word Katharine rhymed with 'wine.'

My hand shook when I put down his coffee cup, upsetting some of the frothy liquid on the smoky glass table when I saw the gold initials on his black leather folder – 'T.M.L.'

To cover my confusion I rushed off to get a cloth, colliding with another waitress, nearly making her spill the Coca Cola floats on her tray.

I felt his eyes on me as I stumbled through my apologies to the other girl. I fetched a damp cloth and mopped the table, my eyes focused on those gold initials. I told myself he'd think I was mad if I asked what the initials meant – and in any case, John who owned the café wasn't too keen on staff getting too chatty with customers.

He was waiting for me outside when I finished work at six o'clock.

"I don't usually hang around and pick up women," he said with a really nice smile." My name's Tony - "Tony Lucas. And I know your name's Fable 'cos I asked."

He steered me down George Street and then left along the High Street until we reached a pub called The Catherine Wheel that had oak beams and no juke box.

"I hate it when you come out of discos," he said, "with your ears ringing and it takes days for them to settle down."

"Do you like dancing?"

He shook his head. "Two left feet, me. I've just got a couple of old school friends who keep trying to match-make and drag me off to these places. I've ended up with some real horror stories…"

"Is your real name Anthony?"

I thought back to those gold initials.

"My mother didn't believe in giving people names she

wouldn't use. So my brother's called Ben and I'm Tony. I had a hard job convincing my boss. We have to wear these stupid name badges and when I first went there they gave me this one with Anthony Lucas on it. 'That's not my name,' I said. 'It is,' said the boss. I had to take my birth certificate in before he'd believe me and make a new badge."

He bought me several gin and tonics and we talked about his job and mine. Our fingers touched when he helped me put my jacket back on. I felt a jolt of electricity and judging from the way his eyes locked on mine, so did he.

He walked me back home, kissing my cheek before he left me at the gate.

*

He invited me out again a few days later. Then, after plying me with several gins, he'd kissed me in the Town Hall Gardens on the way home. I'd smelled cut grass and leaf mould and had felt like the earth was moving, although I may just have been unsteady because of the gin. After that I didn't see him for a few days. Then on Friday morning, he called in at The Office to ask if I'd go out for dinner with him that night.

"It's a do from work," he said, "so you may not want to. Food should be good though – it's at that French place in the High Street – Bistro Parisienne."

We'd sat crammed together in the garlic and herb scented bistro surrounded by images of Paris – the Eiffel Tower, Notre Dame and the Moulin Rouge. The seats were red velvet and the talk was all lawyer-speak.

"So you're young Lucas's intended?" said a lawyer looking at me over his half-moon glasses.

I choked on my coq au vin with shock, feeling conscious that the black lace dress I'd borrowed from one of my house-mates was lower cut than I'd normally wear.

"You look very nice," Tony said as he took my hand and led me onto the tiny dance floor.

"Why do your work colleagues think I'm your intended?" I asked.

"I thought you knew how I felt about you," he said.

I felt as if I was being swept along by a tidal wave that I couldn't stop. That night I drank more than I usually did, leaning on Tony as he walked me home. He was slimmer than Tobias - I could feel his ribs when he put his arms round me when he reached a secluded place sheltered by bushes on the way home.

He held my head and kissed me on the lips and I responded. He smelled of Lifebuoy soap and Brut aftershave. I almost fell over when he released me. The stars were out and there was a crescent moon that looked like a smile. The moon had looked like that when I'd first met Tobias.

We walked a few more paces towards my front gate and then Tony pulled me into the circle of his arms again. He held my head gently as he kissed my lips again, tangling his fingers in my hair.

Then his fingers moved lower, tracing the outline of my breasts, brushing the skin just inside the plunging neckline of my dress in a way that reminded me of when Tobias had first touched me in our willow den down by the river.

It felt like a good omen and I pressed closer to Tony as his hands framed my buttocks, gradually sliding the lacy fabric of my dress further up my legs until he reached the lace edging of my knickers.

A car raced along the road, blasting its horn. Two upstairs lights in my house came on.

Tony groaned. "They'll be sending out a search party."

He readjusted my dress and kissed me softly on the lips,

whispering that he had something special to ask me.

Kirsty was stunned when I rang and told her that Tony and I were engaged.

"Fable – don't. I think you're acting on the rebound."

"Rebound off what? Tobias is dead."

"Yeah I know. All the more reason to…"

"What?"

"That stuff you told me about the omens…"

"That gypsy in Spain told me that I should act on them."

"Lots of people on the planet might have the same initials as Tobias, but you wouldn't want to leap into bed with them."

I wish I'd listened to her.

CHAPTER NINETEEN

I didn't meet Tony's mother until a week after we got engaged and I had a feeling that he wouldn't have bothered to tell her about the wedding if I hadn't insisted on meeting her. It was a cold, grey late November Saturday where the sky settled heavy as a blanket over the Croydon skyline behind us. On the way to his mother's house, we'd passed some big white houses like wedding cakes and as we'd approached each one I'd wondered 'was this it?' But we kept on walking until we turned off into a maze of mean looking terraces at Woodside, finally ending up in a dead end street of two up two down terraced houses with postage stamp gardens front and back.

"We didn't have a bathroom till I was sixteen," said Tony, noticing my shocked expression. He knocked on the door of number forty-six. It was opened by a younger version of Tony who stared curiously at the yellow chrysanthemums I'd brought as if he'd never seen flowers before.

I remembered how Gangan always said you should never visit someone without taking a gift. "Flowers or chocolates," she said, "or better still, something you've made with your own hands."

The front door opened straight into a room crowded with furniture, smelling of mice and damp washing. Ben – Tony's brother – jerked his head towards the cheap looking red plastic sliding door that led to the next room.

Tony raised his eyebrows and let out a deep breath. He walked across the cluttered room in three strides, pulling me behind him, jerking open the sliding door. We were then in what could almost be a decompression chamber between two rooms. There was a small dark space, no more than two small steps wide, with another sliding door ahead of us – grey this time – and a steep, straight staircase on our right-hand side. This second room, like the first, was crowded with mismatched furniture.

Joan Lucas looked sourly at us from where she was sweeping the hearth with a brush that had very few bristles left. She made no response to the flowers I offered her and I stood holding them awkwardly as she carried on sweeping up the birdseed and feathers scattered by a blue and white budgie that chuntered away to its reflection in a small round mirror hung in its cage, angrily dinging its bell when it got no response.

Tony didn't say 'hello' to his mother or give her a hug. He put a cover over the budgie's cage and switched off the blaring radio, causing a momentary silence before he pitched in with:

"This may be a surprise, Ma, but Fable and I got engaged last week."

"Is she pregnant?" were the first words I heard my future mother-in-law say.

I should've left then – but the idea of the right omens being in place was still with me and I ignored that warning voice in my head that told me to walk away and keep going.

"Tea?" Ben edged past us, opening the glass-panelled wooden door that led to the lean-to kitchen, releasing the acrid smell of burnt toast. He made tea, slopping it onto the stained yellow formica table. I wondered where his mother made cakes or bread. Apart from a small space on the table, there was no work surface.

"Tea, Ma?"

Joan ignored him. Then when he'd handed us our mugs of copper coloured tea, she pushed past him and made her own, standing moodily in the kitchen to drink it while Ben, Tony and I perched in the cluttered middle room making awkward conversation.

Banging and crashing in the kitchen, reminding me of the way Sheila used to behave, announced that Joan was starting to prepare a meal. Despite the fact that the oven was on, the whole house felt chilly, damp and unwelcoming.

"Does she want any?" she asked Tony.

"We hadn't planned to stay for more than afternoon tea," Tony said. "Fable and I are eating out tonight."

"Huh, afternoon tea," Joan muttered to herself in the kitchen as she fished out two shop-bought pasties from the fridge, shoved them on a blackened baking tray and put them in the oven. She opened a tin of beans and stood that in the oven next to the baking tray.

She didn't say goodbye.

"She's got a heart of gold when you get to know her," Tony said as we walked back towards the twilit Croydon skyline. I'd never seen him so ill-at-ease.

*

A cold March wind was blowing when I arrived at the Registry Office. There was a hostile atmosphere between Ben and his mother.

"Don't lie, it was your fault," she kept hissing at him, before lapsing into a sulk, her bottom lip sticking out like a shelf.

"What's going on?" I asked Ben, trying to sound brighter than I felt.

"She finks I left the budgie's cage open on purpose," he said, his ears flushing red.

"You did, Ben," interrupted the dragon.

"Well you must've let the bleedin' cat in," he said.

"'Ere, don't bloody swear," said Joan. She was wearing a cream raincoat, a black straw hat and an evil expression and hadn't mentioned the wedding.

"She looks a bundle of laughs," said Kirsty who, as my maid of honour, was dressed in blue velvet. She adjusted the blue satin ribbons on my white lacy hat. "Fable, it's not too late to change your mind."

As my eyes met hers in the waiting room mirror, catching her anxious expression, part of me did want to change my mind – to respond to a weird impulse and run out of the building and leap on the first bus that came along. If Gangan or anyone from my past had spoken at that point I'd have acted on it. I heard nothing, saw no omens in the bleached sky. Instead I went through the brief marriage service as if I was sleep-walking.

We had a small lunch-time reception in 'The Office' – my boss John's wedding present to us. Joan dismissed the place as 'too posh' and said the spicy nibbles would give her indigestion. She got drunk and started singing 'why are we waiting' and flashing her knickers.

Tony looked at me and gave an uneasy tight-lipped smile. "Let's go," he said.

Within minutes he'd grabbed our cases from behind the counter and we'd raced for the station, me almost skidding over in my new white platform shoes.

Soon we were on our way to Brighton – the place had become something of a private joke between us – a number of Tony's clients had their illicit affairs discovered in Brighton. Tony had promised we'd have a more exotic holiday next year.

"If we can get a foot on the property ladder by then," he said. "I don't want to end up like my mother – renting all my life."

The memories came flooding back as soon as we arrived at Brighton and I wished for a number of reasons that we'd never come here.

*

Walking on the pier in the blustery late afternoon I remembered the time I'd come on holiday here with Gangan and Jasmine and how frightened I'd been then looking down through the wooden floorboards to the grey-green sea swirling underneath. Jasmine had laughed at me, alternately scared of falling through the cracks and then glancing nervously upwards at the cold-eyed orange-beaked seagulls that would swoop down and snatch an ice-cream cone or a sandwich crust.

Patrick O'Hagan and Teresa came to spend the last day of our holiday with us and had offered to bring us home. We all sat on the beach together like a proper family, the sun had shone all day and the sea for once was calm and the same turquoise colour as the glass trinket boxes on Jasmine's dressing table. Gangan bought rolls and ham and made us a picnic on the beach. Teresa and I drank ginger beer through straws laughing as we blew bubbles.

We made a pretend tea party for our teddy bears using small stones and seaweed. Patrick bought us fishing nets and we searched the rock pools for shrimps. Later he took us in the sea and we squealed and jumped as the waves leapt over our bare legs. We ate hotdogs on the pier with fried onions and red sauce and played on the penny machines in the amusement arcade.

Later, Patrick and Jasmine left us for a while. Jasmine said she needed to pack and Patrick said he needed to check how he could get all our luggage in the car as well as all of us.

I noticed that Gangan's mouth was set in a disapproving line as they walked away but she didn't say anything.

Teresa and I carried on collecting mussel shells and seeing how many varieties of blue we could find. We ran laughing in and out of the tiny incoming waves.

"Don't you girls go getting them dresses wet," called Gangan. "And them bears of yours'll get wet if you don't come and move them."

The light was fading when Patrick and Jasmine came back for us, exchanging secret looks. Jasmine sat in the front passenger seat as we set off. On the way home we stopped at a pub for a drink and Jasmine changed places with Gangan, sitting in the back of the car with Teresa and I.

I was so lost in my memories as we walked on the pier, that I'd almost forgotten that Tony and I were now man and wife. I walked back to our hotel room, trying to dismiss the thought that I'd done the wrong thing. After all, it must be right – I'd followed the omens like the Spanish gypsy told me to.

*

I'd told Tony about Jasmine, Peggy and Gangan and he'd promised to help me find them after our honeymoon. He didn't keep his word. He went behind my back and contacted Derek.

Tony and I had just finished eating toad in the hole when he dropped his bombshell, spitting the words like bullets, reminding me chillingly of his mother.

"You didn't tell me your mother is an alcoholic."

I nearly dropped the plates I was carrying back to the kitchen. "What do you know about Jasmine?"

"Your father told me about her." Tony looked tight-lipped and angry.

"He doesn't know what he's talking about. She might be better now. You promised you'd help me find her."

"I think it's better that you forget she ever existed. Draw a line under that part of your life. After all, what if she turned up on the doorstep and started making a nuisance of herself?"

"She's my mother." My throat felt stiff and parched.

"Your father tells me you received psychiatric help when you were a child."

"He stole me away from a place where I was happy."

"From what I can gather, he did you a favour. It seems you were in a very unstable situation."

"I was loved."

CHAPTER TWENTY

I tried to leave Tony several times during the first year of our marriage, but each time something stopped me, throwing me back into the quicksand of our relationship like a wave pounding the shore.

Despite what Tony said, there was no way I could pretend that my mother had never existed. I was determined to carry on looking for her, trying hospital after hospital, sometimes getting closer, but mostly having my hopes dashed. These times were bleaker now without Kirsty to commiserate and tell me to keep trying.

It was early December, with frost on the ground and the stars looking sharp as tin in the dark sky. Tony and I had gone to bed early – me because I was tired and Tony because he wanted sex. This led to yet another disagreement. We didn't argue because Tony never would. He'd keep on and on, wearing me down with his lawyer-speak, making out that I was the one being unreasonable until I almost believed it myself. Then, like his mother, he'd lapse into hostile silence.

Tonight Tony had done what he usually did – approximately two minutes of foreplay as if he was twiddling the knobs on a piece of machinery - before climbing on top of me.

"You could look as if you were enjoying it," he grumbled.

"I would if I was," I said. I'd actually been thinking about train times and whether or not I had enough money to get to Moira's in Worcester. I had no idea what I'd do then.

Tony had climbed off, looking grumpy. "You're about as exciting as a sackload of spuds," he said. "Maybe you should see a counsellor."

"Maybe you should think about me a bit more."

"What's that got to do with anything?" His eyes were cold. "Who have you got that idea from?"

"It's just that … well, the colours are only just starting to come by the time you've finished. So maybe we're a bit out of time with each other…"

He snorted. "There speaks Fable, the well-known expert on sexual matters."

He rolled over and immediately fell asleep. By the time I'd woken up the next morning, he'd gone to work.

I'd lain there for ages thinking about that one time with Tobias, knowing that with his death I'd lost something truly precious. I also knew that Kirsty had been right in what she'd said before the wedding· "Never marry a man you haven't slept with, Fable. Without that, you won't know if the chemistry's truly there. It's the same as finding out if you like the same foods or the same kind of holidays."

She'd been right and up till now I'd been too proud to admit it. I'd got out of bed, dusted off a suitcase and was about to pack my things and go when two surprising things happened. The phone rang and I answered it with a sinking feeling that it might be Tony ringing to have another go at me.

"Mrs Lucas?" asked a woman's voice smooth as milk chocolate. "We spoke some time ago about the problems you were having with tracing your mother."

My heart leapt with excitement. "You've found her?"

"Sadly, no, but I do have a positive lead for you. She was last heard of at Foster's Grange, near Malvern. I've got a phone number for you if you'd like it. Mrs Lucas …?"

I rang Moira straight away, thinking as soon as I'd dialled the number that she'd probably be at work, knowing also that Tony would go ballistic at the unnecessary phone call at peak time. Then a sense of relieve flooded me that by tonight I wouldn't be here any more. I'd be on my way to Worcester – and who knows, by the end of the week I could be with my mother again.

To my surprise, Kirsty answered.

"Fable, why didn't you call back? Moira left two messages for you. She so wanted you to be at her wedding. She's on her honeymoon now…"

"I didn't know." I wondered why Tony hadn't bothered to pass on the messages.

"Kirsty – I need a favour."

"You and me both," she said. "My Mum's got a new bloke and he made it clear he didn't want me around. I'm OK here until Moira and Kevin get back… got an offer to follow up at a place in Sidbury. Anyway, how're you doing?"

I didn't know what to say. It felt as if I'd been given something with one hand only to have it snatched away. I looked at the dusty suitcase on the bed. Without money I could go nowhere and it didn't look as if there was anywhere to go. I heard the sound of Tony's key in the front door and quickly replaced the receiver, wondering what I'd say when he queried why I needed to make a long distance phone call first thing in the morning. I shoved the suitcase back under the bed, pulling down the bedspread to hide it.

I went to the top of the stairs, wearily preparing myself for a re-run of last night's bedtime discussion expecting Tony to look tight-lipped like the usually did on those occasions. He'd carelessly shoved his briefcase to the far side of our tiny sitting room and was smiling.

"They've offered me a promotion," he said.

"Where?" I felt a tight knot in the pit of my stomach, knowing that wherever it was it didn't appear that I had any say in the matter.

"Malvern," he said.

It was like drawing The Sun card from a tarot deck. I told myself that despite my feelings about the marriage, it was obvious that I was in the right place because here was yet another omen. I'd go to Malvern with Tony, find myself a job that he considered suitable – he'd made me give up working at the café because that wasn't what lawyers' wives did – and repair the gaps in my friendship with Moira and Kirsty.

*

We moved in January on a day when the Malvern Hills looked as if they'd been glazed with a thin layer of icing into a flat in a Victorian house not far from the library. Then, just as I was about to start a filing job in a local newspaper office, I discovered I was pregnant. Tony's excitement about my news – he was sure I was having a boy – soon disappeared when I was sick for the first few months, combined with a feeling of complete exhaustion that left me only able to lie on the sofa.

"I think you're making things up," he said, when I told him I couldn't cook him bacon and eggs because the smell set off my morning sickness or when the sight of uncooked sausages in the butcher's window had me heading for the nearest public loo.

He turned white with panic that October morning when I woke him to say that my waters had broken and we'd better head for the hospital. As he drove through the dark streets towards the hospital I looked at the stars, remembering the stories of my own birth in the orchard at 'Starlight.'

"I hate hospitals," said Tony. "I can't even visit someone without feeling bad." He passed out before the large midwife with the streaming cold had even examined me. They sent him home.

"Husbands are a nuisance in this situation – you'll be hours yet," said the midwife.

"But my waters went hours ago…"

She was already walking away.

My hair was wet with sweat and my white hospital gown was sticking to me. The pains rose and fell, getting more vicious. I thought I could hear Gangan's voice but she was a long way away.

Another green-gowned midwife examined me. "There's no water here."

I was taken to a side-ward, rigged up to a drip and given an injection of pethedine. Nurses came and went. I asked them questions and fell into a doze before I'd heard the answer, only to be jerked into wakefulness when the pain soared again.

The hands of the clock moved slowly. I heard trolleys clanking up and down the corridor outside, smelled wafts of cottage pie, heard voices as people paused outside the door and moved on. For what seemed like hours, nobody came near me. My window overlooked the car park. It was midday when the drip was put in and now the sun was setting and sullen clouds obscured the moon. Gangan's voice was fainter now.

Once, I thought I heard Tobias. I opened my eyes a fraction and he was standing in the shadows. "Stick with it, Fable. Don't let the angels have you yet."

"Take me with you," I screamed. "Don't leave me here. Nothing's been right since you died." I reached out to him, nearly falling out of bed.

Two pairs of hands pull me back.

I heard Tony's voice – strong and authoritative. "Why has my wife been left in this state? Why isn't someone with her? I'm a solicitor."

"We thought she was just making a fuss."

There was another agonising examination. I reached out to Tobias but he was already fading away. I saw a shadow cross the face of the moon and I was sure my baby was dead.

Tony was sent outside.

In the corner of the room, a nurse made a telephone call. Seconds later, two men in green robes crashed through the double doors. I felt an injection in my leg and then my feet were put into stirrups. I screamed as the cold metal forceps were pushed inside me and then relaxed when I realised that Tobias was with me, holding my hand. I felt as if I was floating through space with him towards a brilliant white light. I looked down and saw my body lying on the bed. A nurse and doctor were trying to restart my heart while another nurse wrapped my baby in a pink blanket.

*

For what seemed like hours, Tobias and I floated weightless in soft darkness. Then his grip on my hand loosened and the white light glimmered and faded.

"Fable, they won't let me take you. The pull from earth is too strong," Tobias said.

I screamed for him to take me with him, I didn't want to go back to earth, but his image faded into the blackness and I tumbled back into my body lying motionless on the bed. I had no idea if my baby was alive or dead and I didn't really care. All I wanted was to be with Tobias.

I had a vague impression of Tony sitting by my bed and of him saying something like: "We've got a beautiful daughter, Fable. Now you just need to get yourself right, draw a line under what's happened ..."

I closed my eyes. The next time I opened them he'd gone.

The next morning, a doctor came into my room carrying a baby with him wrapped in a white shawl.

"You have a lovely little girl, Mrs Lucas – and you're a lucky lady to still be with us."

I could see that the baby had a downy fuzz of blonde hair and that her blue eyes were open. She was making milky nuzzling noises and all I wanted was for the doctor to take her away so that I could sleep. Maybe when I woke up, I'd be dead after all – and with Tobias.

The doctor tucked the baby in beside me for a few minutes. I closed my eyes, not wanting to be bothered. The doctor touched my shoulder gently. "Give your daughter a kiss," he said.

I did so, feeling numb, and he took her away.

We called her Cara because Tony liked the name.

CHAPTER TWENTY-ONE

When Cara was eighteen months old I discovered I was pregnant again. I didn't feel ready to have another child, remembering the horror of Cara's birth.

"Maybe it'll be a boy this time," said Tony, although he didn't sound any more enthusiastic than I was.

We couldn't afford to buy a house in Malvern – Tony dismissed any suggestions I made as 'impractical or downright stupid' – so we looked further afield. I was sorry - I liked being in Malvern, despite the fact that yet another trail leading to my mother had gone cold by the time we got there. One advantage was that I could catch the train to Worcester easily and meet up with Kirsty and Julie, catch up on old times.

Moving to Enderbury – a new town with very few amenities – made that much more difficult, unless I went into Birmingham first.

We bought a house that was one of a line of sentry boxes. There was a garden front and back that was a blank canvas of bare earth. I thought of the garden at 'Starlight' and wondered how I could recreate that without spending too much money in case Tony got upset again. No matter what I did, I never got it right. One minute he'd actively encourage me to buy something extravagant for the house – a painting or a new sofa – and then a few hours later he'd go cold and angry because I'd spent five pounds too much at the supermarket.

As with my last pregnancy, I suffered with sickness and extreme tiredness. I'd never learned to drive but this had never bothered me. I was usually happy to walk. In any case, trying to get on a bus with Cara, her buggy and any shopping I had was a major exercise. Tony had never tried it so he didn't know. He never changed Cara or fed her and didn't even wake in the night when she was at her most fractious.

Unlike most of the mothers I spoke to at the clinic, I hadn't fallen instantly in love with my baby. Although the urge to get away from Tony was still there, the desire to protect Cara and give her a settled environment to grow up in mattered more.

It was a wet July afternoon about three months into the pregnancy when I remembered that Tony had asked me that morning to collect his best suit from the cleaners. It had been a difficult day. Cara was cutting some teeth, I was feeling so exhausted I didn't know how I'd get through the rest of the day and rain was lashing the windows. I knew Tony would complain, but he'd got at least ten beautiful suits in his wardrobe, surely one of those would do for the meeting he was going to. I was upstairs putting some towels in the airing cupboard when he came home. Cara was having a nap.

"Where did you put my suit?"

I took a deep breath. "I didn't get it. It's rained all day and Cara and I would've got soaked."

He glared at me.

"You could go and get it yourself," I said. "They're open till six."

"I've been at work all day so that you can sit on your arse in luxury. All I wanted was for you to get my suit from the cleaners." His voice was low and dangerous. "Can't you manage to do anything? You're completely fucking useless."

I backed away from him, frightened at the tone of his voice. I stumbled and fell awkwardly at the top of the stairs, tumbling down about eight steps to the half landing where we kept a large rubber plant. I'd wrenched my ankle and there was a searing pain in my stomach.

Tony rang for an ambulance. He said he wouldn't come

with me to the hospital because he didn't want Cara left with a neighbour and waking up scared because we weren't there.

I was scared and shivering, remembering that last miscarriage I'd had. Tony was cold and detached. He didn't hold my hand or comfort me while we waited for the ambulance.

"I never did anything against you. Don't tell anyone we argued or they'll take Cara away."

I came home from hospital a few days later feeling cold and empty. Tony's mother had come for a few days to look after Cara. He'd driven down to fetch her from Croydon. She'd only ever visited once before – and that occasion hadn't been a success. She'd left, vowing never to come again.

"She's going back on the coach this afternoon," Tony said as he helped me into the front passenger seat of the car, giving every impression to the nursing staff of being a caring husband.

The first thing I noticed when Tony opened the front door was that the landscape painting that hung in the hall had been taken down. The downstairs cloakroom, which had originally been cream, had been repainted sickly yellow and in the through lounge the dining table and chairs had changed ends with the sofas.

"Looks better like that doesn't it," said Joan as she went into the kitchen to put the kettle on.

I noticed that all my pots and pans had been moved round and that the plants on the windowsill were dead.

Tony looked at me meaningfully.

"I liked it as it was before," I said.

Neither of them took any notice of me. I tried to feel glad to be home.

Cara stroked my face and said "Mummy better now."

After Joan had gone, I asked Tony why he'd moved all the furniture. "I thought you liked it as it was."

"I do. Did" He smiled apologetically. "When she's in one of those moods it's better to let her do what she wants. We can always move it back now she's gone."

Some things never went back as they had been – I never discovered what happened to the painting that had been in the hall.

Tony bought me a diamond bracelet to make up for all the upset.

"Friends again, darling," he said as he fastened it round my wrist.

That night I took it off and shoved it in a box at the back of my wardrobe. I never wore it again.

Despite the fact that I did nothing to prevent it, I didn't conceive again. Tony didn't mention the miscarriage and I never had a chance to grieve for my lost baby. The only thing he did say was that if I ever said anything against him, he'd make sure I never saw Cara again. I didn't want her to go through what I had since Jasmine and I lost touch so for the time being I complied, going through the motions of being an obedient wife.

CHAPTER TWENTY-TWO

Cara is nearly sixteen now – the same age I was when I met Tobias. Up till now, she's felt more like Tony's child than mine. I wonder if things will change as she gets older. Since the Solstice when I heard Gangan's voice again after so many years, I've felt different about my life – more positive. I knew that my life was about to change, I just didn't know how it could.

"Look for omens, mark the signs," said Gangan.

I looked and saw nothing, until at the end of February I felt a surge of excitement when I saw the poster in the library advertising a poetry competition. You see, it felt as if the poster had been written especially for me. 'Dig out those poems you've got hidden away,' it said. 'Show how writing has changed your life.'

How could they have known about the poems hidden away in my drawer upstairs – or that it had changed my life so much. What had prompted me to go into the library just then, just as a lady in a flowing skirt that reminded me of the ones Jasmine used to wear was putting up the poster on one of the pillars near the enquiry desk.

"It's your Wheel of Fortune, Fable dear," said Gangan – her voice sounding so loud that I looked round the quiet library half expecting that other people had heard it.

I wrote down the details – luckily the poems didn't have to be typed – bought paper and ink from the art shop near the library and went home to write out the poems neatly – twenty poems each in its own clean white space written in black ink. I created a title page – 'Childhood Interrupted' and added my contact details, put everything in a large envelope taken from Tony's study, wondering what he'd say if he knew how I'd spent my afternoon. I hurried back to the library with my package before I lost my nerve and just shoved the poems back in the drawer.

A brisk wind was blowing the daffodils in the gardens that I passed and I remembered how Gangan used to call daffodils and white convolvulus 'angel trumpets.'

I took a deep breath as I walked back into the library and across to the enquiry desk. The librarian I'd seen putting up the poster was sitting there. She had a cloud of dark curly hair and gold hoop earrings.

"It takes a lot of courage to put your life on paper," she said when I handed her the envelope.

I looked at her, startled, wondering if she was clairvoyant and could see through the envelope. She had kind brown eyes and I suddenly thought how long it had been since I'd had a proper friend. I didn't count the wives of Tony's work colleagues as friends and he'd discouraged me from keeping in touch with Kirsty, even though she was only an hour's bus ride away.

"Now that you've begun, you must keep going on your journey," said the librarian.

"I hadn't thought of it as a journey," I said, "but now you mention it, my life has changed so much since I began."

"Try to write something every day," she said. "And keep faith with what you're doing."

Another librarian called out "Linnet, you're wanted on the phone."

She smiled apologetically. "We'll talk again soon, I'm sure of it. Call in and see me next time you're in town."

I hugged the secret of my new friendship as I walked home in the gathering darkness, hurrying to get there before Cara wondered where I was and started asking questions about where I'd been and what I'd been doing.

Later that night I awoke from a dream where I'd been wandering along a moss-green carpeted corridor in a stately home I'd never seen before. There were large oak doors on each side of the wide corridor and I wasn't sure which one I was supposed to go through.

I spotted a house-maid dressed in black with a white cap and apron and she curtsied as she pointed out the right door. I pushed it open and found myself in a room lit by a large, glittering chandelier and packed with people I'd never seen before sitting on spindly-legged gilt chairs around a large wooden lectern with a carved eagle on it.

Linnet was waiting for me. She took me by the hand and led me to the lectern.

"We've been waiting for you," she said.

I'd woken up then, feeling cheated to find myself in bed with Tony. Rain was lashing the windows next to me on one side, and on the other, Tony was lying flat on his back, snoring his head off – a thing he maintained he never did. Trying to make sense of the dream, I went down to the kitchen to make tea and then sat at the table with my notebook writing down every detail.

There was a full moon outside the window and I could clearly see the three stars of Orion's belt in the midnight sky.

When I heard Cara's light footsteps on the stairs, I flipped the page over, pretending that I was writing a shopping list.

"Couldn't sleep either, huh?" she asked as she poured herself a mug of tea from the pot. She seemed in a good mood for once and I was reminded of Gangan and Jasmine and some of the late-night conversations they had when I was a child. I pointed up the stairs.

"I'd defy anyone to sleep in that."

Cara giggled, spurting tea all over the pine kitchen table. "Oops, sorry." She fetched the dishcloth. "Reminds you of whale love songs, doesn't it? Maybe I could get some of the boys from school to come round with their guitars and do a recording."

"You could design the cover for it."

She giggled again. "Yeah – all waves and whale-spouts. Whale-spout'd be a good title."

She talked about the artwork she was doing for her GCSE and what the art teacher had said about the artist Georgia O'Keefe. "Like, when she moved to New York and she painted flowers, she thought it was no use doing them the usual size because New Yorkers just wouldn't take any notice. So she painted them so big it looks like you could almost walk inside them."

Her violet-blue eyes shone, reminding me of Jasmine when she was carried away with a dress design. "This journalist came to interview her and they were walking towards some trees. He said to her, 'what can you see?' and she said 'what can you see?' He said 'leaves against sky' and she said 'sky against leaves.'

I thought of the poem I'd written, now in the envelope I'd handed into the library, called 'Handful of Leaves' about that time by the river at Isbourne when I'd first met Tobias, wondering what Tony would say if he ever read it.

I put our empty mugs in the sink and kissed Cara goodnight.

"See you in a few hours," we told each other as we went back upstairs, stifling giggles because Tony was still snoring.

At breakfast time I joked with Tony about how Cara and I had heard him snoring. Tony was eating toast and marmalade, cutting the toast into slices like he usually did. He'd propped the Telegraph against the teapot on the kitchen table and was reading the sports page.

He'd been in a good mood when he'd first got up, whistling while he was shaving in the bathroom. Now he shot a sideways look at Cara and glared at me.

Cara was staring at her bowl of cornflakes as if she couldn't quite work out what she was meant to do with it. There were dark circles under her eyes and she was fussing with her hair at the table, something Tony usually disapproved of.

"Is this true?" he asked Cara. "Maybe I ought to get up and join you for one of your little midnight feasts."

Cara's face was smooth as alabaster as she looked coolly back at him. "Nah, Mum's making it up," she said.

"As I keep saying, she's been acting oddly lately," said Tony. He and Cara exchanged a conspiratorial look and I felt a stab of unease, wondering if I'd imagined the events of last night.

*

Later that day, as I was passing the library on the way back from the shops, I met Linnet on her way back from lunch. "Call in for a few minutes," she said. "I wanted to ask if you wanted to join my new writing group. The first session's tomorrow."

Even before we'd gone through the heavy doors into the library, I'd said yes. After all, there was no reason why Tony should ever find out about it. I was so excited that night that I could hardly sleep, hoping and praying that Tony wouldn't suddenly decide to work at home or that Cara wouldn't be ill and need to stay off school.

During that first session the group of six sat round one of the tables at the far end of the library where there was a large window that looked out onto a few bushes starred with Coke cans and chocolate wrappers. The path into town was on the far side of that, but very few people walked past, and in any case I was so interested in what was going on I wasn't worried if they did.

Linnet gave us a series of ten-minute exercises and the time flew by. We wrote about colours, we wrote about seasons and we wrote about childhood memories. She did a visualisation where she took us on a tour of a magical garden, asking us to hold the memory of what we saw. I saw a rainbow border of flowers - hot pink, acid yellow, indigo and purple. I felt the warmth of the sun on my skin and through the soles of my feet as I walked barefoot on the hot marble pathway. I saw glittering diamonds in the droplets of water in the fountain, smelled lemon and almond blossom and touched the damask silkiness of rose petals.

I opened my eyes, preparing to write all this down but Cara's face was all I could see, framed by the window opposite me. I blinked and she was gone. My excitement about the class evaporated like a burst balloon and I dreaded going home. It was only when I'd nearly reached our house, the tight feeling in my chest growing worse with each step, that I wondered what she was doing playing truant from school.

Cara waited until tea-time before she said anything. I'd just served up toad-in-the-hole and baked beans – one of Tony's favourites. Cara sat picking at hers, taking all the skin off her sausages and eating just the crispy bits of batter. I wondered how it was she always managed to make it look as if there was more on her plate when she'd finished than when she'd started the meal.

"Don't mess about with it, Cara," said Tony crossly.

His meeting hadn't gone well today and he'd barely

spoken since he got home.

"What were you doing in the library with all those weirdos today, Mum?" asked Cara as she took her plate out to the kitchen. I could hear her scraping her left-overs into the bin. She came back and sat at the table, resting her elbows on it and leaning her chin on her hands.

She looked at Tony. "It was really embarrassing, Dad. There she was sitting round this table with a load of people who looked like they were on a day out from the local nut farm. They were closing their eyes like this - she squinched her eyes shut - while some woman was talking to them."

I touched the small piece of rose quartz Linnet had given me after the workshop and prayed for someone to help me.

Tony looked at me with one eyebrow raised. "Would you care to enlighten us, Fable?" He sounded like he was cross-examining a witness in court.

I took a deep breath. The food I'd just eaten felt like it had settled as a solid lump just below my breast-bone. "I was attending a writing group."

They both collapsed laughing. "*You* were?" said Tony.

"Don't you know how to write yet, Mum?" asked Cara.

"Fable's fables – that's a good one," spluttered Tony wiping his eyes.

I picked up Tony's plate and took it to the kitchen. By the time I'd returned with the apple pie and custard he and Cara were talking about something else and the writing group wasn't mentioned again.

CHAPTER TWENTY-THREE

The week after Easter, the whole country was devastated by thunderstorms and torrential rain that battered the daffodils in our front garden to scraps of yellow silk.

The news reports on the radio carried story after story about power lines being down, people disregarding flood warnings and drowning in freak accidents and homes and businesses being wrecked.

When the phone rang very late one night I didn't recognise the quavery voice on the other end of the line.

"Fable, is that you?"

"Who is it?"

"Sheila."

My first instinct was to slam the phone down. She was the last person I wanted to speak to and I felt irritated that she'd still got our address. I thought Tony had understood years ago why I no longer wanted anything to do with Derek, but I was wrong. I know Tony had gone to see Derek after our wedding, but I'd not seen him since that day long ago when I'd left Isbourne. Tony had obviously disregarded my feelings and had sent change of address cards each time we'd moved. For all I knew, he could've taken Cara to visit him.

The one time I'd challenged Tony as to why he'd contacted Derek, he'd said: "He is your father. He's got a right to know where you are and how to get in touch when he needs to."

"As far as I'm concerned he's got no rights at all," I'd said.

Sheila was still on the other end of the phone.

"What do you want Sheila?"

"It's your father. He wants to see you."

I looked out at the torrent of water pouring from the sullen skies and greying out the houses opposite. "Why?"

"Please, Fable. He may not have long. The doctor's trying to find him a hospital bed – the Infirmary's flooded and they've had to airlift some of the patients. He doesn't want to leave the Vicarage in case she's out there waiting for him. He's been having those nightmares again…"

"Sheila, you're not making any sense."

Tony had come home and was making a lot of fuss about taking off his wet coat and mopping his briefcase dry. He'd only come from the car. He looked enquiringly at me and pointed to the phone. I scribbled 'Derek' on a piece of paper and he shook his head. I saw him go into the kitchen and pour himself a glass of whisky before he looked through the cupboards to see what he could eat. I hadn't bothered cooking anything because Cara had gone to a friend's for the night and Tony had said he'd be having a cooked lunch at his meeting and wouldn't need anything.

"What can I eat?" he asked loudly, seeming oblivious to the fact that I was talking to someone.

"I'll get you something when I've put the phone down," I said, putting my hand over the receiver and wondering why he always had to bang around and make a noise when he could see I was busy. If he was the one on the phone he'd go ballistic if anyone so much as whispered.

I heard Sheila take a deep breath that was more like a sob.

"He was doing a wedding on Saturday," she said. "As you can imagine it was a terrible day for it. They had to have the lights on in church it was so dark and dismal. The ceremony was going all right. He'd got to the last few minutes of it. And then he went most peculiar – as if he'd seen a ghost.

Nobody else appeared to see the woman he was babbling about, but one of the flower arrangements in the porch had been shredded and a letter 'J' created in flower petals…"

I felt a surge of hope. "Expect me sometime tomorrow," I said. "I hope the buses are still running."

Tony, clutching half a pork pie in one hand and his glass of whisky in the other, glared at me from the other end of the hall. "How are you going to get there?" he asked as soon as I put the phone down. "Wouldn't it be more sensible to wait until the floods subside?"

"Derek may be dead by then."

Tony didn't say anything. I went upstairs to pack a small suitcase. He followed me, watching my every move, but didn't say anything.

"As I said before, Tony, if you hadn't bothered sending them a change of address card, then they wouldn't be able to contact me. As they have, and it's his dying wish that I should be there, then I'm going. If you're not prepared to take me, then I'll catch the nine o'clock bus."

I wasn't bothered about seeing Derek. What mattered was that my mother was still alive. She'd been in the church on Saturday. If I got there before her trail went cold, there was a chance we'd find each other this time.

CHAPTER TWENTY-FOUR

As the bus pulled in to Isbourne just after ten o'clock, I gazed through the curtains of rain as we passed the station, remembering how I'd hidden in the Ladies Waiting Room that first time I'd tried to escape, with my few possessions crammed into my brown leather school bag together with all the money I'd owned. I remembered the anger and disappointment I'd felt when Derek had prevented me from getting on the train to Paddington and how I'd vowed never to come back here once I was free.

Taking a deep breath, I hauled my suitcase off the bus when it pulled into the town centre. The air smelled of a mixture of chocolate cake from Sunset Foods and engine oil. A blast of rain and wind hit me as I reached the one remaining taxi parked near where the buses pulled in. The driver pulled a face when I told him where I wanted to go.

"Worst end of town, love. Shops in Waterside are flooded and the river's right across the road. People in them houses opposite must be shitting 'emselves. Still, hop in. I'll take you as far as I can." He tossed his newspaper onto the back seat, got out and put my suitcase in the boot and held open the front passenger door for me. He set off, sending plumes of water spurting upwards from the edges of the road.

Rivulets of water ran down each side of the High Street. I looked from side to side, noticing familiar shops and those that had changed hands. The Indian shop that Kirsty and I had loved was now a beauty parlour – white walls and pictures of immaculately groomed women replacing the Taj Mahal posters and orange and purple banners with elephants on them. The windscreen wipers of the taxi were on full, making little impression on the water pouring down.

The taxi driver was still chatting away, not noticing if I answered or not.

"… some silly bugger got swept away crossing a ford. You'd think folks'd look before they drive into tack like that."

We passed red warning triangles saying 'Flood' as we crossed the bridge near Waterside and turned right. Then I saw the dark brooding shape of the Vicarage ahead of us and began to have doubts as to whether I should've come.

"Here we are then."

I paid the taxi driver. He unloaded my suitcase and handed it to me, then got back into the car, speeding back the way we'd come towards the town centre.

I pushed open the creaking front gate and made my way down the dripping overgrown pathway to the door. I rang the bell, hearing its echo inside the house. It was ages before anyone answered and I pulled my waterproof more tightly round me, wishing again that I hadn't bothered to make the journey.

"Oh it's you." Sheila peered at me from the dark recesses beyond the front door.

"Who did you expect?" I felt irritated. "Sheila, let me in. It's sopping wet out here." I stepped into the hallway, breathing in the never-forgotten smells of bleach, damp and musty books.

Sheila stood in front of me looking as if she didn't know what to do next. I dumped my suitcase at the bottom of the stairs, feeling as if I wanted to shake her.

"It was terrible," she began. "You have no idea the torments he's been going through… the nightmares…"

"He's always had those," I said sharply. "The funny thing is when I mentioned them years ago, he accused me of imagining what I'd heard."

I'd never seen anyone wring their hands before. Sheila's

were like pale fish swimming one over the other in an endless circle.

"He was good to you. You shouldn't speak ill of him."

"Wouldn't we be warmer in the kitchen?" My jacket and boots were soaked and my teeth were chattering.

Sheila seemed to gather herself a little. "I could put the kettle on."

I followed her along the hall and into the dismal kitchen, watched her fill the kettle, put it on the stove and light the gas. She peered in the cupboard, looking for the coffee jar. I had no doubt it would be the same as it always used to be – a jar of the cheapest available from the supermarket and just a scraping of coffee in the bottom of it.

"I'm still waiting for the doctor to call," said Sheila. "There have been so many injuries over the last few days – so many people needing help. I didn't like to be too pushy."

I went to the window, looking out at the river, oily black under glowering skies.

"How seriously ill is he?"

She didn't meet my gaze. "The river's already swallowing up the graveyard – just like he feared it would." Sheila pushed a cracked mug of weak coffee towards me, wrapping her pale hands round her own.

I didn't say anything. Suddenly the memory of hearing about Tobias's death, here in this kitchen, surfaced like something washed up by the flood and I couldn't stop shivering.

Sheila didn't appear to notice. "It was your mother's fault," she went on. "She was here, dressed in red at the back of the church when he was conducting a wedding last Saturday. Taunting him. That's what he says. But I said, how could she be? She was supposed to be in that hospital for life."

"Which hospital?"

Sheila didn't answer my question.

"You always were ungrateful, Fable. After all your father did for you."

"I never asked him to take me away from my mother. I was happy then. Don't you understand that?"

There was the sound of someone banging on the ceiling with a heavy object. Sheila hurried out of the kitchen.

The gas ring was on, providing a minute spark of light and heat in the dank kitchen. I got up and started moving around. The floor felt sticky as I walked on it and the air was chilly and damp. I looked in the pantry. There were patches of mould on the walls and a film of damp on packets and tins.

I switched on the radio. The crackling voice of the newsreader spoke of flood warnings being issued for the Avon and Severn. "The police urge drivers not to use the roads unless your journey is absolutely necessary and to exercise extreme care when driving through surface water. Water levels are likely to rise during the night as rain falling in the Welsh mountains ..."

I heard Sheila's footsteps returning back along the landing, down the stairs and along the hall. She came into the kitchen carrying a bundle of sheets that reeked of vomit and stale urine. She pushed the bundle into the ancient washing machine, added a meagre amount of powder, slammed the door shut and switched it on. It started up with a jagged cough.

Sheila fetched a glass of water and hurried back upstairs, appearing to forget that she'd asked me to come here.

I wandered down the gloomy hallway and into Derek's study. The notes for his next sermon – something to do with Noah's ark, the rainbow and God's covenant to man – were on scraps of paper on his desk together with the familiar row of pens and sharpened pencils.

The telephone rang making me jump.

It was Tony. "You didn't ring to say you'd arrived. Cara and I were worried."

"Tony I've only just got here."

"What're we supposed to eat? You didn't say."

I gritted my teeth. "Anything in the fridge or freezer."

"Cara and I couldn't see anything we liked. I thought you were supposed to have done the shopping this week…"

I felt tired and irritated. A membrane between my ears felt like it was twanging a single note. "If you don't like what's there Tony then go and get fish and chips or a pizza."

He went quiet and I could picture the cold expression on his face. "What's this about you entering a poetry competition?"

I felt as if someone had emptied a bucket of ice down my back. "How do you know about that? Have you been opening my post?"

The silence on the other end of the phone made it obvious that he had.

"I'm cross with you for doing something like that."

For once I didn't care what he thought. "Then you'll just have to be cross. Enjoy your dinner."

I slammed the phone down.

CHAPTER TWENTY-FIVE

I switched on the brass lamp Derek had on his desk, thinking how Tony had been adamant that he and I should never argue in front of Cara. The light cast shadows in the corners of the room as I remembered how Gangan and Jasmine had disagreed sometimes but it was clear that they'd always loved each other, whereas continually backing down for the sake of peace had eroded any feelings I'd ever had for Tony.

I realised that while I'd been talking to him, I'd switched off completely and had idly pulled a thick cream coloured envelope out of Derek's waste bin and had been doodling on it with one of the black felt tips in the pot on his desk – repeating spiral patterns around a daffodil, a star and a crescent moon.

After I put the phone down, I turned the envelope over. It had been delivered by hand a few days ago and was addressed to 'Derek Mitchell, Child Stealer, Isbourne Vicarage.' The scent of jasmine emanated from it and I felt a spark of excitement.

I sorted through the rest of the waste bin, like a dog digging for a bone. Most of it was rubbish, thin brown envelopes that had once contained bills, begging letters and circulars for double-glazing and house insurance. Wedged at the bottom was a catalogue for an art exhibition. It had been slashed with scissors, reminding me of those letters Jasmine used to receive when I was a child.

The catalogue was on thick glossy paper and also smelled of jasmine. It must've been in the envelope I'd just been doodling on and was advertising an exhibition in the Arts Centre which was now housed in what used to be Graingers Pie Factory – a building that looked as if it was standing on stilts over-looking the river.

I heard Sheila's footsteps outside and hurriedly shoved the catalogue under my sweater.

She looked annoyed to see me in Derek's study. "I hope you haven't been messing with anything, Fable."

"Just why did you ask me to come, Sheila?" I asked.

"It was your father's idea. But now he's in such a state he doesn't know what he wants. And the doctor says it'll be several hours before he can get here."

My stomach growled with hunger and I realised it was nearly seven hours since breakfast. I knew from experience that Sheila wouldn't have anything worth eating in the cupboards.

"I need some air," I said, heading towards the kitchen to collect my jacket.

"In this weather?" squeaked Sheila looking at me as if I was mad.

I felt the sharp edge of the catalogue under my sweater. "There's something I need to do."

Sheila didn't try to stop me.

CHAPTER TWENTY-SIX

Picking my way along the wet pavement, I eventually reached the café on the other side of the bridge. In my teens it was called The Place, and the owner – a man who reminded me of pictures of Humpty Dumpty – had tried unsuccessfully to create a London style coffee bar. A juke-box blasted out music by Black Sabbath and Deep Purple, and was always surrounded by bikers and their girlfriends. The café had a back room where it was rumoured people smoked pot and dealt in drugs and the police made several raids, always retreating empty-handed. I'd often seen Nathan in there.

It was now renamed the Cosy Corner Café and had red gingham curtains at the window. I pushed open the door, and was hit by a wall of fragrant steam. I sat at a corner table by a radiator near to where two old men – ex market gardeners by the sound of them – were talking about plums, and ordered coffee and a bacon sandwich.

"Frost got the blossom last year, Cyril. Looks like the floods'll wash it away this'n yew."

"Ah," said the other one, siphoning tea through toothless jaws.

Photos of men holding huge marrows or rounds of asparagus and silver trophies had replaced the ones I remembered of racing cars and electric guitars.

I relaxed in my corner, feeling warm for the first time since I arrived. The windows were too steamy to see anything properly and I ate my sandwich slowly, allowing the years to roll back and the memories to flood in.

I'd nearly come in here once, standing near to the always-open door, enveloped in a purple fog of cigarette smoke looking for a boy Kirsty was keen on. He had long dark hair and he played lead guitar in a band called Night Train.

"Come with me, Fable," she'd said. "You can ask him if he wants to go out with me."

"What would I say?"

She shrugged. "You'll think of something. Look how good you are at finding excuses for not doing your maths homework."

I'd trailed slowly behind her towards the café, praying that he wouldn't be in there and I wouldn't have to do it.

In the finish, when we peered in through the doorway, Nathan was in there, leaning on the grimy stainless steel bar, talking to two bikers, so I didn't go in. By the following week, Kirsty had fallen for someone else…

I sipped the last of my coffee, paid my bill and put my jacket back on, now warm from the radiator, and made my way towards the Arts Centre that had once been Graingers Pie Factory. When I was living here, it was the place kids used to go to ask for bits of waste meat – ham or bacon – to use for fishing bait.

The place looked more like a Victorian workhouse, red brick with high barred windows, built on what looked like cast iron stilts to protect it from flooding. When I'd gone to Tobias's caravan that day, we could just see the pie factory sticking up behind the trees on the far side of the river.

Then, the smell of the pies cooking used to permeate the air. Some days it'd be beef and onion and at other times veal and ham or sausage. Sheila used to buy broken ones for our tea sometimes, queuing up in headscarf and boots with the gaggle of old women who worked at the local fruit and veg market looking as if she hadn't got two halfpennies to rub together.

I stood for a few moments, breathing in the smell of rain, river water and leaf mould outside the building, feeling as if I was inside one of those kaleidoscopes, where my memories and senses were churned and disrupted.

From the sloping entrance-way into the Arts Centre I could see the farm on the other side of the river where Tobias used to work. Today, the meadows where cows used to graze looked more like an ornamental lake. That copse of ash trees was the one that framed his caravan on the one side and I wondered what happened to all his things. I'd found my way there early one morning only a few days after he'd died, hoping that by some miracle it'd be a mistake and he'd be there waiting for me.

Mist was rising eerily from the fields and the sun was only just coming up – a golden ball bouncing just above the horizon.

When I reached the caravan, the whole area was surrounded by yellow and black tape and there was a policeman on duty, looking bored and eating a Mars Bar.

I'd felt scared then and hadn't gone any further, walking home and getting back into bed before anyone had noticed I was missing, wishing I'd been stronger and made Tobias take me away with him whether my exams were done or not.

Today, the cast iron supporting the Arts Centre was freshly painted gleaming liquorice black. There were large glossy posters attached to the railings advertising the exhibition 'Travels With The Gypsy Queen – a journey through madness' by Jasmine de Costanza.

I pushed open the double chrome and glass doors and came face to face with a portrait of my mother. Her hair was iron grey but there was no mistaking her dark eyes or the pink lipsticked curve of her mouth.

I stood in the entrance hall, looking out at the endless

water, thinking of the poem I'd always loved at school – Tennyson's 'The Lady of Shallot,' breathing in the smell of roses and jasmine from a large round glass bowl of potpourri standing on a black wooden table by a sign on a paint spattered easel that said 'Your journey begins here…' A series of arrows led exhibition visitors into the next room, which was dimly lit, like a room preparing for sleep or a night nursery. The black walls were crammed with collages created from paper and fabric, words, faces and flower patterns jostling for space. Lines of poetry spiralled round a border of sky blue morning glories on one side, balloons came from open mouths spouting fragments of memory and fairytales.

On the ceiling she had created a roof of stars above a full moon smiling down from one wall. I stood for a long time reading the fragments of story hidden amongst the collages, absorbing light and colour, knowing that this was a coded message for me, hoping and praying I'd turn the next corner and come face to face with her, then wondering how I'd feel if that happened.

In the next room was a sign that said 'touch me, feel me' and a collection of exhibits that pierced my heart. I touched crimson velvet that reminded me of Jasmine's bedspread when I was a child. I touched rabbit fur, which reminded me of the piece Gangan gave me as a pram cover for my favourite doll. There were dolls' clothes tacked together with large white stitches that reminded me of the ones Teresa and I used to make. We'd beg scraps of fabric from Gangan or Jasmine's ragbags and create dresses for our dolls with what Peggy called 'Saturday night stitches.'

"What does she mean by that?" I'd asked Gangan once.

Gangan had chuckled.

"She's thinking of when Jasmine was young. Years

before she met your father she got this invitation to a local hop at the village hall. She spent ages rooting through her cupboards before she said she'd got nothing to wear. So she went and bought some material and a pattern and ran up a dress in no time at all to wear to the dance that night. The only trouble was, she hadn't fastened off the threads properly so she had to borrow a coat from someone to cover her modesty on the way home. Peg never let her live it down."

The last room of all was dark, the blinds drawn against the rain, the painted images bleak – a lonely figure in what looked like a barred cell, endless corridors stretching to nowhere and a feeling of emptiness and despair.

On one wall was a screen that danced with crackling images like an early talkie, reminding me of old films featuring Rudolph Valentino and Mary Pickford. There was a smell of perfume and face powder in this room and a re-creation of Jasmine's dressing table at Starlight – littered with trinkets, dusty and patterned with spilled eye-shadow, surrounded by a pyramid of empty gin bottles.

I stood there, watching the film over and over again until the receptionist came to tell me they were about to close, not wanting to walk away from these images binding me to the past, knowing for certain that my mother still loved me.

CHAPTER TWENTY-SEVEN

The wind and rain hit me with full force as I left the shelter of the Arts Centre, walking away from the light and colour but carrying with me the threads that bound me to my childhood. Before I'd left the Arts Centre, I'd left a note in the comments book in the entrance hall with my address and telephone number. 'I'm Fable. I'd love to see you. With all my love. '

At the reception desk on the way out, they were selling a book that supported the exhibition. "The artist only created a limited edition. This is one of the last copies," the bleached-blonde receptionist told me as I handed over my last ten-pound note. "No I'm sorry I don't have contact details for the artist. I can leave a note for the curator if it's urgent?"

She put the book in a plastic carrier bag and I hugged it under my jacket all the way back to the Vicarage.

When I arrived back at the Vicarage, Sheila was looking out for me, her face ghostly in the fading light. "Your father's been calling for you this last hour," she said crossly. "I didn't know where you were."

"He didn't want to see me earlier," I said.

"He needed to compose himself – to think about what he needed to tell you. To pray before he saw you."

I didn't say anything. I was feeling hungry again and there was no sign of Sheila cooking anything, no smells from the kitchen or clanking of saucepans. "Your husband phoned again," she said.

We stood awkwardly in the hallway. Sheila held the study door open as if she expected me to rush in and phone Tony. I didn't move.

"Derek wants his papers carried upstairs," said Sheila. "He's agitated because the emergency people have been round asking if we want to be evacuated to the local leisure centre. They think the river levels might rise again tonight. I told them we're waiting for the doctor and I don't think he's well enough to be moved. He keeps going over what happened in church – and how he's afraid she might be waiting for him with a knife…"

"I'll help you sort the papers and carry them upstairs," I said. "Put the kettle on and we'll make a start."

Sheila looked doubtful but she moved towards the kitchen.

Handfuls of rain mixed with hail hit the window and forsythia twigs tapped like bony fingers as I carried a box into the sitting room and started work, sifting through dusty yellowed paperwork, uncertain of what I was looking for.

Sheila was back, hovering in the doorway with two mugs of weak tea on a grubby white tray.

"The man on the news just said river levels are rising six inches every half hour. Maybe I should think about going to my sister's once Derek's seen the doctor."

"What did he want just now?"

"He keeps babbling like he's got a fever, the same thing over and over. He keeps saying 'while we have time… while we have time we should set the record straight.'

The phone rang and Sheila went into the study to answer it.

I looked at some of the papers that were already stacked in smaller boxes inside cardboard crates and made a start with moving them upstairs, trying to move quietly so that Derek wouldn't hear me.

The dimmest of bulbs flickered lazily from the half-landing and the stair carpet was the same threadbare one that had been here all through my childhood. In the process of sorting the papers, I'd seen some letters from the Archdeacon saying that the Diocesan office would be 'sending workmen to effect essential repairs and would Derek please be good enough to allow them access to the property this time.'

I caught my foot in a hole in the carpet and tripped, letting go of the crate enough so that some of the papers spilled down the stairs.

I noticed as some of the papers fell that they were unopened envelopes with my name on – the postmark some twenty years earlier.

"He only did it for your own good," said Sheila looking up at me.

"Did what?" My voice was sharp.

There was a loud crash upstairs.

Sheila pushed past me, screaming "Derek!"

"Phone an ambulance," she yelled a few minutes later. "And tell them to please hurry."

The ambulance arrived within minutes but it felt like hours. The two paramedics went upstairs and Sheila went with them. I heard the low rumble of their voices and Sheila's higher pitched one.

My tea had gone cold and had a greasy skin on the top of it.

After what seemed like ages they carried Derek downstairs.

He tried to reach out and touch me when he saw me, his face agitated. "I only did it for the best reasons, Fable."

"Take it easy, mate," said one of the paramedics.

I didn't say anything or offer him any sign of forgiveness.

He and Sheila disappeared into the gathering darkness. I heard the ambulance siren start up and fade into the distance and then all I could hear was the lashing of the wind and rain and the endless tapping of the forsythia twigs on the study window.

CHAPTER TWENTY-EIGHT

Not long after they'd gone a van with a loud hailer came slowly down the street advising people to move valuables upstairs and to leave their properties while there was still time. The Vicarage stood higher than most houses along this stretch of road and as far as I knew had never flooded, but I'd looked out of my old bedroom window and could see that half the graveyard was under water, the very tops of some of the stones still visible and a few stone angels looking as if they were walking on water.

My stomach rumbled with hunger – I'd had nothing since my bacon sandwich earlier – so I searched through the pantry, checking the dates on the tins before finding one that contained sausages and beans. I opened the tin with the rusty can opener and heated the contents in one of Sheila's thin saucepans.

I made myself a mug of coffee, using a week's worth of granules by Sheila's standards, and sat by the uncurtained sitting room window looking out at the ravaged garden. As the newsreader had said, the rain had stopped although the wind was still strong. The sky looked clearer and I could see a dark patch freckled with stars and the edge of the moon sliding out from below a cloud, its silvery light highlighting the slowly creeping dark water.

When I'd finished eating I washed up the dishes and then carried a large saucepan and an electric kettle full of water upstairs. I came back down, being careful not to trip on the worn patch of stair-carpet again and searched through the pantry for anything edible, finding teabags, digestive biscuits, half a loaf of bread and some cheese that hadn't gone mouldy. I'd listened to the warnings and they'd spoken about people being marooned in their houses without food or water. Strangely, I wasn't frightened of the thought of being alone here. Just imagining it gave me a wonderful sense of freedom.

I went into my old bedroom, which didn't look as if it had been touched since I was last here. The same pictures were on the walls – mawkish ones of cats and dogs chosen by Sheila - rather than the Rolling Stones posters I would've preferred. The purple curtains I'd found in a junk shop still hung at the grimy window, matching the bedspread Kirsty had given me.

I slid my hand under the bedspread, feeling the dampness of the sheets and blankets. As usual, the heat coming through the radiators was virtually non-existent. I went along the landing to the airing cupboard, opening the door and turning the dial to a level that would give Sheila an apoplexy. I found all the thick blankets I could and hung them in the airing cupboard to warm. Then I switched on the water heater intending to have a long hot soak in the bath – something I'd never done all the time I'd lived here.

The heating pipes banged and clanked in protest but gradually more heat began to filter through. I stripped off the sheets and blankets from my bed, putting them on radiators in other rooms determined to make myself warm and comfortable.

Derek's room was usually cell-like in its tidiness, reminding me of Peggy's room at Starlight. The only furniture in the room apart from the bed was a dark oak wardrobe, two bedside cabinets and a reading lamp.

Today was different. The bedclothes were rumpled, the sheets stained and dirty. The room reeked of vomit and stale urine and I shut the door quickly. Sheila could sort things out when she got back.

Her room was a complete contrast to Derek's. She

didn't believe in throwing anything away and carried on wearing clothes long after they should've gone for jumble.

She'd turned Nathan's room into a shrine. A photo of him, blurred at the edges, and obviously taken on a school trip, was in a silver frame on the mantelpiece. His football boots – hardly ever worn because he rarely went to school – hung on a nail on one wall. His favourite jeans and sweat shirt lay on the bed as if waiting for him to come home and change. All that remained that was familiar was a faint smell of sweaty socks and mouldy biscuits.

I closed the door on the unpleasant memories conjured up by the sight of the photo and went to the bathroom. In the airing cupboard I'd found thick towels that had never been used so I draped these on the radiator ready for when I got out of the bath. While the bath was running, I went downstairs and poured myself a generous measure of Derek's medicinal brandy and carried it back upstairs, placing it on my bedside table. I went into his room and borrowed the reading lamp from beside the bed. Then I remade my bed, looking forward to the feel of warm sheets and blankets.

The bath was deep and I stretched my tired limbs in the hot water, noticing how the steam was making rivulets down the white tiles. No doubt Sheila would have something to say about this when she came back, but I didn't care any more.

The phone rang again while I was enjoying a long soak, but I felt too relaxed to get out and answer it. Every bath I'd had here prior to this one had been in a few inches of tepid water so I was determined to enjoy it.

As I was relaxing in the hot water, I remembered the bracelet Tobias gave me for my birthday – the one that had reminded me of pieces of pink coconut ice. I got out of the bath, wrapping myself in one of the large white fluffy towels. A howling draught came through the ill-fitting window frame, making me shiver. I dried myself as quickly as I could, putting on my pyjamas and dressing gown and adding socks and a thick sweater.

Back in my bedroom, I rummaged under the bed, lifting the rug and feeling for the loose floorboard. The bracelet was still there, its condition as good as the day Tobias gave it to me. I kissed it and fastened it round my wrist, trying to remember the look on his face when he'd given it to me.

I got under the warm blankets, taking a sip of the brandy and reaching for the carrier bag that held the book I'd bought from the exhibition. There in my old room, safe from prying eyes, I began to read Jasmine's story.

CHAPTER TWENTY-NINE

The book is printed on hand-made paper the colour of thick cream and the cover has a raised pattern of Persian roses on it.

JASMINE'S STORY

My nightmares always come back to the same thing – the knowledge that something precious is about to be taken from me and I am powerless to stop this happening. It always ends with me trying to escape from a locked room or a journey along a corridor that I never reach the end of.

My dreams are always full of people I don't remember but who appear to know me, like the woman with bobbed dark hair who wears a butterfly brooch.

"We're doing our best to help you," she says.

The way she says it makes me feel savage, makes me want to beat on the bars of this place they put me in until the walls crack under the pressure.

Every night when I close my eyes, it's as if I'm watching a re-run of the same film – those ones with Rudolph Valentino or Mary Pickford in them. The early talkies with jerky figures on a crackling background and sinister music that suddenly comes to an end…

Most nights a woman in a brightly patterned headscarf and gold hoop earrings who calls herself the Gypsy Queen is there waiting for me.

"I'm your mother," she says. "I've come to help you find your daughter."

Night after night her broken-toothed smile haunts me as she shuffles a greasy pack of cards under the light of a full moon.

She always deals me the same cards – Death, The Devil and The Tower – but I can't remember what they mean, any more than I can remember where my daughter is.

The nights when there is no moon are the scariest. I'm left in the thick shit-scented darkness surrounded by creatures that slither and creep, drawing their slime-filled bodies over mine hour after hour of eternal night. Sometimes I hear other voices screaming and smell the stink of their fear. I call to them but they never answer back.

A few nights were good. Once Lily came to me. I don't know how, the door remained locked and the woman who unlocked the next morning said no one had been there.

"You're wrong," I said. "Her name was Lily."

She carried the scent of lavender and fresh bread.

"You remember me," she said. "I looked after you when you was a little girl."

"Think," she said as she started to fade away. "Think of your baby."

And I tried to remember.

"I do remember," I said as the image faded. "Her name was Fable and she was born under a roof of stars. Help me find her…"

My voice ends on a wail as I realise she's gone and I'm left in here in a room with a metal framed bed and high windows you can't see out of.

"What time of year is it?" I ask the woman with the keys. "Are the roses out?"

For a brief moment I thought I could smell them and then the image faded and all I could sense was the antiseptic stink of this place.

Outside my room is an endless corridor that seems to stretch upwards, on and on. They take me that way sometimes for treatment. And I think, today I'll escape. I tried several times, but I'm so un-used to walking that after a few yards I slump with exhaustion.

I know then that I'll have to become as crafty as my captors. Stop taking the little white tablets they give me. Do exercises to strengthen the wasted muscles in my legs.

I must've slept again.

For a while I was dreaming about a man who was like a tall column of black marble. His face is a blank but words spout from his mouth in a torrent of fire.

"Failure, drunkard, loser... failure, drunkard, loser...failure, drunkard..."

I can't remember his name but I know I will. He's the one who stole my baby. If I'm not watchful, he'll get in here and kill me.

I try to warn the woman with the key but she makes out she doesn't know what I'm talking about.

For a few days now, another man's been watching me. I've tried to ignore him. Mostly in this place if you close your eyes or ignore something they've gone when you open them again.

Not this time.

I wonder who he is and why he's so interested in me.

I steal a quick look from under half closed eyelids, carefully, because he hasn't shifted his gaze from me.

He's got a bald head like a vulture and his dark eyes are hooded and watchful.

"Do you like drawing, Jasmine?"

"He's noticed that I've drawn over the white wall of my room with shit."

I ignore him but he doesn't go away.

He's able to go far longer than anyone else I've ever

known without saying a word.

"Look at the light patterns on the floor," he says, pointing to some golden squares and triangles. "What do they remind you of?"

I stared back at him. I know their tricks in this place and how they try to worm information out of you and then find a way of using it against you.

"Your artwork could release you from here," he said. "Wouldn't you like to be free, Jasmine?"

I didn't say anything.

The next morning a nurse led me along the corridor to a large white room where he was waiting with several easels set up, each with a primed canvas on them. There was paint in white plastic pots and a large box that held brushes. There were several other people in the room, all dozing in armchairs.

I didn't look at him or say anything.

There were bars of light on the grey lino floor, but the most amazing thing was you could see outside from here -green trees, clouds, blue sky and a crow making a cut out pattern – black on aquamarine. I hadn't realised how much I'd missed seeing these things.

The man saw the direction of my gaze.

"Could you draw that?"

An old woman was wandering about – rats' tail grey hair, nicotine stained fingers and a lopsided gait. She looked at me and her face contorted spitefully.

"You couldn't do that," she cackled in a raucous seagull's voice as she moved slowly in the direction of the tea trolley.

I looked at the paint and the brushes but couldn't remember what I was supposed to do. In frustration I threw the canvas off the easel onto the floor, hurling paint onto the *surface – a river of blue, dollops of green, a pantomime moustache of black. He didn't try to stop me as I worked it with my hands, scraping shapes into the thick paint with my nails, collapsing exhausted amongst the mess.*

"That's better," he said calmly. "You'll be well now."

It was a slow climb out of the depths.

There were days when I stared at the wall not wanting to be bothered and others when I edged forward a little, experimenting with colours and ideas, being aware of feelings and memories coming back...

Franco – the art teacher – and I fell in love. He told me how his painting saved him when his wife died and he wanted to know how someone like me ended up in a place like this.

I found it hard to put it into words until the day I started painting an orchard under a roof of stars and the memory of that special night returned.

This book is dedicated to my husband Franco de Costanza who has never given up on me and the exhibition is dedicated with love to my daughter Fable Rose. May I find her again one day.

CHAPTER THIRTY

The next morning I telephoned home. Cara answered, sounding off-hand and moody as if I'd woken her up.

"Everything OK?" I asked, trying to suit bright and breezy.

"Dad's in a mood," she said. "Why didn't you phone last night like you said you were going to? That's all I heard last night …"

"There were a few problems here. Derek was taken to hospital. There were severe flood warnings and I had to move a lot of stuff upstairs in case the river got in overnight."

Cara didn't answer.

"I'll be back on the two o'clock bus," I said.

"Dad's in the bathroom. Shall I get him?"

"No," I said hastily. "Don't disturb him. Anyway, why aren't you on your way to school?"

"Mum …" she dragged the word out and I could imagine her rolling her eyes, comic fashion. "We've got a teacher training day. Don't you remember anything? Jade and I are going to Birmingham. I told you."

"Have fun," I said.

She put the phone down.

I looked out of Derek's study window at the scud of grey clouds across the small patch of sky I could see through the overgrown foliage. There was the sound of steady dripping from the bushes in the garden and the overflow pipe.

I went into the kitchen and looked out at the garden. Despite the gloomy predictions, the flood waters were nowhere near the Vicarage but they must've covered at least half the graveyard.

I made coffee and toast, finishing up the scrapings of a

jar of marmalade wondering why Sheila never stocked the cupboards properly, then realised that as it was Lent, she and Derek probably didn't eat breakfast anyway – they never used to. I shuddered, remembering the plainer-than-usual food – and how Sheila wouldn't allow any chocolate in the Vicarage from Shrove Tuesday until Easter.

When I'd finished breakfast, I telephoned the hospital and after a long interval of 'push this button' and 'dial this number' I eventually got through to the ward Derek had been taken to. The nurse I spoke to had a Scots accent.

"Are ye a relative?"

"I'm his daughter," I said through gritted teeth, crossing my fingers behind my back.

"I'll find out for ye." I heard the sound of her footsteps moving away from the phone.

A few minutes later she was back. "He had a comfortable night but there's no real change in his condition. Doctor thinks there won't be until we get to the bottom of the wee nervous upset he had."

I put the phone down and prepared to leave the Vicarage, knowing that I wouldn't ever come back.

I went to the kitchen and made more coffee, using the last of the jar, and tipped in some of the medicinal brandy as I sat at the table, sorting the papers from Derek's study that I wanted to take home, including those envelopes with my name on that had never been opened until last night.

After I'd read Jasmine's story, I'd opened the envelopes. Most of them were from Gangan – the contents of each very similar.

"Dearest Fable

I'm not much of a one for letter writing. You know that. But this comes with much love and hopes that you are well. I miss you and will not stop trying to get you back. We'll meet again one day. Fondest love. Gangan."

Some of the envelopes contained letters from me to Gangan, written in my childish scrawl.

"Dear Gangan

Please come and take me away from here. I want to be home with you and Magpie. I miss you and want to be with you.

Love from Fable.

My heart broke, imagining her waiting for a letter that never came, thinking I didn't care about her.

By the time my taxi came to take me to the bus stop, it had stopped raining, but a squally wind was blowing. I spent the entire journey looking out at the landscape, watching how the flooded fields gave way to ones with black and white cows amid fields of buttercups, followed by villages and industrial estates, red brick overtaking green fields as we got nearer to Enderbury.

Despite the fact that I'd told Cara which bus I was catching, Tony hadn't bothered to meet me at the bus station. Feeling weary, I picked up my suitcase and started walking. I'd spent all my money and couldn't afford another taxi.

Tony's car was on the drive when I finally got home but he didn't bother to greet me when I opened the front door. He was sitting on the sofa watching a football match and didn't offer to make me a cup of tea. In the kitchen, the sink was full of dirty crockery as if he and Cara hadn't washed up all the time I was away and the surround was sticky with toast crumbs and spilled orange juice.

I put the kettle on to boil, throwing a handful of teabags into the pot.

Tony stood in the doorway, his eyes cold with anger.

CHAPTER THIRTY-ONE

Tony didn't ask me what had happened at Isbourne. He sat watching the news while I cleaned the kitchen and prepared a stew for dinner. At one time his behaviour would've bothered me and I'd have thought it was my fault. Now I just felt irritated and no longer prepared to tolerate it.

"You said a letter had arrived for me," I said, hoping it was something to do with Jasmine.

He grumbled and rooted it out from where he'd stuffed it onto the magazine rack. I wondered how he'd have liked it if I'd done that to one of his letters. I smoothed it out and read it, feeling a surge of excitement. It was from Linnet, inviting me to attend the awards ceremony for the poetry competition the following week.

"What's all this about?" asked Tony. "Who is this Linnet woman?"

"She's a librarian," I said. "She organised the poetry competition. I entered it."

"You don't write poetry," he said.

"I bet it's the one who was talking in the Library," said Cara. "When Mum and the others were all going..."

She closed her eyes and pretended to look spaced out.

Tony snatched the letter off me. "I don't know what you're looking excited for Fable. All it says is that you've been invited to some 'awards ceremony,' which you'll probably have to pay to attend. It's highly unlikely that you'll have won anything." He screwed the letter up and tossed it into the waste paper basket.

I waited until he'd gone upstairs before I rescued the letter from the bin, smoothing it out and re-reading it, not allowing his attitude to prick the bubble of excitement it had given me.

When we'd eaten dinner and I'd cleared away, Tony sat watching a football match and I spent the rest of the evening sorting out the contents of my suitcase, wishing I'd stayed away longer and spent some time looking for Jasmine, particularly as Tony didn't seem particularly pleased to see me now that I was back. He hadn't hugged me or said he was glad I'd got home safely.

I sat up half the night writing, feeling torn between excitement about the poetry awards – although as Tony correctly pointed out, the letter didn't say I'd won anything – and frustrated because I'd been so close to Jasmine and yet we'd still not made contact.

At breakfast time the next morning, Cara and Tony were treating my poetry as a joke. So far, neither of them had asked to read it – for which I was thankful.

"Written any good odes, Fable," said Tony looking meaningfully at Cara, who collapsed in fits of giggles, spluttering tea all over the table.

"Did you tell Mum about that weird woman who phoned yesterday?" asked Cara as she buttered another slice of toast.

"What weird woman?" I nearly choked on my cereal.

Tony shrugged. "Sounded foreign."

My throat felt so tight I could hardly breathe. "Did she give a name?"

Tony didn't answer but I knew she had and that he'd told her to go away.

*

As soon as Cara and Tony had left the house I started sorting all the papers I'd brought back from Isbourne. Amongst the bundle of letters were emotional ones from Peggy who'd obviously been told a different set of lies from the rest of us. "…When we met, you promised we'd be together. You promised me marriage. I thought you wanted us to be together. How could you treat me this way?" she'd written over and over.

There was a solicitor's letter addressed to Derek asking if he knew the whereabouts of Fable Rose Mitchell. It was dated three months ago and as far as I could tell, Derek hadn't replied to it. I found pen and paper and wrote a reply to the solicitor, enclosing my birth certificate. I went out to post it, taking deep breath as I passed the library, noticing the posters for the awards night feeling a fresh tremor of excitement, only marred by the fact that my mother had obviously been in touch and Tony had sent her away. I hoped with all my heart that she'd get in touch again and that this time I'd be the one who answered the phone.

CHAPTER THIRTY-TWO

Tony came home early on the night of the Awards Evening instead of playing squash like he usually did on a Thursday.

"I thought we'd go out for a meal tonight," he said. He hung up his jacket in the cupboard and came down the hall to the kitchen where I was scraping potatoes and rinsing salad ready for an early dinner.

I took a deep breath. "Maybe we could go tomorrow night instead. I'm going to this Awards thing at the Library tonight." I hesitated nervously, wondering how he'd react.

"You could always cancel. You don't sound that bothered about it."

I started to feel flustered. "I don't want to cancel. Anyway, what's wrong with going out tomorrow night instead?"

He looked at me as if I was a complete idiot. "There's a Man. U match on tomorrow."

"Then we'll have to leave it to the night after. I'm going to the Library tonight."

"Please yourself."

I knew he wouldn't bother to take me out on a different night.

"Don't expect me to come with you though," he added. "If it's a poetry event you can guarantee all the blokes'll be gay and I've no intention of spending all night with my back pressed against the wall, thanks all the same."

I felt relieved that he didn't want to come with me – I knew if he did he'd find some way of spoiling the evening.

"I don't like the idea of you going on your own, though. Maybe Cara'll go with you."

Cara looked up from where she was sitting at the

kitchen table going through some of my recipe books looking for ideas for her Food Technology project.

She rolled her eyes. "No thanks. I'm going to Vicky's later. We're doing a maths project together and we've got to give the book back tomorrow."

"You've had that book for a week," said Tony severely. "What've I said to you about taking your studies seriously? You only get one chance with qualifications..."

Cara walked out in the middle of the lecture, sparing me the next bit when he usually went on about how much more choice I'd have had with jobs if I'd stayed on longer at school.

"You can meet Cara at Vicky's on the way back," said Tony, organising my time for me like he usually did. "That'll save me having to miss the last part of the news."

Later, I left the house feeling self-conscious in my new turquoise velvet skirt and top. It wasn't brand new, of course. I'd bought it from Christabel's charity shop in the High Street – the one she runs to help the animal sanctuary. Christabel is like an old black spider. When the shop bell rings, she comes out from the room at the back clutching her large white coffee mug. There's always a smell of whisky coming from it, no matter what time of day you visit.

The shop itself always looks as if it needs a good sort out – not to mention a cleaner who looks above eye level. The grubby white walls are festooned with cobwebs above head height that are so big they look like hammocks for mice. Below them, crammed into every inch of space, clothes are piled onto racks, sorted by colour not size – with Christabel's colour theme for the week taking priority.

When I went in the chosen colour was blue. Coats, hats and dresses jostled for space with abstract paintings, curtains, enamel pots and pans and a giant papier mache model of a seahorse.

The place reminded me of the junk shop in Isbourne that Kirsty and I used to explore – the one where I once found my purple bedroom curtains.

As I browsed, Christabel watched me, her eyes dark as elderberries above the rim of her white coffee mug. As soon as I touched the soft turquoise fabric I fell in love with it, praying as I pulled it off the rail that it would fit, watching the colour change as the light caught it, reminding me of a shaft of sunlight on a summer sea.

"Try it on dear," urged Christabel.

I squeezed into the curtained area behind the till, sloughing off my jeans and sweatshirt and easing the soft fabric over my body. I walked out of the changing area feeling self conscious in my bare feet so I could see the full effect in the long mirror near the door. I was amazed at the difference it made – I looked younger and more confident.

A man in a black tracksuit, browsing through the dusty collection of LP records looked up and whistled.

"If I wasn't meeting my wife in half an hour, I'd offer to take you out to lunch," he said in a strong Birmingham accent.

"A new dress can change your life dear," said Christabel as she wrapped the outfit in crumpled tissue paper and put it in a carrier bag. "Now have you got a piece of jewellery you can wear with it?"

On a stand that said 'jewellery 50p' I found a heart shaped pendant made of mother-of-pearl.

Tony made no comment about my new outfit as I left the house. I'd half expected him to carp and complain about the waste of money and was ready to retaliate by saying I'd spent less than six pounds and maybe he should ask his work colleagues what their wives spent when they went clothes shopping for a special occasion.

The closer I got to the Library, the more nervous I felt. It was a warm night, with a soft breeze carrying the smell of newly mown grass. I'd put on a thin black jacket over the outfit and a pair of strappy sandals that I wasn't used to walking in.

"Don't forget – you're meeting me at Vicky's at ten," said Cara. "Her Mum and Dad are very strict about bed times."

"I don't know what time this thing finishes," I said, feeling irritated at Tony for setting this up and thereby making sure I'd be on edge all evening.

"You'll just have to slip out," he said. "It's not like you're a main player after all."

When I pushed open the Library doors, I could hear voices and music coming from the meeting room upstairs. The entrance hall had been decorated with posters and yellow balloons.

I followed the yellow arrows pointing upstairs. As I went through another set of doors, one of the library assistants pressed a glass of white wine into my hand and behind them I could see a large table loaded with food. Further down the room, rows of dark grey chairs with numbers on had been arranged in crescent shaped rows in front of a small platform with a lectern on it.

"The drink's the only thing that makes these things worthwhile," said the man standing next to me. He had a soft Irish accent, reminding me of Patrick O'Hagan and eyes the colour of cream sherry.

"And beautiful women," he added sweeping those topaz coloured eyes over my body.

I felt myself blushing. "I've not been to anything like this before," I confessed.

"Have you not? Then you've a treat in store."

Something about the way he raised his eyebrows and gestured towards the group of business-suited men and women on the far side of the room made me laugh.

"That's better. You looked scared to death. Just think of them without those grey suits…"

He was wearing black jeans and shirt and a leather jacket lined with dark blue silk. His hair was long and sun-bleached, tied in a ponytail and he smelled of lemon and coconut. He took off the jacket, hanging it on a nearby clothes stand. "Only got the jacket yesterday at Christabel's – it's probably not quite right for the occasion, but who cares?"

"My outfit came from there too."

"There we are. They say if you dig down a bit everyone's got something in common." He had long fingers and fine golden hairs on the backs of his hands. There was a triangular scar on the back of his left hand that showed white.

"Liam, you bugger. Didn't recognise you without your storyteller's coat."

Liam touched my shoulder gently. "I'll catch you later. Duty calls."

I felt nervous again after he'd gone. The room was crowded now and people were searching for their seat numbers. I was sitting in the front row and the seats on either side of me were empty as a woman with short iron-grey hair and wearing a navy two-piece suit and a badge saying ' Head Librarian' rang a small handbell and called us all to order.

Liam flopped into the seat on my left side. The seat on the other side was still empty. The atmosphere in the room was sweltering and I wished I had a glass of water. Some people were fanning themselves with the yellow single-sheet programmes that had been left on each seat, folding them zigzag fashion, like I remember doing when I was a child.

"I'm very pleased to welcome you here tonight," began the Head Librarian, her face looking flushed. "I'm glad that so many of you have been able to attend."

"Get on with it," muttered Liam.

"We're also pleased to welcome our guest judge, Slade Sinclair. Stand up, please, Slade. Let everyone see you."

A petite woman, who only looked about sixteen, with dark hair falling in ringlets to her shoulders and wearing a long red velvet dress and a matching pillbox hat with a tiny glittery veil stood up.

"Slade has published three poetry collections and two non-fiction books on ghost-hunting in Cornwall, and I'd like to hand you over to her for the prize-giving."

"I bet Slade's a made up name," muttered Liam, making me want to giggle.

Slade tottered on impossibly high heels towards the lectern and prepared to speak.

"Wait till you hear my name," I whispered to Liam.

Slade shot an irritated glance towards us.

"We've received a number of entries," she began in a silvery voice, "and the final decision was far from easy. I was intrigued by the variety of subjects people chose to write about." She smiled in a sickly sort of way.

"There was a charming poem about pussy's favourite chair at one end of the scale and then a spine-chilling one about someone wanting to kill their mother-in-law at the other. I'm going to try to explain why I awarded the prizes as I did."

Liam sighed.

Slade paused for dramatic effect, her long-lashed gaze sweeping the arcs of chairs. "Fable Lucas's poems…"

I nearly fell of my chair when she mentioned my name.

"… had an interesting combination of real emotion

mixed with fantasy and fairytale. You get an idea of there being a real person behind the stories. Stand up, Fable. Let everyone see you."

I stood up, feeling as if my legs were about to give way, thinking it was like those times at school when you were in trouble with the teacher.

"Now, Fable, if you'd like to come and collect your prize for now, we'll ask you to read one or two poems for us in the second half of the programme."

"Brilliant name," said Liam when I came back with my certificate and a copy of my poetry book. "How did you come by that?"

"And next we have Liam Flynn," Slade went on. "Well done Liam."

I noticed she gave him a peck on the cheek when he collected his prize.

I looked in disbelief at the cover of my small collection of poems. The title – 'Childhood Interrupted' was picked out in raised silver letters on the lilac cover and I ran my finger over the shapes like I used to do with the numbers on the liquorice black weights that went with Gangan's scales.

Liam held his book loosely on his knees. It had a red cover and was called 'The Storyteller.'

"Sounds like a fascinating story," he said looking into my eyes and making me feel hot again. "You must tell me one day."

"Our third prize winner, Charlotte Miller has been delayed," said Slade, "so we'll now have a short break and continue with our readings in a few minutes when hopefully Charlotte will be with us. Please have something to eat, mingle and chat and we'll reconvene in about fifteen minutes."

I felt sick. "I've never done anything like this before," I

said to Liam. "I can't get up and read my poems in front of all these people."

He gave a lazy smile that made his eyes light up. "Sure you can. Remember to take a deep breath before you start. Wait till everyone's quiet. Speak slowly. And if all else fails and you feel you're making a complete janders of it, just imagine everyone sitting here without their clothes on."

"Liam darling." A girl with a waterfall of blonde hair and dressed in a long black fur coat had just made an entrance. She got the attention of the whole room as she rushed up to Liam and enveloped him in a hug that nevertheless failed to disturb her immaculate make up.

"I haven't missed my reading have I?" She gazed up at him with china blue eyes.

"No, you're fine Charlotte."

Charlotte swept me a look that said 'keep off, he's mine.' "Come and look at this poem on the wall, Liam darling. It's the one with that photo of us when we stayed at that castle."

My throat felt dry. I sipped nervously at a glass of orange juice, but even that made me feel queasy.

A few minutes later, Slade rang a bell and everyone returned to their seats. I was a bit slower getting back to mine – I'd gone in search of the Ladies – and by the time I came back, Charlotte had taken my seat next to Liam and I was sitting next to her. She'd taken off the coat by now to expose the long black lace dress she was wearing underneath. It had wide sleeves that almost covered her slim gold-ringed hands.

"I'm hoping the photographer from 'The Advertiser' will be here soon," said Slade importantly. "But in the meantime, I'd like to ask our third place winner, Charlotte Miller to come and read a selection of her work."

Charlotte got up and undulated across to the lectern,

giving a theatrical performance in a sexy, husky voice.

Everyone applauded. Liam went next, looking as if he wasn't bothered if he was there or not. "I'm better known as the man in the storyteller's coat," he said in his soft Irish accent. "So it's nice that I can say I'm the man in the leather jacket who writes poems as well."

Everyone laughed and Charlotte beamed proudly at him.

His reading made everyone laugh too, but I sat there feeling a shaft of dread that in a few moments it would be my turn. I wondered what would happen if I tried to stand up and nothing happened.

I walked slowly across to the lectern, clutching my book, the pages I was going to read from marked with small pieces of yellow ribbon taken from one of the balloons.

I looked at the sea of faces in front of me, aware of isolated images – the reflection off someone's glasses, Slade's red dress and the barley sugar coloured streetlights outside.

"I'm Fable Lucas," I said. "And this is the first time I've read in public. These poems are brief snapshots of my life." After a few moments, I relaxed a little, finding that I was enjoying myself. I had the feeling that the audience were with me and every so often there was a ripple of interest. When I finished the last words, I got the biggest round of applause of the night.

Liam mouthed "Well done" to me as I made my way back to my seat. Charlotte turned her body to block my view of him.

There was a flurry of activity near the door as I sat down and a man carrying a black bag rushed in.

"How bad was that?" asked Liam.

I smiled at him. "Better than I expected."

It was then I noticed the clock on the wall. It was nearly ten o'clock.

"I should go," I said.

"Can I have you three over here please?" asked the photographer.

I hesitated.

"You can't miss your moment of glory," said Liam taking me firmly by the arm, despite Charlotte almost hissing at him to put me down.

The photographer took his time, positioning and repositioning us until he was satisfied.

"Right now, ladies and gentleman. Big smiles. Say cheers. That's the way."

He clicked the shutter over and over, then took his time writing down our names and addresses with a blunt pencil.

By the time we'd finished the library clock said ten-fifteen.

I raced out, walking so quickly round to Vicky's house to get Cara that I nearly turned my ankle a couple of times.

"About bloody time," Cara said. "I've been waiting outside Vicky's for ages. I thought you'd forgotten."

She maintained a moody silence all the way home, reminding me of Tony's mother. I gazed up at the stars and the delicate curve of the new moon, determined not to let Cara's moodiness destroy the magic of the evening.

CHAPTER THIRTY-THREE

Fired with enthusiasm, I decided to find out about writing courses at the local college. Linnet from the Library gave me some brochures and I looked through them, feeling determined to get a job so I could earn the money to pay for one. I knew that Tony and I had agreed that I should stay at home to look after Cara, but she was sixteen now and no longer needed me like she did as a young child.

I left the brochures in the sitting room, intending to talk to Tony about them. The next time I looked for them, he'd put them in the bin.

I wrote my feelings of frustration into my notebook. Our marriage felt like being in one of those horror films where the walls were closing in and there was no escape.

It was hard not to be depressed looking at jobs that required the person appointed to be computer literate, but there were other things like cooking and cleaning that I knew I could do. It was just a matter of finding the right job.

Cara got a Saturday job in a jeweller's and came home most weeks with silver rings on her fingers and toes or a new bracelet. One Saturday she came home with her ears pierced and Tony hit the roof.

"Did you know about this?" he demanded.

"I didn't."

Cara looked mutinous.

"But it does suit her," I added, "and anyway, most of the girls have had their ears pierced."

I heard an echo of Gangan's voice saying 'you may as well be out of the world as out of fashion.'

"Thanks Mum," said Cara, giving me a rare hug.

*

That night I had a dream about a walled garden. It was early morning and the air was frosty. The sky was blue with wispy clouds, diaphanous as a silk scarf and there were snowdrops and miniature daffodils everywhere, their fragile beauty masking a feeling of menace that overwhelmed me as I walked the gravel pathways.

I reached a gap in the wall where some bricks had crumbled and squeezed through to the place beyond where there was an old fashioned outdoor swimming pool with stone steps leading down into it, surrounded by statues of angels and Greek heroes all tarnished with green moss.

Some unseen force was drawing me towards the edge, urging me to look into the thick green water.

I was startled by the alarm call of a blackbird and as I turned, that's when I saw the body in the water. She – it was a young girl – wore a white nightgown and held a bunch of dead roses in her clasped hands reminding me of that painting of 'Ophelia Among The Flowers.' She looked like me.

*

The next day I missed the writing workshop at the library because Tony decided to work at home. I thought I'd be able to go under the pretext of fetching some shopping from town, but he insisted on taking me in the car, and waiting outside while I took my books back.

"We need to spend some time together," he said.

I left a message for Linnet, hoping she'd understand.

Later I heard Tony talking to Cara. "That writing thing's a passing fad with your mother – she's not the type of person who ever sticks at anything."

That night I wrote a poem that described how I felt.

Visions

I am in a box
buried alive
by your jealousy

thoughts churn
and dance
like butterflies

you squash them
with your indifference
feet stamping
hands clapping

through a crack
in the lid
I see sunlight
golden as honey

the lid falls
I am enclosed
in endless night

The poem was published a few weeks later in a magazine called 'Spectator'. A few days later I got a note through the post. It was written on a heart-shaped scrap of shiny red paper.

'Why didn't you tell me you're so unhappy? Come to the Library on Thursday and lighten my day. L xx'

There was no address or telephone number, but the tiny message made my heart leap.

The following day, Thursday, I went into the Library to look at their job vacancy list. I could see Liam in the Children's Library talking to a noisy group of children. He was wearing a patchwork velvet coat – the colours as vibrant as a stained glass window. I moved closer, pretending to look at the information board. He was surrounded by a collection of stuffed animals and musical instruments – drums, tambourines and triangles – and was telling the children a story about how the world was made.

There was a red and yellow poster on the wall that said 'Storyteller in Action.' I listened, still trying to make out I was interested in the entire contents of the Library notice board, as he told the story of 'The Lion Who'd Lost His Roar.' He made the children help him play an introduction to the story, strumming gently on his guitar. I glanced at him, noticing his long fingers and the golden hairs on the backs of his hands.

The children were spellbound as he began the story. It was one of those where the lion had to travel the world – going from forest to desert to farm to try and find the missing part of him.

"So off he goes, loppity loppity, along the forest path," said Liam. He took a finger puppet from one pocket of his multi-coloured coat and put it on his finger, making it move in the way he'd described.

"I thought only rabbits went loppity loppity," said a little boy with round glasses and sticking out ears. "This story's really stupid."

"With that level of scepticism you've a great future in stocks and shares young man," said Liam. "This lion went loppity loppity because he got fed up with striding like lions are supposed to do. All he wanted to do was find his lost roar…"

Liam reached the end of the story and the children chattered excitedly as they went to find a space at one of the tables to draw a picture of the lion's adventures for the display board.

Liam's voice had been hypnotic to listen to, but now I realised he'd finished the story and his eyes were fixed on me. I looked away first.

Liam got a toy wand out of a pocket in the indigo silk lining of the coat as the children gathered round him for the next story. I started to walk away, unable to think of an excuse to stay any longer.

"Right," said Liam, "I'm going to tell you a story about this magic wand."

The children stared at the wand.

"This wand once belonged to a princess who was born under a roof of stars."

I turned round and stared at Liam, amazed that he'd remembered. He held my gaze as the children began asking questions and squabbling for attention.

"What was her name?" asked the boy with glasses and sticking out ears.

"Her name is Fable," said Liam, winking at me and making me feel hot.

"That's a silly name," said four-eyes-sticking-out-ears.

"It's a very good name," argued Liam, "it means magical story."

"I wish my name was Fable instead of Elizabeth," said a little girl with fair curly hair.

"Perhaps you could pretend. Now go and draw me what you think a roof of stars looks like and then I'll tell you the story about the princess."

He smiled at me.

"Looks like you've got your hands full," I said as he took a gulp of water from a plastic bottle.

"It's one way of earning a living. Beats busking in Dublin in the pouring rain."

I laughed.

He shrugged. "Work's work. I don't get too precious about what it is. How've you been? I've been thinking about you."

"OK." I tried to sound bright, but failed miserably.

"Thought so. Why d'you put up with him?"

"Who?"

"Whoever's making you look like that."

"I'm just tired."

"And I'm the Archbishop of Canterbury."

"Mr Storyteller – Nathan's just taken my red crayon and he won't give it back," shouted a little girl with a black ponytail.

"It's mine," said Nathan.

"It's not yours – it's the library lady's. I'm telling of you," said the little girl.

"I'm telling, you're smelling."

"I think we've done enough drawing for now," said Liam, shepherding them all onto the carpet again. "Now I'm going to tell you about Princess Fable. She was born under a roof of stars. She wore a silver crown and pink ballet shoes in bed because she always needed to be ready to dance…"

He winked at me and I choked back a fit of the giggles as I headed towards the exit. "She spent time in Archie's Coffee House from three o'clock every day making a young man very happy," he went on. "Archie's Coffee House was near the market square…"

I looked at my watch – it was nearly one o'clock – wondering whether to take the last remark as a serious invitation.

As I walked into town a few kids from Cara's school were out on their lunch break. I bought a bar of fruit and nut chocolate and a bottle of orange juice and sat in the park. From what I'd seen at the awards night, Liam and Charlotte Miller appeared to be an item, so what did he want with me?

I walked slowly along the crowded streets until I reached the Victorian Market Hall. It was on two floors and had a glass roof – some of it was stained glass that bled squares of colour onto the concrete floor below when the sun shone. I wandered round the market stalls, looking idly at second hand books and clothes, tantalised by the smell of fresh bread and hot sausage rolls.

Archie's Coffee House was next to the market, as Liam had said, and as I walked past it I met Linnet. She gave me a hug..

"It's good to see you, Fable. Liam says we're all meeting for coffee."

"I thought he was teasing me when he mentioned it."

"Why would he do that?"

I shrugged.

Linnet was wearing a long black skirt with fringes on it and a black velvet top. Round her neck was a turquoise beaded necklace with a feathered dream catcher on it.

She pushed me into the steamy warmth of Archie's café. I'd never been in here before. Big fans hanging from the high ceiling turned the air slowly, looking like something out of the Indian Raj. My stomach growled with hunger as I smelled fresh coffee, toast and frying bacon.

Liam was sitting in a corner on the far side. There was a large sketch pad on his raised left knee and several empty cups on the table in front of him. He was sketching Archie, dressed in a striped shirt, stomach overhanging his trousers and white teeth showing through his black beard reminding me of a pirate, as he cleaned the chrome and black coffee machine behind the bar.

"He won't be very flattered with this one," said Liam as he greeted us. "He always says don't waste the paper, but it's one way of paying him for his hospitality."

The eggshell blue walls were crammed with paintings done by other regulars – some with price tickets on.

Liam ordered cappuccinos for us.

"This man," grumbled Archie in an accent that sounded Italian. "This man – he wait till I clean machine and then he want more coffee. I ask you."

Most of the tables were occupied. Some customers were reading newspapers, a woman in a navy trouser suit was painting her nails and a scruffy looking man was sitting in the opposite corner to us scribbling in a notebook.

"That's Wilf," said Liam, following the direction of my gaze. "Writes poetry that'd break your heart. Those pictures over there – the female nudes – are his wife."

"They don't exactly go together do they?" I said. "She's beautiful."

"She left him for another woman and he went to pieces.

All his paintings and poems are for her."

I couldn't imagine Tony going to pieces if I left him – or writing poems for me in a steamy café.

"So why aren't you writing?" asked Linnet, her eyes keen as a blackbird's. She took a sip of coffee, looking at me over the rim of her cup.

"I didn't say I wasn't."

I hesitated, not knowing how to describe my situation without being disloyal to Tony.

"It's hard to make the time."

"Tell me about it," said Liam. "Putting those storytelling workshops together took ages. All that bloody fuss about being politically correct – making sure you don't touch the kids, being careful not to swear. I hadn't planned that story about Princess Fable, but it actually worked better than the ones I spent more time on…"

"Have you written a story about Charlotte?" I asked, wishing I could bite back the words when I saw his face darken.

"Why would I do that?" Liam's eyes narrowed like a stalking cat's.

"You just seemed like an item when you were at the reading – that's all."

"She dropped me like a hot potato when she found someone with a bigger bank balance." He sounded bitter and the light had faded from his eyes.

I didn't say anything.

A group of school kids were walking past the window, staring in. I hoped Cara wasn't amongst them.

"So what do you think, Fable?"

I realised Linnet had just asked me a question.

"Sorry, what did you say?"

"I was asking if you'd like details of a writing workshop

based on crystal healing."

I looked at the large chrome rimmed clock that hung above the café door. It was quarter to four and I was supposed to meet Cara at the dentists. "Send them to me," I said. "Sorry, got to go."

By the time I reached the dentist's Cara had already left and I walked home with the sinking feeling of having failed again.

CHAPTER THIRTY-FIVE

By the time I got home, Tony had made me a doctor's appointment.

"You've been behaving oddly lately," he said. "It's all the weird people you've been consorting with – people Cara and I haven't met. I think you've got some kind of mental problem. Hardly surprising with your background."

"You'd have had the chance to meet them if you'd come to the Awards Evening."

"You know my views on that."

We were standing in the hall and I could see Tony from three different angles in the mirrors that hung at either end.

I caught sight of my own reflection – my face was pale and there were panda-dark circles under my eyes. I tried to phrase the words in my head to try and tell Tony how unhappy I was, but they wouldn't organise themselves sensibly. My chest felt tight and my throat burned but the words wouldn't come.

"You look hunched," Tony went on. "When you're out with Cara and me, you look as if you don't know what you're doing. You're an embarrassment."

I didn't say anything.

"Are you just going to stand there with a silly look on your face?"

The words came out in a rush. "Things aren't working between us, Tony. I'm not happy. I don't feel valued. I want us to go to Relate for counselling."

The silence that followed was terrifying.

"So what you're saying is I haven't been a good husband and father?" Tony's voice was quiet and menacing. "You're in such a state you don't know what you want. You go to counselling if you want to – you're the one with all the problems."

"If one of us has a problem with the relationship, then we both do." My voice trembled and my mouth felt dry.

"You're the one coming home with all the weird ideas. If you gave up seeing these so-called friends and just stayed here where you're supposed to be, then we wouldn't be having this conversation now. All this silly writing nonsense has gone to your head. Things were fine till then."

I stood there, trying not to show how scared I felt.

"Look at you." Tony turned me to face my reflection in the mirror.

I could see Cara's reflection too – she'd crept half way down the stairs and looked as scared as I did.

"Now get in the car," he said. "Once the doctor's given you some medication, we'll all have an easier life."

When we got to the health centre, he gave my name to the receptionist and helped me into the crowded waiting room as if I was senile or heavily pregnant. He sat down next to me, his face a mask of silent anger. The doctor called me in and Tony came as well – looming over the desk as I sat in the other available chair. The room was painted pale green and smelled of antiseptic and furniture polish.

"What can I do for you, Mrs Lucas?" The doctor was Egyptian with liquid brown eyes.

"She needs something for her nerves. She's been behaving oddly recently."

The doctor looked keenly at me.

"Perhaps you'd like to wait in the waiting room, Mr Lucas."

Tony went out, slamming the door.

"Now Mrs Lucas, I don't think there's much wrong with you is there?"

I tried to laugh and ended up choking and then bursting into tears.

"Perhaps you can try to tell me what the problem is? I would like to help you."

I sniffed, taking a tissue from the box on his desk and dabbing my eyes. Tony always said how ugly I looked when I cried. "I just told my husband I wasn't happy – that I feel like I'm shut in a box I can't get out of…" The tears flowed again and I mopped at them with my now soggy tissue.

"It is good that you let the feelings out," he said. "I will give you tablets to help you sleep. You will feel better for some rest. And I will arrange for you to see the counsellor."

I left the surgery on shaky legs, relieved that somebody understood.

"I told him to give you some tablets," exploded Tony. "Why won't you ever speak up for yourself? And you're not seeing any trick-cyclist. Once you're labelled, you're a nutter for life. You never think of how your behaviour affects my career prospects."

"You were the one who insisted on taking me to the doctors, Tony," I said wearily.

Cara was waiting anxiously when we got home. She'd made tea and corned beef sandwiches and I tried to force some down, past the lump of unshed tears lodged in my throat. I went to bed soon afterwards, taking one of the little white tablets the doctor had given me. I soon fell into a deep, dark sleep, not stirring until Tony came up a few hours later.

He reached for me. "Not tonight," I mumbled sleepily.

He grumbled and turned away.

CHAPTER THIRTY-SIX

I woke the next morning, feeling as if my head was full of wet cement, relieved to find that Tony and Cara had already left the house. I got out of bed slowly, feeling the strange silence of the empty house, and went to the bathroom where I went to the toilet and washed my face, neck and under my arms, not feeling strong enough for my usual shower. I sprayed on Charlie Silver and put on yesterday's blue sweatshirt and jeans, noticing that they were crumpled from being left on the bedroom floor, but not feeling bothered enough to dump them in the wash basket and find something else.

When I got downstairs, Tony and Cara's breakfast dishes were dumped in the sink and the table was a mess of sticky toast crumbs and slopped tea. A crumpled copy of The Telegraph was left open at the Sports page.

Feeling weary, I switched on the kettle, put a teabag in the pink mug with white daisies Cara bought me for Mother's Day and got the milk out of the fridge. Tony had already opened the post and had dumped the envelopes in the kitchen bin. Linnet's letter to me, about the writing course, was on the top, splattered with tea. I took it out of the bin, smoothed it and read it, wondering why Tony was so threatened by my writing.

I couldn't face anything to eat and wandered about restlessly with my mug of tea gazing at the small white clouds scudding across the expanse of blue sky. I couldn't think clearly in the house, so I went out intending to go for a walk, wondering if Tony was right and I was losing my mind.

As I reached the path that led to the Library, I was startled to see Liam standing in front of me. His guitar was slung over his shoulder and he was wearing torn jeans and a black t-shirt with the slogan 'Peace or I'll thump you' written on it in white letters.

"What's been happening to you?"

"What do you mean?"

"I mean what's that bloke done to make you look like a road accident?"

"I'm not supposed to be outside talking to people," I said. "I should be at home doing the housework." I felt as if I wanted to put my head against Liam's chest and burst into tears.

"So he's got you under house arrest?"

"He says it's for my own good."

"And I'm a chimpanzee. Don't let him do this to you, Fable."

"The doctor's given me some sleeping tablets. I'll be better soon."

"Bollocks."

I burst into tears. Liam moved forward to comfort me. He smelled of coconut and fresh lemons and I wanted to stay there forever, but I pushed him away dreading what would happen if Cara or anyone else saw us.

He looked huffy. "I'm trying to help you, darlin'," I heard him say as I hurried back towards home, feeling a sick sense of dread.

I could feel the tension in the air as soon as I opened the front door. The message button on the phone was flashing. I checked 1471 and Tony's office number came up. He hadn't left a message.

I hung up my jacket and put my handbag in its usual place by the kitchen table. The phone rang again.

"Where were you?" asked Tony. He sounded suspicious.

"I was asleep."

"I don't believe you. I thought I told you not to leave the house."

"So I'm under house arrest now?"

"I'm only trying to protect you from yourself. You're obviously not able to cope out in the big wide world. You've only got to look at how strange you've become since you started all this writing business…"

I put the phone down with a feeling of hopelessness, looking out at the red and yellow tulips in our flower borders, wondering what it would be like to be dead. After all, my husband and daughter didn't really love me and I'd lost all hope of getting back in touch with my mother. The bright hope of a new life I'd felt only a matter of weeks ago had faded to ashes.

The phone rang again

I burst into tears when I heard Liam's voice.

He listened as I poured out my torrent of feelings.

"… and I was just thinking wouldn't it be easier for everyone if I wasn't here any more."

Liam listened patiently. "I'd miss you darlin'."

"What did you say?"

"It may have escaped your notice, but I love you, you silly woman, although it's probably not a politically correct thing that a wild rover like me should be saying to a married woman."

CHAPTER THIRTY-SEVEN

Tony was white with fury that evening when I said I wanted our life together to be different.

"Who's put this idea into your head? Why are you always so stupid and gullible, Fable?"

"I'm not stupid and I'm not gullible," I said, trying to keep my voice steady and my hands from shaking. "I want us both to go for counselling. For our marriage. Surely you can see things aren't right."

"As I've said before, you're the one with all the problems. And they're all inside your head. Nobody else thinks there's anything wrong with our marriage. If you'd stop getting involved with these weird ideas and talking to people who are a few bricks short of a load, then we could all get back to normal."

"What other people think doesn't matter. I'm saying I'm unhappy. Therefore we both have a problem."

"The problems are all yours, Fable. And for your information, if you ever do think of doing something stupid like leaving me, I'll make sure you don't get a penny to live on. Earning money's not exactly your forte is it- and you'll find a vast difference scraping by on the dole. So think about it."

I lay awake most of the night thinking about it, not knowing what to do next. I didn't even dare get up to write in case Cara or Tony found out. In fact, it was difficult to know what I could do that Tony didn't consider weird. If I looked out of the window, he said I was acting strangely. If I didn't take exactly the same route round a shop when we went out together, then that was wrong too.

I got up that morning feeling gritty eyed and exhausted. After Tony and Cara had left the house, I spent most of the morning curled up on the sofa under my old pink fluffy dressing gown, staring listlessly out of the window at the dying tulips. There was a layer of dust on the furniture, but I didn't have the energy to deal with it. I hadn't written anything for several days – all the stories and ideas in my head felt like they'd turned into cotton wool.

About halfway through the morning, when I was trying to summon up the energy to get up and make another mug of tea, the phone rang. I hesitated before answering it, certain that it would be Tony checking up on me again.

It was Linnet. "Liam says you're not well. He's worried about you."

"I'm doing OK."

"No you're not," she said gently.

"Sorry," I sniffed. "Once I start crying I can't stop."

"It's better not to bottle things up."

I didn't say anything.

"Look, tell me where you are and I'll come and get you. A change of scene might do you good."

"Tony won't like it if he comes back and I'm not here."

"He goes out without your permission doesn't he? You can leave him a note. You're not a child, Fable. Stand up for yourself – and your life."

"You're right," I said. "I can't think properly here."

"Great," she said. "I'll come and get you."

Half an hour later, Linnet's purple Volkswagen Beetle pulled up outside. I picked up my handbag, left a note for Tony on the hall table and hurried out to her. When I opened the car door I was hit by the smell of roses (good for stress, Linnet said). There were purple velvet cushions on the back seat and soft music playing on the stereo.

"When I was with my husband, he always worried that

I'd get too relaxed when driving and have an accident," said Linnet. "We laugh about that now."

"You still see him?"

"Every couple of months we have dinner together. We thought it was important to put our differences aside for our son Barnaby."

"So does Barnaby live with you?"

"Like most kids he's out for the main chance. He goes wherever he gets the best deal. At the moment that's with his father."

"And you don't mind?"

"He's happy and confident and we're always talking on the phone. Why should I mind?"

I looked out of the car window and saw a woman with a little girl who looked like Cara when she was small. I felt sad that those years had passed so quickly and I thought about the babies that weren't born at all. We turned down a small lane with a field of sheep on the corner and a copse of trees on the hill in the distance. At the end of the lane was a row of four three-storey Victorian villas that Linnet said once belonged to the local farm.

"The bus stops at the end of the lane so Barnaby's fine when he comes to visit," said Linnet. "Sometimes I come home and find he's taken up residence again, just like the bats that spend the winter in my loft."

"You know where I live now," she said as we got out of the car, "so you can come whenever you like." She unlocked the kingfisher blue front door.

There was a tiny lobby where coats and shoes were kept and from there a door led into a big living room with open stairs going off it. The walls were covered in paintings – mermaids and seahorses and vibrant abstracts in pinks, purples and blues.

A black and white cat that reminded me of Magpie dozed on a torn cushion by the inglenook fireplace.

"That's Delia Smith," said Linnet, stroking the cat's ears. "She's always out in the kitchen with me when I'm cooking. Barnaby thinks she's probably written her own recipe book."

I followed Linnet out to the kitchen when she went to make coffee. As predicted, Delia Smith followed, her black tail hovering like a question mark.

Light poured in through the green-tinted windows onto butter yellow walls and the scrubbed pine table.

"I should really clean these windows," said Linnet ruefully. "For the last six months I've been pretending they're stained glass instead of moss-stained. Trouble is there always seems to be so many other interesting things to do."

"I used to tell my husband I wasn't born with a dishcloth in one hand and a broom in the other," she added as she made strong coffee and toasted some teacakes.

I laughed.

Delia Smith climbed onto my lap as I drank my coffee, licking the last vestiges of butter off my fingers.

"Cupboard love," said Linnet. "She'll love you till the end of the teacake."

There were piles of paperwork everywhere – lists and lesson plans, timetables and scraps of paper covered in Linnet's round handwriting.

"How do you keep track of it all?"

"With great difficulty. The thing is, one idea leads to another – a bit like when you paint with watercolour and allow one colour to bleed into another."

I stared at her in amazement.

"You can paint, can't you?" asked Linnet.

"It's years since I tried."

"You should try again. You're an artist – it shows in your handwriting."

"Tony doesn't approve of my writing – he'd have a fit if I started painting as well."

"Maybe the only answer is to leave him."

"I've got no money."

"You can achieve anything if you're determined."

"Gangan used to say that."

"Look, Fable, I've spent years looking at healing techniques and teaching people the benefits of positive thinking. I wasted time years ago, stuck in the wrong life. I wouldn't want you to do the same."

The hours passed as Linnet showed me her ideas on colour healing, her collection of crystals and the paintings she was in the process of framing for an exhibition she was doing later in the year. We'd gone back to the kitchen (Delia Smith following as usual) for pate, salad and crusty bread and before I realised it was nearly four o'clock and Cara would be home from school.

"I should go. Don't worry about driving me. I can get the bus."

"Why don't you stay?" Linnet looked eager. "Just tonight? The breathing space might do you good."

Heart thumping, I phoned home. Cara answered.

"There's some housekeeping money in the bread bin. Get a pizza for you and Dad."

"Yeah cool," she said.

I gave her the telephone number and said I'd see her tomorrow.

The phone rang almost as soon as I'd put it down.

Linnet answered it and I felt my heart plummet coldly in my chest as I imagined Tony's voice on the other end of the line.

"I'll think about it," said Linnet. "I'll call you back in ten minutes."

"What's the problem?"

"A friend – she's a writing tutor – is poorly. She can't take her class tonight and wondered if I could stand in for her."

"Of course you can."

"But I've invited you here for respite care. I can't go out and leave you."

I raised my hand as if making a Brownie promise. "I promise not to put my fingers in the sockets or leave the taps running."

She laughed. "OK. I'll put Anne out of her misery and say I'll do it then. So long as you're sure?"

"Sure," I said.

"We'll eat when I get back."

After Linnet had gone, I made myself another mug of tea and wandered round the living room, gazing at the paintings on the walls, drinking in the vibrant colours. I was just doing a third circuit when there was a knock at the door. I stood for a few moments, my heart hammering in my chest, worried that it might be Tony standing on the doorstep.

I opened the door cautiously, keeping the chain on. Liam was standing there, wearing faded blue jeans and a black sweatshirt.

"Linnet asked me to keep an eye on you. God, woman, you look terrible. You're all bones."

I smiled weakly as I held the door open for him.

"How come you escaped old rough balls?"

"Linnet asked me over for the day. I thought I'd be

home by now."

We were in the kitchen now, with Liam making another cup of tea.

"You'd be better off without him," he said lifting my chin and looking into my eyes, stroking the dark circles under them.

"It's not that simple."

I remembered what Tony had said once about a divorce case he'd dealt with where the wife had left the husband, taking the children with her. The wife had taken the husband to court and had won a large settlement.

"If that were you, Fable, I'd make sure you never got a penny. You'd never see Cara again. You'd cease to be her mother."

"What're you thinking about?"

I told Liam about the things that Tony had said.

"He can't do that. OK. Trust me, it'll be OK. In a year's time you'll wonder what all this was about."

Sobs tore at my throat and chest.

The phone rang and Liam answered it.

"Sure. No problem," he said. "See you later." He put the phone down and strode across the room, putting his arms round me and holding me tight. I smelled that almost-familiar scent of coconut and lemon again and could hear the beat of his heart through the soft black sweatshirt. He stroked my back in wide circles until I calmed down.

A shaft of evening sun filtered through the kitchen windows, casting green shadows on the tiled floor.

"Sorry," I sniffed.

"There's nothing wrong with a few tears, Fable. When my wife died I walked for two days along the coastal path in Ireland yelling at the top of my voice, raging at the wind and the seagulls. And I'm not ashamed to say I cried, threw myself down in the mud and howled. There was a priest once in our village and he always said a weepy funeral was better for everyone than a stiff upper lip one. What is a stiff upper lip anyway? Sounds bloody uncomfortable to me."

"Better ask my husband. He's got one." The tears were flowing again. "I'm sorry, I didn't know your wife died."

"It was five years ago. I loved her but she's gone. Life has to go on."

I think that one day I'll be able to tell Liam about Tobias and he'll understand. But then, he'd said nothing about any of his plans for the future including me.

"Linnet's been delayed. I'm to get dinner for us both. There's some pasta-something-or-other in the fridge."

He bent down and rummaged in the fridge, taking out the remains of the salad Linnet and I ate at lunchtime, a bowl of pasta in a meat sauce and some garlic bread. He lit the oven and put in the bowl of pasta, before going back to the fridge and pulling out a chilled bottle of white wine.

"Linnet won't mind," he said as he uncorked the bottle.

The smell of spicy meat and garlic made my mouth water.

When everything was ready, we carried it outside to a white-painted wrought iron table on a tiny patio. Liam had wiped the table and chairs with a flourish and lit a candle, pretending to be an Italian waiter. The metal chair felt cool through my jeans as I gazed at the rampant garden where the elderflowers and hawthorn reminded me of those months with Tobias.

The evening sun was going down behind the clump of woodland at the end of the garden and large pale moths were drawn to the candle flame. We sat in the fading light and Liam told me about his childhood in Ireland, the stories he'd been told and how worried he was about his mother.

"She lives in a cottage by the Atlantic where salt spray cakes the windows most of the year and she's a dear soul. I'm catching the ferry to Dublin in the morning – see if I can persuade her to see a doctor…"

He took my hands in his. "Promise me though that if there's any trouble you'll come and stay at my place. I've had a key made for you and you can stay as long as you want."

His eyes looked like liquid topaz.

We took the plates and glasses indoors. As I reached the sink, I dropped my glass, cutting my hand on the jagged edge. Blood spurted from a small cut and I felt panicky. Liam held my hand under the cold tap until the bleeding stopped, wrapping a piece of kitchen paper round it while he searched in Linnet's cupboard for plasters and ointment.

When he'd put the plaster on, he kissed it like I used to do with Cara, pitching me onto the edge of tears again.

"The first step's the hardest," he said, putting his arms round me again. "The first bridge is always the most difficult. Once you've made the first move you can only go forward. Never go back, Fable, remember that."

CHAPTER THIRTY-EIGHT

Linnet took me home.

"See you soon. Call me if you need me." She blew me a kiss as she drove off.

Tony came downstairs after she'd gone.

"Why didn't you come down and meet Linnet?"

"Why would I want to do that? She looks odd – how can you be taken in by someone like her after all we've said lately?" His voice was dangerously quiet. "Cara and I didn't know what was going on. The poor kid's really confused. All she got was a garbled phone message from you saying you were staying at some weirdo's house. We were left with no tea and no idea where you were."

"Cara was fine when I spoke to her yesterday. I told her there was money for a pizza and I gave her Linnet's phone number. "

"I thought we agreed that family comes first?"

"I needed some time to sort out how I feel."

The memory of Liam's arms cradling me made me feel desperate to be with him again.

"How you feel about what for Christ's sake? That woman you spent the night with?"

"What are you talking about?"

"I know you're naïve, Fable, but even you know what a lesbian is."

"Linnet's not a lesbian."

"If you leave me, I'll make sure you never see Cara again – even if it takes all the money I've got. It'll be like you never existed. The choice is yours."

"Where is Cara? I want to talk to her."

"You're not talking to her unless I'm present. For your

information, she's staying with friends at the moment. The poor kid's traumatised by your behaviour."

"Who is she staying with?"

"That's none of your business. Now get us some dinner and see if you can start to behave normally."

Linnet telephoned me the next day.

"Everything's fine," I told her through frozen lips. I'm going to stay here and give things another try…"

"Fable, wake up and smell the coffee! Tony's a controlling bastard. If you don't escape you'll just fade into the wallpaper. He'll chew you up, spit out the bits and not think any more of you."

"He won't let me see Cara if I leave him."

I could hardly speak for crying.

"I've got to go, Linnet. If you speak to Liam tell him I'm sorry - I wasn't able to cross the first bridge."

CHAPTER THIRTY-NINE

Tony had always blamed me for acting 'strangely' but as I was cooking dinner on the night after I came home from Linnet's I realised how much his own behaviour had changed recently. He'd had a lot more phone calls than usual and would never say who'd called. Yesterday I heard him talking on the phone upstairs.

"Who were you talking to just now?" I asked when he came downstairs.

"I wasn't talking to anyone, you must've imagined it." He sprinkled salt and pepper on his cottage pie as if closing the subject.

He'd also had several late meetings at work and once he came home smelling of another woman's perfume. He got angry when I mentioned it.

"Some woman must've hung her jacket up next to mine. I suppose this is the next turn in your neurotic fantasies, Fable. You'll be accusing me of having an affair next."

I wondered if the way he'd behaved towards me was his way of trying to force me to leave. I wasn't bothered about money or possessions – as long as I could find some way of supporting myself and Cara. The problem was, it was so long since I'd had to support myself, I didn't know if I still could.

One thing was certain, though, there was no way I could go on with this marriage as it was. I was sure that Cara would take Tony's side if I left him and I wasn't sure if I could bear the heartache of losing touch with her. I hadn't managed to talk to her properly because Tony made sure we were never alone together. She'd been very moody lately, spending a lot of time in her bedroom, saying she'd got homework to do.

This morning, the sky was dark as a bruise and

thunderstorms were forecast. I wandered round the house looking at furniture and ornaments that had been part of my life for so many years, trying to decide what to do. I could see that coming back here had been a mistake. I'd been sucked back into Tony's regime and was gradually losing the power to think for myself. If I left it any longer – till Cara was eighteen, say – then I'd lose the power to act at all. I thought about what Liam had said:

"You have to make this decision for yourself. If I had my way I'd come and rescue you, but you need to take the first step for yourself."

I wandered into Cara's room, instantly hit by the smell of vanilla body spray and mint hair conditioner – the smell of mint reminding me of Linnet's garden, the greenish light that flooded into her kitchen, the meal Liam and I had eaten together and the feeling of being in his arms.

Cara loved the old black and white films and her room was lined with posters of 'Arsenic and Old Lace', 'Rebecca' and 'Wuthering Heights.' I gazed at them, realising how much they reminded me of the film that Jasmine had made as part of her exhibition, feeling sad all over again that she hadn't tried to get in touch with me again.

I heard Gangan's voice in my head, telling me that nothing would change unless I took the first step. "Sometimes difficult things are like pulling a wobbly tooth," I remembered her saying once when I was worrying about telling my teacher I'd lost my library book. "Best to do it quick, Fable, before you have time to think about it."

My mouth felt dry and sour and my legs felt heavy as I dragged the brown leather suitcase out from under the bed and began to pack my most treasured things, changing my mind every few minutes and starting again. I remembered how a teacher had read 'Treasure Island' to us at school and how anxious I'd felt when Jim and his mother were at the inn, with the dead body of the Captain and the threat of the pirates returning, and yet Mrs Hawkins was insisting on making sure she'd got all the money due to her. I felt the same edginess and need to escape, but at the same time didn't want to leave anything important behind.

Heavy rain and hail stones lashed the bedroom window and thunder rumbled like a concrete mixer as I packed and unpacked, reminding me of that journey to Isbourne and the discoveries I made there. Several times, I almost abandoned my idea, feeling that the bridge was too wide to cross.

"What the hell do you think you're doing, Fable?" I hadn't heard Tony come back and silently climb the stairs and felt sick with dread that he'd try to stop me.

"Where's Cara? Why isn't she at school today?"

"I thought that's where she was. How do you expect me to know if you won't let me see her?"

Tony sneered at me. "What sort of a mother are you? The head teacher rang me to say she'd seen Cara walk out of the school gates at nine thirty this morning."

"Why did they phone your office and not our home number?"

He didn't say anything.

"What've you told the school about me, Tony?"

"The truth – that you're not behaving rationally and would they please refer any problems with Cara to me personally."

I placed the last few items of clothing in my suitcase and zipped it up.

"Making a pathetic display of independence won't get you anywhere Fable. And you know what the consequences will be."

"Do what you like, Tony. I'm fed up with your bullying." My lips felt dry and stiff and I was sure he could see my knees and hands shaking.

"Where can you go anyway? What will you live on?" His voice was smooth as milk chocolate. "You won't get a penny from me. You'll end up in a cardboard box in the gutter…"

He moved towards me, knocking me off balance so that I fell sideways, hitting my head on the corner of the dressing table. Blood spurted from a cut on my forehead and I crouched for a few moments feeling sick, giddy and disorientated.

Then anger surged through me. "That wouldn't have happened without your threatening behaviour. I'm going to the police this time like I should've done before."

"Nobody will believe you. It'll be your word against mine and who d'you think they'll believe?"

He looked at the splashes of blood on the cream carpet. "You'd better get that cleaned up. I'm going to contact some of Cara's friends and see if I can find out what's going on."

I got unsteadily to my feet, holding onto the windowsill for support. Someone had parked a scruffy white van across our driveway.

"I'm phoning an ambulance," I said, "and I'm telling the police about you."

"Nobody will believe you, Fable."

I heard footsteps on the stairs and turned, expecting Cara to be there. There was a flash of lightning and then the room went dark, like a scene change in a play.

"I believe Fable and so will the police." Jasmine had appeared in the room like a ghost or a figment of the storm. Her long wavy hair was silver instead of black but the fire in her eyes was the same.

"Who the fuck let you in? Tony's voice was as cold as a stone dropping down a deep well.

"Cara of course," said Jasmine. Her voice was a little huskier than I remembered it, but still lively and musical. The lightning flashed around her, making the tiny mirrors on her lilac dress glitter like rainbows.

Cara walked into the room. She looked pale as she leaned her head against Jasmine's shoulder.

"Why aren't you at school today, young lady? What are you doing with this woman?" Tony's voice was cold.

"She's not 'this woman.' She's Jas – my grandmother – and I'm going to live with her."

"Over my dead body."

"We'll see about that," said Jasmine grimly. "Now get out of the way so I can take my daughter to the hospital since you don't care enough about her to do so yourself."

She took my face in her long slim hands. "Come on, Fable. Everything's going to be fine. You'll see."

She left the bedroom first, carrying my suitcase, with Cara and me following.

I didn't look back.

CHAPTER FORTY

Tony didn't attempt to follow us out of the house.

It was still pouring with rain as Cara and Jasmine settled me on a mattress in the back of the battered white transit van. Jasmine put a clean rag on the still-bleeding cut and covered me with a soft pink blanket. Rain drummed on the roof and I dreamily took in the smell of turps and new wood.

Cara sat on the front passenger seat next to Jasmine for the short journey to hospital. When we got there, Jasmine made Cara wait with me while she went to find a wheelchair.

"I can walk," I said, but when I sat up I felt sick and giddy.

Cara was pale and quiet as we sat in A & E waiting for me to be called to see the doctor. There was a large telly in one corner that nobody was taking any notice of, a pile of dog-eared magazines and a snack machine that did crisps, chocolate and cans of drink. The large room smelled of antiseptic overlaid with sweaty socks and a faint smell of vomit.

"I think you should be checked over too, Cara," said Jasmine looking concerned.

"Not now, Jas, I'm fine." I noticed that although their colouring was different, they had the same expressive hands and infectious laughter.

"What's going on?"

Cara flushed and shot a glance at Jasmine.

"Nothing that can't be sorted out," said Jasmine. "We've all got years of catching up to do – and this wasn't the way I imagined our first meeting…" She was silent for a few moments, fiddling with her collection of silver rings. "I never stopped loving you whatever they told you, Fable."

"I always knew that," I said, touching her hands gently.

"It's like Gangan's stories never really went away." I hesitated, feeling a lump in my throat. "She's – dead, isn't she?"

Jasmine laughed. "Whatever gave you that idea? No, Fable love, she's very much alive and waiting at Starlight for us all to celebrate her ninetieth birthday with her."

"Mrs Lucas, the doctor will see you now," called the nurse. She pushed my wheelchair into the first available cubicle and helped me to get onto the couch. I lay there, wondering if I'd heard Jasmine correctly, feeling a bubble of excitement that I'd very soon see Gangan again.

When the doctor came he felt my head, examined the cut and shone a light in my eyes.

"Quick stitch needed in that cut, Mrs Lucas and then I think you can go home to your nearest and dearest." He was young and skinny with short dark hair.

"I'm not sure if I've got a home to go to," I said, my eyes suddenly filling with tears. "You'd better ask my mother, she's in the waiting room."

There was a mumbled conversation between the doctor and a nurse and I was told to wait there for a while.

"We'll move you back out into the waiting area, Mrs Lucas, while we try to find you a bed."

Cara and Jasmine were waiting for me. It was evening now. The rain had stopped and the setting sun had created mottled patterns of crimson, orange, pink, gold and lilac in the darkening sky. The streetlights were on outside the hospital and an ambulance man brought in a young man on a trolley. He looked deathly pale. While the ambulance man was checking him in at the desk, the young man tried to sit up, lurched sideways and vomited a yellow stream all over the grey lino.

"Great," said Cara. "At least I've stopped doing that now."

Jasmine shot her a warning glance.

"Will one of you tell me what's going on?" I said.

A nurse came over to us. "Mrs Lucas, your husband's on the phone. Do you wish to speak to him?"

I looked at Cara and Jasmine. "No," I said. "Not at the moment."

I looked at Cara. She swallowed and took a deep breath. "I didn't mean it to happen, Mum, but I'm pregnant. Martin – that lad I was seeing a few months ago – doesn't want to know."

"We'll help you," I said, taking hold of her cold hands in mine. "Jasmine and I will help you." I felt close to tears again.

"Remember that day Dad took you to the doctors?"

I nodded. "How can I forget?"

"Well, that was the day I found out Dad was having an affair. Martin and I had wagged off school to go round the shops and we saw Dad's car outside the Phoenix Hotel. He and a woman came out – they looked extremely friendly. When I challenged him about it, he said I'd imagined everything and then got really shitty and said that if I mentioned anything to you he'd make sure I didn't go to France with the school. Anyway, I got a bit upset and confused, Martin tried to comfort me and …"

The nurse came to take me up to the ward. "Can your mother or daughter collect some things for you?"

"See what you can find in my suitcase," I said, feeling exhausted.

Jasmine was back in no time with a collection of offerings from her and Cara. They sat on each side of my bed – the ward sister said they could stay a few minutes to settle me in – holding my hands not really wanting to leave each other.

The sky outside the window was inky black now and a crescent moon hung like a blade in the soft darkness.

"Where will you stay tonight?" I asked Jasmine.

"Cara and I will manage fine in the van – it's not quite the gypsy caravan I always imagined but it's the next best thing."

"Tell me about Gangan," I said. "Why wasn't she home when I went to find her years ago?"

"She did what I always talked about – went off and travelled the world – the Great Silk Road and all the rest of it, which was why she wasn't there when you tried to find her."

"You should leave Mrs Lucas and the other patients to get some rest now." The ward sister's voice was soft, but didn't brook any argument.

"We'll be back for you in the morning," said Jasmine "and I'll tell you the rest of the story then. Sleep well."

CHAPTER FORTY-ONE

"Get some sleep, Mrs Lucas," the ward sister said gently. "From what your mother has said you've had a trying time over the last few months and it's what you need most."

I tried, but I couldn't sleep for wondering what else Jasmine had to tell me. I sat up, gazing at the crescent moon hanging like a blade amongst a cluster of stars, thinking about the strange journey that had been my life so far, wondering what would happen now – and trying not to feel anxious about what Tony might do. I'd half imagined that he'd come to the hospital, say that I was making everything up and insist that I discharge myself immediately.

Jasmine had obviously thought the same thing. "I don't think he'd be stupid enough to do anything like that, but if he does, stick to your guns and don't ever go back," she'd said as she kissed me goodnight. "Whatever he might say about things being different from now on, you and I know that with someone like him it never will be."

I lay in my starched white bed, fidgeting and thinking how it reminded me of waiting for Christmas when I was a small child or when Gangan called me in for bedtime when other children were still outside playing and there was warm air and the smell of cut grass from summer lawn mowing coming in through the open windows.

Thinking about those times eventually made me drift off to sleep and I didn't wake until a young nurse in pale green cotton trousers and top woke me with the breakfast trolley. I managed to eat a bowl of Cornflakes and drink a cup of strong sweet tea.

Now it was daytime, I felt anxious again, wondering what would happen today and where I'd be by this time tomorrow.

Cara and Jasmine came to collect me after the doctor had done his rounds.

"You're staying with Linnet for a few days," Cara informed me. "She says she's been going frantic wondering what had happened to you. Dad wouldn't tell her anything – just said you weren't there any more. Is she that weird woman from the Library?"

"Here, no more talk of weird now you're with me," said Jasmine, punching Cara's arm playfully. "Do you know what the kids used to call me when I lived in Germany? They called me Hexe – meaning witch."

This morning, wearing a long, layered red dress, she looked more like a silver-haired gypsy. Cara, by contrast, was wearing a candy pink track- suit and, with her blonde hair loose, looked much younger than sixteen.

So why can't we go straight to Starlight now? And who's looking after Gangan?

"She's got a live-in companion – a lovely woman called Karen who cooks and cleans. Believe it or not, Gangan still potters in her herb garden and does the odd tarot reading. It's all the rage amongst the young ones now apparently. And we can't go immediately because I've got an art exhibition in Paris."

"Paris?"

"And I'm going to help her," said Cara excitedly.

"We'll take you to Linnet's house," said Jasmine. "Cara and I'd like to meet her before we go to Paris."

After I'd washed and dressed, the three of us made our way down to the car park. The sun was shining, and the sky was full of small fluffy clouds, reminding me of sheep grazing on blue grass.

"When're you back? We've only just met up again and now you're leaving me."

"We'll be back in a couple of days – and then we'll take you to Starlight for Gangan's birthday. You can sleep in your old room if you like. For now, the best thing you can do is rest and get your strength back." Jasmine gave me a warm hug. "It'll all be fine – you'll see."

Just then Tony's silver BMW swept into the car park, blocking our exit. He got out of the car, his lips compressed with anger.

"This nonsense has gone far enough. Fable and Cara, you're coming with me. You – Jasmine or whatever your name is – you can be on your way. I blame you for all that's happened."

"I can't move. You've blocked me in," said Jasmine sweetly.

"I'm not going back." Cara and I sounded as if we'd rehearsed the words.

"What d'you mean you're not going back? Where else can you go?"

"I don't see that's any of your business," said Cara.

Tony seemed to swell to twice his usual size. "You don't want to be taken in by a charlatan like her. I thought you were more discerning, Cara."

"I'm pregnant," said Cara coolly.

Tony's face turned white. "This is your fault," he said, jabbing his forefinger towards my face. "If you hadn't got involved with those weird people at the Library none of this would've happened. If you'd stayed at home and been a proper wife and mother like we agreed then we wouldn't be having this problem now."

"We would be having this 'problem' as you call it,

Tony," I said, "because the truth is, as I tried to tell you before, I don't love you any more. I'm not sure if I ever did. Now please move your car as Jasmine asked you to do. There's nothing else to say."

Tony didn't move. "If you leave me, then it'll be like you never existed. You'll get nothing from me – not a penny. You'll cease to be Cara's mother and I'll make sure you're punished for daring to leave me."

"They don't lock women up for leaving their husbands any more," said Jasmine, hands on hips, glaring at Tony.

"You can't stop her being my Mum," said Cara.

"She's wrecked your life," hissed Tony, "don't you understand that?"

"No, she didn't. If anyone's to blame, it's you. If I hadn't been so upset when I saw you come out of that hotel with your arm round that woman…"

"I never did any such thing," said Tony coldly, as a red Mazda MX5 pulled in behind his BMW, causing even more congestion in that section of the car park.

A woman in a charcoal grey suit with shiny chestnut bobbed hair got out of it. "I've been waiting for you for the last twenty minutes," she said in a pseudo-posh voice. "And here you are chatting to some women in a car park. You have no idea how I felt when I called your office and they said you'd gone to the hospital."

She swept us all a look with cold grey eyes. "Are these clients of yours?"

"Not exactly," said Jasmine looking dangerous. "And who might you be?"

"I know who she is," said Cara. "She's Dad's mistress."

CHAPTER FORTY-TWO

The next morning when I woke in Barnaby's attic room at Linnet's house, I lay there for ages absorbing the peaceful atmosphere, gazing up through the sky-light at ravens wheeling on the air currents like cut out black shapes on blue paper. The smell of roses and cut grass came in through the partly open window opposite the bed.

Linnet had left me a note together with a tray containing croissants, fresh butter, black cherry jam and a glass of orange juice.

"Back later – sorry to abandon you as soon as you got here. We'll talk later. P.S. Help yourself to coffee downstairs."

I sat up against the pillows, relishing the luxury of breakfast in bed. The croissants were just right – crispy on the outside and soft inside, the jam rich and dark and full of fruit. When I'd finished eating, I went to the bathroom for a shower and put on yesterday's jeans and a clean lilac t-shirt. I carried the tray downstairs, washed the dishes and stood gazing out through the greenish windows to the sunlit garden.

I unlocked the back door and wandered out to the tiny patio, remembering as I did so that evening with Liam and how he'd unleashed passionate feelings I thought had gone forever. I half closed my eyes, wondering where he was now and feeling sad that he hadn't bothered to contact me. He'd promised to give me a key to his house but nothing had happened and I had the uneasy feeling that he didn't really mean what he said.

I stood watching two peacock butterflies spiral in the jam-scented air above a purple buddleia bush, feeling the warm sun on my bare arms, hearing the murmur of bees in a clump of lavender and thinking of how all this reminded me of Gangan's garden and I felt a bubble of excitement knowing I'd soon see it again, quickly followed by a feeling of exhaustion when I remembered how angry Tony was when I last saw him. I knew he couldn't take Cara away from me but I did worry about what he might do in retaliation.

I heard the metallic click of the latch as someone tried to open Linnet's side gate and my stomach turned over with fear. The hedges on each side of Linnet's garden were overgrown with bramble, nettles and convolvulus. There was nobody in either of the gardens that I could call to for help.

Whoever was out there tried the gate again and I heard it shudder as it opened with a creak. I had a few seconds to take refuge indoors before the intruder reached the place where I was standing. Fear galvanised my shaking legs and I flung myself into the kitchen, slamming the back door and locking it, before leaning against it for support.

I strained my ears listening for any sound of intrusion. There was silence. I put the kettle on feeling that I needed a strong cup of coffee. Then I heard it – the sound of banging at the side of the house just inside the gate. My first thought was that Tony had turned violent and was damaging Linnet's property.

Picking up a heavy brass ornament, I opened the back door quietly and crept out, remembering the games Teresa and I used to play spying on Peggy or Gangan from the shelter of a thick clump of hollyhocks. It was funny how Gangan always knew we were there, but Peggy never did.

To my surprise, Liam was there. He'd finished hammering in a fence post with a wooden mallet and was now hacking at a clump of nettles with a scythe and singing 'Carrickfergus' at the top of his voice. He was wearing jeans and sandals and his hair was tied back with string. His back looked suntanned and his hair shone with golden highlights. Looking at him, I felt suddenly shy, remembering our last meeting. I crept back to the kitchen, trying to still the frantic hammering of my heart, wondering what to say to him.

I made two mugs of coffee and carried them out to the garden, watching the ripple of his muscles as he worked for a few moments before I spoke. Unnoticed by him, a peacock butterfly had landed on his shoulder, drinking the salty sweat.

"Liam."

He turned, looking wary. He didn't come towards me and I wondered what I'd done wrong.

"Husband let you out for a few hours has he?" He sounded hostile.

"Didn't Linnet tell you what happened?"

"Tell me what? She's not here half the time."

"Liam – what's the matter with you?" My hands were shaking so much I was spilling the coffee. I put the mugs down on the table, remembering that last occasion when we'd eaten together.

"What's the matter with me? That's rich. I offered to help and you didn't bother to take up the offer. You didn't even bother to answer my letters."

He picked up a mug and took a large swig of coffee, wincing as the hot liquid burnt him.

"What letters?"

Liam looked angrily at me. "What letters, she says." He slammed his coffee mug down on the fence post, spilling hot liquid on ripening blackberries. "Fable, why didn't you come to my place like you said you would if you needed help? How d'you think I felt when I came back from Ireland and didn't know where you were?" He put his coffee mug back on the table. His eyes were like liquid fire and his voice was breaking with emotion.

"I even went to your house for Christ's sake. That husband of yours said you'd gone off with someone. I thought you'd got another man. Have you any idea how I felt?"

He flung down the scythe and stormed off.

"Liam, let me explain…"

He didn't turn round. I heard the click of the gate and then silence. I went indoors and sat on Linnet's sofa hugging a cushion thinking that I didn't have an address or phone number for him so how did he expect me to get in touch with him. If he'd written me letters – where had he sent them? Obviously not to my old house or Tony would've had a ready-made divorce petition and would've lost no time in telling me so. The only thing I could do was leave a note for Linnet and explain what had happened – unless he came back before then.

As if conjured by my thoughts, there was a knock at the door – more of a heavy thumping really, just like a frustrated Irishman in a temper.

I opened the door, reeling with shock when I saw Tony standing there.

"Get your things," he said. "You're coming home with me."

"No, I'm not."

"You won't manage any sort of life without me, Fable. You're naïve, stupid and gullible. I'll give you a fortnight and you'll be in the same state as your mother."

"I do hope so – she's a very successful artist with an exhibition in Paris at the moment.

Tony goggled at me.

"Think what you like about me, Tony. I know what you are. You're a lying, destructive control freak and you're having an affair."

"You drove me to it."

"You're welcome to each other. I don't suppose she'll put up with you like I have. Goodbye Tony, I'll see you in court."

I slammed the door, feeling weak and shaky for all my brave words. I poured a nip of Linnet's gin, topping it up with orange juice from the fridge, wincing at the barely-concealed flowery smell and wondering how Jasmine had drunk so much of it for so long.

"What's this, party time?" asked Linnet as she came home a short time later. "I was a bit worried. An angry looking man in a silver car drove past me and I thought you may've had some trouble."

"It's been nothing but trouble here this morning," I said wearily. "Liam was here…"

"And…"

"He got angry and now he's gone. He said he'd written to me and got all upset because I hadn't stayed at his place when I was in trouble. But he didn't tell me where it was so how was I supposed to know?"

Linnet was laughing.

"What a lot of misunderstanding. I thought you knew where he lived – at the other end of this terrace… Did I not tell you that?"

Relief flooded me. I could sort things out. Make him listen. "No you didn't say."

I hurried out of the door, racing along the cobbled path that led along the front of the houses until I got to the one at the far end. The paint was flaking off the front door showing layers of dark blue, red and black. I knocked and shouted through the letter-box but the house had that empty feel. Liam had gone.

I walked wearily back to Linnet's, realising how empty

my life would be without him. By the time I got back to Linnet's, Jasmine and Cara had arrived to take me down to Gangan's house. Jasmine's white van was crammed with canvases, bedding and boxes of food for the party.

"I'll sort Liam out," whispered Linnet. "He'll cool down and be back soon – when he's walked the frustration out of himself."

I remembered then what he'd said about what happened after his wife died.

"When you see him," I whispered, "tell him I've crossed the first bridge and my life is empty without him."

*

The front door was open when we arrived at Starlight. The house looked as different from the last time I saw it as it could possibly do. The front door was freshly painted shocking pink and a riot of scarlet sweet peas and yellow and orange nasturtiums covered the bushes in the small front garden.

With Jasmine leading the way, the three of us went indoors. The hall had been freshly painted with a colour-wash of pinks, beginning with darker pink nearer the skirting board and going up to pale pink that almost faded to white on the ceiling.

"Wait till you see your bedroom," said Jasmine. "I've done a lot of the repainting here and it's been great fun – like creating stories in paint.

There was the sound of voices and laughter coming from the kitchen and the smell of chocolate, hot lemon and spices hung in the air.

"Wow," said Cara, her eyes like saucers. "Is this really where you grew up, Mum? Why didn't we ever come here before? It's really cool."

"Your Dad didn't approve."

"He's weird."

Gangan was sitting in her usual place by the fire. It was summertime, so there was just a token fire of pine-cones and a few seasoned apple logs burning. A black and white cat that looked like a reincarnation of Magpie dozed on a red cushion by Gangan's feet.

"Your turn next, Fable," said Gangan indicating the cards on the table in front of her, acting as if it was only a few days since she'd last seen me and not thirty years. She was a bit thinner and her hair had turned completely white but other than that, she looked the same as she'd always done.

I hugged her and gave her my birthday present to her – a copy of my book of poems.

"I've missed you, Gangan," I said.

"Stuff and nonsense child, I said we'd meet up in this life again and we have. Now sit down and let's see what the future holds for you."

On the table near the window was a huge pink and white birthday cake with '90' on it and a ring of candles round the edge.

I shuffled the pack, selected my ten cards and waited.

Gangan laid out the cards in the familiar pattern and sat studying them, her eyes sparkling behind her round glasses.

"The Knight of Cups is waiting for you," she said. "And you're the Queen of Wands – just like I always said you'd be. Did you bring this new man with you, Fable?" she looked eagerly round the room.

I shook my head. "There was someone, Gangan, but he's gone away."

"He'll be back," she said firmly. "It's in the cards. But don't expect life with him to be an easy ride."

The candles were lit on Gangan's cake and she blew

them out. Then Cara was clamouring for me to show her the rest of the house and Jasmine was keen to show off the way she'd decorated my old bedroom – a colour-wash of blue this time, light at the bottom and dark on the ceiling with fluorescent stars added "so you can imagine what it was like on the night you were born."

Karen, Gangan's live-in companion, called me back to the kitchen to say goodbye to the last of the guests. Cara and Jasmine announced their intention of going to bed. When I looked out of the bedroom window that used to be Peggy's I could see a crescent moon surrounded by a scattering of stars like freckles. I turned the coins in the pocket of my jacket over and whispered a prayer for luck.

Karen pressed a silver goblet of mulled wine into my hand after the last guest had gone. "Blow me if that isn't the door again," she said. "Who can it be at this time of night?" She hurried along the hallway, her feet pattering softly on the polished floorboards in their black ballet slippers.

From her fireside corner, I noticed Gangan nodding quietly to herself as if she knew. She was wrapped in a scarlet shawl now and announced her intention of going to bed soon. "One more reading to do," she murmured to herself. "I'll sleep easily then."

I heard Karen pattering back along the hall, followed by a set of heavier footsteps that I recognised like my own heartbeat. Carrying my glass of mulled wine and leaving Gangan alone in the kitchen, I escaped into the garden.

Ghostly looking moths hovered around Gangan's herb bed and I could smell lavender, rosemary and mint. I sat on a blue and white striped cushion watching the stars until he came to find me, as I knew he would.

"You believe in making things difficult for me don't

you?" said Liam.

"You can talk, storming off like you did and not giving me a chance to explain."

"Explain what exactly."

"That I didn't read your letters because I didn't know where you'd sent them. You never told me your address. I didn't even have a phone number for you."

He was wearing black jeans and a clean white shirt, which made him look more sun-tanned than ever.

"I left the key under the mat for you. I thought everybody did that."

"I didn't know where you lived until Linnet told me earlier." I felt close to tears, worn out with the emotion of the day. "I just thought you weren't interested in me any more."

"And I've been torturing myself thinking you weren't bothered with an Irish peasant like me and wondering how I'll get through the rest of my life without you." He took a step towards me.

"So why are we arguing when we both want the same thing?" I stepped into the circle of his arms, feeling the frantic hammering of his heart and his warm breath on my cheek. He smelled of sweat and coconut suntan lotion and his lips were soft on mine.

"I love you, you silly woman," he whispered. "I've felt the same since I first clapped eyes on you in that Library. I'm not going to change my mind. And Gangan – wonderful lady that she is – just read my cards and said that you were my Queen just like I always knew you were."

We walked slowly down the garden towards the orchard. I could see a circle of little lights in coloured glass jars and wondered who had put them there.

"She said everything's ready for us – whatever that

means," said Liam, holding me close.

"I was born here," I whispered as I sank down on the soft cushions left in the circle of lights.

Liam produced a bottle of champagne from a bucket leaning drunkenly against a plum tree.

I felt a sudden flash of despair, knowing what was to come, remembering what a disaster my sex life with Tony had been.

"What is it?" he asked, pulling me down beside him..

"What if I'm no good for you? What if I'm a disappointment?

"And how could that be?" His hands caressed my body, teasing away my clothes. His lips were raising me to heights of passion that I'd thought were gone forever. I saw an explosion of magical colours and the echo of our twin cries rose towards the heavens.

We fell asleep under a roof of stars in the orchard where my life had begun. The Wheel of Fortune was beginning a new circle and I knew it would be an exciting journey.